To J. D. Douglas

Aye giean thanks at ilka
thocht o' you.

The Doomsday Connection. Copyright © 1986 by Sherwood Eliot Wirt.
Published by Crossway Books, a division of Good News Publishers, West-chester, Illinois 60153.

Book Design by Karen L. Mulder

First printing, 1986.

Printed in the United States of America.

Library of Congress Catalog Card Number 85-72914

ISBN 0-89107-380-9

DRAMATIS PERSONAE

Crew and passengers of Flight 803

Captain Frank Medeiros, chief pilot
First Officer Bill Garrett, copilot
Flight Engineer Barney Bricklebine
Lead Flight Attendant Sally Carstairs
Flight Attendant Kristen Rountree

Reverend Jordan Foster
President-elect Raymond Phillips of P.I.T.S.
Mrs. Colleen Phillips
Charlotte Embree
Alison Pitt-Barr, secretary to Miss Embree
Ralph Epstein, attorney
Arvie Erickson, captain, U.C.L.A. tennis team
Mary Zlibin
Maybelle Lewis
Reginald St. Columba Tibbets, her grandson
Vasily Mechikoff of the U.S.S.R.
Gus Krieger
Nick Gavrilovich
Saint Columba

Commissioner Peter Hilliard, The Salvation Army
Jack Denlinger
Rick Ramsey, Linda McDowell, Rennie Lopez, students

Other Characters

Mrs. Van Roux, librarian
Diane Finlayson, friend of Sally Carstairs
Irwin Embree, brother of Charlotte Embree
Major Sebastian McCorkle, The Salvation Army
Mrs. Major McCorkle
Gary, Frances, Clarence, Salvation Army soldiers
Doug Prucha, weather officer
Mrs. Arlowene Foster
Mrs. Vivian Foster
Danny Foster
Paula Marie Ives
Roger Gillespie and Gordon Pfaff, FBI agents
Robbie Cronk, TV host
Eli Pixley, musician
Deacon Leroy Warburton
Dr. McMurtrie
Yakob Malof
Zoltan
Arturo, bellman
Jerry and Tony, river men
Jennifer Cochran
Brenda Cosgrove, president, Chi Omega
Mrs. Tracy Medeiros
Calvary Bible faculty: Professors Oberholzer, Nilsson, Baum,
   Chernowith, Arleigh, Langham, and Dean Mallory

SAYING OF CHRIST LINKED TO ADVANCE NOTICE OF RETURN

New York Times News Service

AMSTERDAM, Sept. 13—The librarian of the Free University of Amsterdam today announced the discovery of a reputed fragment of the long-sought "Gospel of the Hebrews," containing a previously unrecorded saying of Jesus that he intended to announce in advance his return to earth.

Mr. Franz Oosterbaan, at a press conference here, stated that the quotation from the noncanonical Gospel was found in a rare first edition of the "Medulla Sacrae Theologiae," written and published in Holland by a seventeenth-century English controversialist named William Ames. The volume was a recent gift to the library by an anonymous donor.

According to the passage in Ames (missing from a later edition), the Latin extract from the lost Gospel was contained in a letter supposedly written by the legendary medieval priest-king of Abyssinia, Prester John, to the Holy Roman Emperor, Frederick Barbarossa, about 1150 A.D. Ames quotes the letter as saying:

" 'I would share with Your Highness a remarkable incident that occurred last year during my coronation visit to the beloved

Abbot Gelasius of the sacred monastery of Saint Epiphanius in the western mountains. I was personally presented by the Abbot with a single page, torn and almost illegible, from the uncial Greek codex of the lost Gospel of the Hebrews, which the Holy Apostolic Church has not seen for a thousand years.

" 'In this brittle fragment, which I now hold in my hand, our Lord is recorded as saying to his disciples, "And before the Son of Man cometh with the clouds of heaven and all his holy angels, is it not written in the Testament of Daniel that his appearing for his church shall be portended to an assemblage chosen of the Father's own pleasure?" ' "

This passage, as translated by Oosterbaan, seems to refute statements in the canonical Gospels, such as Matthew 25:13 and Mark 13:32, in which Jesus states that neither men nor angels, "nor the Son himself" knows the time of his return to earth.

The Gospel of the Hebrews was highly regarded by Jewish Christians living in Egypt in the second century, although several early authorities branded it as heretical. Only a few remnants of it have survived, and they do not include the new discovery.

The Ames volume has been placed in a government vault in The Hague, awaiting there the convocation next month of an international group of New Testament Greek scholars. In a statement released today by the Vatican Press Service, Monsignor Guglielmo Tellori, chief archivist for the Vatican library, repudiated any suggestion that the discovery was authentic. . . .

PROLOGUE

Reginald St. Columba Tibbets lay twisting on his pad, an antique brass bedstead that matched the Dutch colonial decor of the Tibbets' suburban home. He was into his first PCP trip and was terrified by the images floating through his mind. Streaks of color, fiery sparks, and menacing shapes that alternately blurred and sharpened made it impossible for him to focus on anything. A fishbowl appeared before him, and the fish began talking, assaulting his ears with a cacophony of strange dialects. Now he was inside the fishbowl, swimming with the creatures and being chased by a spiny shark.

Jeff, the classmate and dealer who lived on the other side of Schenectady, had assured Reginald that the drug would open up his mind, would enable him to decipher passwords, crack spy codes, penetrate computer combinations at top levels, and give him access to secret data from the great corporations. He could even predict coming events. But instead of reveling in such elusive powers, Reginald found himself half-awake, tormented by fears that his parents would discover his condition, that his brother Dick would give him away, that he would be removed from the house and placed in some rehabilitation holding tank where drug-crazed addicts would assault him.

He tried to remember the directions Jeff had told him: "Stand in front of your mirror and keep staring at it. After a while the mirror will split in two and the monkey demon will jump through." Reginald slipped out of bed and turned on the light. He put on his thick prescription lenses and walked to the full-length mirror on his bedroom door. As a rule Reginald spent little time examining his countenance, for it was not particularly attractive. Behind the spectacles his eyes appeared owlish, one being more owlish than the other. Both were dilated and inclined to wander. The nose was well-formed, but the mouth and chin seemed to fall away, due partly to the contrivances of an orthodontist. A ring of zits circled his hairline. He was fifteen years old and small for his age.

Once before, that evening, Reginald had stood before the mirror, but nothing had happened. This time it was different. The first sign was when Baxter, his water spaniel curled outside the door, began to growl. The mirror did a split, and there on the floor before the boy was something small, dark, and wriggling. It pulled back its lips and displayed two ugly rows of teeth. His body tingling, Reginald stooped to hear what the chattering creature seemed to be saying: "You name it. You name it." Reginald was speechless until it added, "You want girls to come sit on your lap?"

"No!" The question broke through his reticence. Girls weren't nice to Reginald. Daringly he said, "I want to set up an interrogation system for coding data about the future. How do I do it?"

The shriveled monster began dancing about. "What for?" it asked in a cracked voice. "What for? What for?"

Hardly realizing what he was saying, Reginald blurted out, "I want to know when Jesus Christ is coming back."

The monkey demon turned two somersaults and gave a screech. "He wants to know! He wants to know!" It leaped on the mirror and scrambled up, scratching the glass as it went, and perched facing the boy. "We know," it hissed. "Angels don't, but we do."

Reginald felt a tightening at the roots of his hair. A month earlier, before he quit Sunday school for good, they had read something in the Bible—in Matthew, it was—that said the demons were expecting a "time."

"All right," he whispered, "when?"

"When?" echoed the creature. "When? When?" It showed its teeth. "Pick a date," it said. "Pick a date."

"Pick what date?" asked Reginald incredulously. But the monster disappeared the way it had come, and the mirror snapped back to its original shape. Reginald found himself lying on his bed in the dark, tossing feverishly, while outside Baxter continued to growl.

The first experiment with PCP was the last. Reginald never touched the drug again. It was while he was packing for the trip to southern California that he came across the scratches on the mirror.

ONE

FRIDAY

At the moment, 2:30 P.M., the sky over Nebraska was clear and the gauges on the deck of Intercontinental Flight 803 were looking good. Captain Frank Medeiros was wishing he could put the weather stats on hold the rest of the way to Los Angeles. As the engines hummed on the rather airworn Boeing 727, images of country clubs and private beaches were dancing lazily through the skipper's mind. For today, Friday, September 13, his name was up for review before a special board of Intercontinental Airlines for the position of assistant director of operations.

Ten minutes later everything had changed. A report came in from Denver Center, informing the cockpit that Las Vegas was reporting heavy rain and Phoenix possible flooding. Frank Medeiros' satisfaction vanished along with the fairways and beaches. The W.W. (weather warning) he had received at John F. Kennedy Airport in New York had hinted at trouble. Now the number two generator loomed up in his mind like a spook, but he dismissed it; the decision had been his and he was prepared to live with it.

Whatever lay ahead, with fifteen thousand flying hours under his belt, plus the wiry build of an Air Force major and the mustache of an expensive dentist, Frank Medeiros was not about to lose his cool. This flight would end as the others had.

Back of his self-assurance was the strong feeling that in spite of a precarious career that had etched deep lines in his face, life had not been all that rough on Medeiros. His second wife, eighteen years his junior, was shaping up nicely; his luck was holding. In the company he was so respected professionally that it had taken some fancy footwork to avoid being elected to a union office that would have threatened his standing with management.

At 5 o'clock that morning Medeiros had awakened in a New York hotel room with the pain on the side of his neck sending out a caveat, reminding him that he was no longer young. As he stood under a hot shower in the tub, he thought about the bubbling spas at Desert Hot Springs, and the doctor who was claiming 80 percent success in his arthritis treatments.

Then when Medeiros arrived at Kennedy Airport he faced the generator business and the W.W. At the time he wondered if somebody was trying to tell him something. He desperately wanted Flight 803 to touch down on runway two-five at LAX before dark and on time. If it did, and all went well, it would be his last line operation. But competition was fierce; a question mark—even an exclamation point—on his record could tip the scales against him. Today he wanted anonymity and a smooth run. Then roger, over and out.

On this particular Friday a million souls, more or less, were airborne over the planet in some eighteen thousand planes, each passenger somehow seeking to make his life more abundant—or less unendurable—by traveling from Menominee to Wauwatosa or from Omsk to Tomsk. Cabin conditions on Flight 803 were fairly typical. Attendants were putting away the last of the dinner trays. A movie was entertaining a few travelers with a fantasy about the destruction of Europe from outer space, the pea-sized brains of the green galactic invaders quite possibly exceeding the cranial capacity of the sci-fi writers who created them. Other passengers were dozing or had moved their seats. It was a long, boring flight, the sooner ended the better.

On the flight deck a light banter camouflaged the awareness of the crew that big stakes were in the pot. The good-humor man of the crew was First Officer Bill Garrett, a lean, curly-haired bachelor who was monitoring the automatic pilot. He stopped humming a country-western number long enough to crack, "See, we gotta lay down this bird real sweet so Don Casanova can put his feet under that mahogany desk."

To which Barney Bricklebine, the young flight engineer, added, "I see it as romantic. 'The Last Ride Together.'"

"'The Last Ride Together.' Who wrote it, Professor?" asked Garrett. "Come on, give it to us."

Bricklebine was a recycled English major who was gaining notoriety around the company as "the poet." He said, "It's Browning.

> *'I and my mistress, side by side*
> *Shall be together, breathe and ride. . . .*
>   *Who knows but the world may end to-*
>   *night?' "*

"What's he spoutin' now?" demanded the chief pilot.

"Says it's 'The Last Ride Together.' "

Medeiros snorted. "He must be bucking for grease monkey."

"Comes from eating too much chicken and rice," opined Garrett.

"Tell him to shut up or he'll be sorry. We're opening Tonopah out in the desert next month. . . . I hear they love poets. They have a reading every Friday the thirteenth."

Garrett glanced amusedly at the pilot. Glossy dark hair, neatly combed, topped a classic profile. As he sat quietly with his eye on the on-board radar, Medeiros could have been a Brazilian general. He seemed the essence of imperturbability.

"You nervous?" Garrett asked.

"I'm always nervous," replied the pilot grimly. "Look at that radar!"

"What's Denver sayin'?"

Medeiros chose to ignore his copilot. "Here we go," he said, selecting the P.A. switch to the cabin. "Ladies and gentlemen, this is your captain speaking. At this time I will ask you to return to your seats and fasten your seat belts securely. It seems we're expecting a little turbulence over the mountains, that's all. Thanks."

From the cockpit, sensational cumulus activity could be seen spreading southward from Pike's Peak. Billowing clouds literally covered the western skyline. The pilot was uncomfortably aware that inside some of those clouds violent winds were moving vertically at 60 to 80 miles an hour, generating flashes of lightning that could knock a larger plane than his out of the sky.

Medeiros looked at his new wristwatch, a six-months' anniversary gift from his wife. It was close to 3 o'clock, the usual time for thunderstorms in the area. Denver had brought him down from 39,000 to 35,000 feet. He now resumed his dialogue with the air traffic controllers and asked for vectors. Denver informed him that since Phoenix and Las Vegas continued to report weather problems, no suitable alternate route was available.

"But," the tower added with that serenity that comes only when the speaker's feet are on something solid, "don't worry, we'll get you through. Our radar coverage is complete."

Denver did not know, of course, that at Kennedy Airport Medeiros had ordered one of the aircraft's generators to be disconnected—a normal procedure for which FAA approval was automatic. To repair the mechanical nuisance on the generator in New York would have delayed the flight, which Medeiros certainly did not want. Because better maintenance facilities were available at Los Angeles, Flight 803 was dispatched from Kennedy with the number two engine's generator inoperative.

Now the plane was over Colorado Springs and beginning to penetrate the clouds. They proved more extensive than Denver had reported, confirming the captain's apprehensions. He advised that he was slowing the plane to 280 knots, the optimum turbulence penetration speed, and asked again for vectors. The monitors responded with a broad picture that somehow failed to isolate the larger storm cells.

As he sought to take the aircraft through the thickening murk, Medeiros found himself forced to rely on his own weather radar. Just as he felt he had navigated the worst of it, and was congratulating himself on avoiding this latest threat to his professional future, he brushed the edge of a sullen, menacing storm center embedded within the cloud formation.

With a blinding flash and tremendous clap, a bolt of lightning struck the 727 on its black plastic nose, splitting open the radome and shearing off a piece of the radar antenna. As the piece flew off, it was immediately sucked into the intake of the plane's number three jet, disabling the engine and causing it to flame out.

Frank Medeiros found his eyes quickly readjusting following the strike. He attempted to contact Denver, but discovered the lightning bolt had caused a complete electrical failure and all radio contact was disrupted. The radar had been wiped out and the automatic pilot disengaged.

"Barney," Medeiros called out sharply, "we've lost essential. Switch to number two." At the time the captain issued his command, Bricklebine was busy resetting circuit breakers in an effort to restore electrical power. Two seconds later a microburst sucked the aircraft into a violent downdraft that dropped it two thousand feet within the next forty seconds. Garrett, desperately attempting to get the nose up, found that the plane's performance had been seriously impaired by the downdraft and the dead engine.

As the aircraft continued its drop, Bricklebine felt his stomach giving way. He managed to reach the selector and turn it to the number two engine. Nothing happened.

"I said switch, Barney!" yelled Medeiros, sitting helplessly.

"I did, Frank," Bricklebine shouted back. "The generator's out!"

Medeiros cursed the day he was born. Why had he neglected to fix that generator in New York? "Well, don't sit there with egg on your face. Go to number one!"

Several more seconds of confusion elapsed before Bricklebine managed to throw the switches that restored essential electrical power to the still-plummeting aircraft. Garrett was finally able to maneuver his ship across and out of the downdraft area and into the corresponding updraft that began buoying the plane toward its former altitude. By now Medeiros was using his VHF radio to request a lower altitude, citing the totaling of his weather radar and the loss of his number three engine. He asked for immediate authorization to fly at 24,000 feet.

During a break in the chatter with Denver, Barney ventured to ask, "How are we doing now, Captain?"

"Try and get us some more power," Medeiros replied. "We can't stand another electrical failure." His voice softened. "If our hydraulic system goes, the girls can't make their coffee."

Garrett picked up the change in timbre. "So—do we push on to L.A.?"

Medeiros stretched his arms above his head while his eyes flickered over the dials. Even though they had come through the worst, he knew more storm cells were in the area. He was really thinking about the meeting in the Los Angeles airport where his fate might be hanging on a split vote. "All the safety factors are being weighed," he said at last in his best professional voice, remembering that he had turned on the voice recorder at the start of the turbulence. "We're not going back—not through that gunk. Get Sally in here and we'll find out if we have injuries. Barney, get into your charts and give me a flight level. Set the throttles for maximum until we get our new altitude."

Garrett, who had reset the automatic pilot, got on the intercom as the authorization came through to start down. Bricklebine waited a moment, then spoke up. "Hey, did you fellows hear a voice say something back there when we were dropping . . . ?"

2

Until the captain's announcement of "a little turbulence" called the passengers back to their seats, the state of affairs in the cabin had continued stable. For Sally Carstairs, the lead flight attendant, Medeiros' timing was perfect. His seat belt order came as she was locking up the last of the luncheon equipment in the galley. She responded by flashing the amber light that alerted the other three attendants.

Sally wore her authority lightly, but as her assistants well knew, her attractive smile masked a will of carborundum. With eleven years' flying experience behind her, a farm upbringing in North Dakota to undergird her, and a marriage that went pfft! to chasten her, Sally had set herself to win career recognition at Intercontinental, and she had made it. In her own words, she had seen everything and still liked her work.

The girls soon cleared the aisle and looked to see that all eighty-five passengers were properly strapped in. Kristen, one of the attendants, checked the two rear lavatories and found one of them locked. She reported this to Sally, who replied, "I'll take care of it." Walking quickly down the aisle, Sally reached the rear of the aircraft just as it gave a heavy lurch. She rapped sharply on the door that read, "OCCUPIED."

"Return to your seat!" Sally called out. After a few seconds she rapped and repeated the order.

A further delay followed. Finally the door opened and a large, well-dressed black man emerged, holding a paper towel to his head. "Sorry," he said, "I just banged my head against the mirror."

"Please buckle up," said Sally. "Are you all right?"

The man examined the towel in his hand. "Didn't break the skin, ma'am, but it took care of that mirror!" He smiled, showing white, even teeth. Sally followed him to his seat.

"You're sure you're O.K.?"

"I'm in better shape than your airplane."

Sally hurried back to her seat. When the lightning struck, few in the cabin saw the flash, but everyone felt the jolt. A thumping underneath told Sally that the locked-up wheels were reacting to the turbulence, and she quickly became aware that the number three engine was no longer functioning. Neither Sally nor anyone else was prepared for what happened next— the microburst that pulled the aircraft earthward at a rate of three thousand feet per minute. During the terrifying descent, everything loose in the cabin—coats, scarves, magazines, purses, coffee cups, cocktail glasses, decks of cards, cigarette butts, even flight bags and briefcases—flew toward the ceiling. The movie screen rolled up with a snap. Newspapers were blown apart and floated everywhere.

Prevented by their seat belts from mingling with the debris overhead, the passengers increased the pandemonium by verbalizing on various levels of angst. Several screamed for help; cries of "O God!," "Jesus!" and "Get me out of here!" punctured the air. Some immediately became sick, with olfactory results that mingled with the aromas created by bad consciences, weak kidneys, and the fear of death. Only Sally, of all the occupants of the cabin, fully understood that the aircraft, having been drawn into the vortex of a downdraft, would soon fly out of it. What frightened her was not the plunge, but the silent engine.

After forty seconds the plane's continuing forward movement brought it out of its precipitous descent, and the associated thermal sent it soaring back up.

From her seat Sally shouted to the passengers, "Everyone bend over! Watch your heads!" as the barrage of papers, purses, magazines, and paraphernalia descended from the ceiling. The effect was chaotic, and accompanied by screams, but amazingly the passenger complement emerged with only minor bumps and bruises.

A blond young man wearing a blue-and-yellow sports jacket stepped into the aisle holding up a briefcase in his hand. "Anybody lose this?" he asked in a rather disagreeable voice.

Kristen, who by now was on her feet, responded quickly, "I'll take it. Did it get you?"

He nodded. "In the shoulder."

"I'm sorry. I'll get back to you in a moment." He was, Kristen noted, quite tall and smoothly handsome, but not very pleasant.

Once the aircraft was stabilized at near normal speed and power was restored, Frank Medeiros' voice again came over the P.A.: "This is your captain speaking. I want to apologize on behalf of the crew for the discomfort you experienced during the turbulence we just came through. As you probably know, we lost our number three engine when we took that lightning strike. But we still have two healthy engines, and are proceeding according to flight plan." The captain paused. "To show you how much we appreciate the way you came through like champions, I am asking the attendants to serve champagne on the house for the rest of the flight. Now please sit back and enjoy yourselves. Thank you."

Following the captain's lead, the cabin crew sought to convey the impression that the crisis was over and further explanation was unnecessary. Three of the attendants served the champagne, then set about restoring belongings to owners and putting loose articles into plastic bags. In fact, Kristen was so busy that she forgot about the young athlete's shoulder.

As Sally Carstairs prepared to answer a call from the flight deck, she realized that in some ways the crisis was not over and that more explanations were in order. For during that descent she and every other person on the plane had heard a voice speaking in plain English, loud and clear, and saying something that had nothing to do with aeronautics.

3

*E*ntering the cockpit during flight was for Sally like visiting a rock star's dressing room. She could have assigned the duty to any of the other attendants, but preferred to take it herself. The flight deck in transit was an exotic world—a mysterious globule of panels and dials and pointers and gauges and always, like an unseen presence, life and death. Sally loved it. Sometimes in her fantasies all three flight officers would be stricken with stomach cramps, and she, Sally, would then take the controls and gracefully land the mighty jet in her father's cornfield. . . .

But today was different; electric tension was in the air, and her job was to face the moment. As she paused to knock, Sally glanced out a porthole and spotted far below them the natural spire of Ship Rock, solitary in the desolate landscape. The vibration of the two engines kept forcing itself into her consciousness as she kept listening for a miss. Perhaps she ought to put in for a ground assignment.

"Enjoy the ride?" Barney inquired as he admitted her.

Sally grinned, then addressed Medeiros directly. "Nobody seriously hurt, Captain. One bruise from a falling briefcase. A broken mirror in the head."

"How's the champagne going down?" was Medeiros' response.

"Like gangbusters. We had to stop our cleanup to keep the glasses filled."

"Captain says we're taking it on in," said Garrett.

"Great."

"Have to," said Medeiros, "the way we are."

"What's the—"

"Vegas is still being soaked, and a gullywasher took out half the runway in Phoenix."

Medeiros lifted his hand in a gesture intended to wave Sally back to her cabin. Instead she leaned back against the door. "Can I ask a question?"

"Shoot," said Bricklebine.

"Did any of you guys say something over the P.A. while we were going through that business?" No one replied. "I mean, at first I thought it was a message from up here." The silence became embarrassing. "Everybody heard it."

"Heard what?" asked Medeiros calmly.

Sally watched the ragged clouds whizzing past. "I'm not sure. It was some weird kind of warning."

"I heard it." Garrett was tight-lipped.

"Well, I heard something," admitted Bricklebine.

When Captain Medeiros spoke, his voice carried a note of irritated authority. "All right, get this. I want everybody to use his head. Here's where we are and here's what we've got. And everything else can wait until we put this baby on the ground at LAX."

"Right," agreed Garrett heartily.

"Give us half an hour and we'll be out of this system," Medeiros continued. "What we've got to face is that there may be some joker on board, and we've got to find the guy. He may be a hijacker."

The words whipped through the cockpit like a chill draft.

Garrett whistled softly. Sally felt the perspiration on her palms. "Maybe it was somebody using a tape recorder," she suggested.

"Negative," answered Medeiros crisply. "More like a freak transmission, or else a plant. We've got no security on board."

"You know," said Garrett speculatively, "Operations was telling me the other day about some propjet that was getting stuff from down below—in New Mexico, I think. Seems the length of the fuselage was tuned into a frequency and was acting as a receiver, so the passengers listening on earphones were picking up police calls." He laughed. No one else did.

"I wasn't wearing a headset, and I heard it," objected Sally.

"That couldn't happen on a jet anyway," said Medeiros, "but almost everything else could."

"Like someone in the washroom, maybe, loosening the panels and cutting into the wiring?" asked Garrett.

"Right." Medeiros pointed to a toggle switch connected to one of the auxiliary radios. "And it's possible that lightning could have fused these wires together. We don't know what it did to the lower forty-one."

"We had a man in the washroom," said Sally quietly.

————
4
————

When Sally Carstairs returned to the galley she learned that the other girls had accumulated a vast fund of misinformation. Some of the passengers thought the voice sounded ominous; others said it was rather pleasant. Some thought it was a male voice; others said female. Those watching the movie said they heard it through their earphones; the others said it came over the P.A. As for its content, some declared it a warning about the end of the world; others thought it conveyed hope. Some claimed they could not hear or did not understand the message; still others refused to discuss it. No one seemed particularly elated or disturbed by it, the only distress of the moment being a few bruises and airsickness.

Sally related the cockpit instructions to her assistants, then opened a bottle of champagne and set out on a fact-finding mission. The first passenger she spoke to was a tall, impressive, bearded man of about forty, whose black hair fringed a growing bald spot. He told Sally his name was Columba, and seemed quite knowledgeable as they discussed the lightning hit, the downdraft, and the enigmatic voice. To Sally's astonishment, he took out of his windbreaker pocket a sheet of paper on which he had printed the words of the announcement.

"I made notes as soon as we leveled off," he said with a disarming smile. "You can keep it."

"Let me make a copy," Sally said.

"No, that's all right. I thought somebody might want it . . . but I am feeling a bit queasy. Do you have something? I lived too long on Irish potatoes and Scotch haggis, and when I'm on assignment it sometimes flares up."

"I noticed your accent." Sally smiled. "Are you from—?"

Columba shook his head. "That was some time ago."

She flagged Kristen for some aspirin and then, standing in the aisle, read the odd Irish lettering: "LET THE PEOPLE KNOW THAT AFTER TWO DAYS I SHALL EXECUTE JUDGMENT AND JUSTICE IN THE EARTH. BUT LET THOSE I HAVE FORMED FOR MYSELF COME INTO THE ARK."

"I'll show this to the captain if you don't mind," Sally said. "You're not security?"

"No."

The plane's remaining engines increased their tempo and caused the fuselage to shudder. Sally scanned it again. "I guess it's the kind of thing you expect on this job. Reminds me of those old Cecil B. DeMille movies that scared me when I was a kid. You know—" She raised her voice and lifted her arms. "—BEWARE! JUDGMENT IS COMING!"

A woman sitting across the aisle unbuckled her seat belt and bolted for the lavatory.

Leaving Columba, Sally found the next few passengers were

in emotional stages ranging from unhappy to distraught. But when she reached Maybelle Lewis, a white-haired doll collector from Schenectady, she was unprepared for what she heard. Maybelle, who seemed to have survived the turbulence fairly well, had rosy cheeks and ultramarine blue eyes that matched those of the antique doll in her lap. She spoke in a high, lilting, musical voice that reminded one of a doll with a music box in its stomach.

"That voice was either the Lord Himself or it was His angel," she announced. "I'm as sure of it as I am of sitting here." And Maybelle was strapped in and quite sure of where she was sitting.

"Did you hear something about judgment?" inquired Sally.

"Not for me, dearie," responded Maybelle as she carefully removed the tiny slippers from her doll. "Didn't you hear what it said? We're invited to go on a boat ride."

Sally stared at her, then at the paper in her hand. "A boat ride?"

"Maybe you didn't hear it. I caught every word, in spite of all the bouncing around." Maybelle examined the slippers and gently returned them to the doll's feet. "Poor little Henriette almost hit the ceiling. I just managed to grab her as she was going up."

"But how could the same voice say two things?" persisted Sally. "This man heard it say the world is up for judgment and you heard something about a boat ride. Do you mean the ark?"

Maybelle batted her blue eyes. "He that hath ears, let him hear!"

5

Kristen was waiting for Sally when she returned to the kitchen area. "A woman in 17A broke her glasses," she said. "They were on the seat beside her and—whoof!"

"Did you explain about compensation?"

"What do you think? She says she has an extra pair in her suitcase. And there's another woman waiting in line who asked if we had a Bible."

Sally placed her bottle on the counter. "A Bible? What does she think—"

"Why not?" retorted Kristen airily. "I think it's cute. FAA emergency regulations—Bibles and booze on every airline."

"Don't knock it," said Sally. "The booze keeps us flying."

"Well, that champagne was a stupid idea when we're still picking up bags. The whole cabin stinks."

Sally cut her down with an order. "You tell that woman it's not our airline policy to carry religious materials." Then she hesitated. "No, wait. I'll go. Which one is she?"

"I think she's back in her seat now—24C."

As Sally was detailing the "airline policy" to the middle-aged woman in 24C, the man in the adjoining seat interrupted her. "Excuse me," he said, "I happen to have a Bible with me if you'd like to look at it." Both women stared at him, surprised—Sally in particular, for it was the black man who had banged his head in the lavatory. Seeing their expressions, he laughed. "I'm a minister of the gospel," he explained as he reached in his pocket and handed a business card to Sally.

"May I keep this?" she asked.

"Of course."

She read aloud, "The Reverend Jordan Foster, D.D., senior pastor, Rose of Sharon Church, Bellflower, California. A Church for All People." Looking up, Sally inquired politely, "Is your head feeling better, Reverend?"

"Oh, sure," Foster chuckled. "I'm just sorry about the—"

"No problem," interrupted Sally, "we're just trying to check on that mysterious voice that came over back there. Did you—"

"I heard it," nodded Foster. "Yes, I surely did."

"Could you tell me what you heard?"

"It was—well, I'm not sure. You know, there was a lot of commotion going on."

Sally pressed hard. "Could you just give me an idea? Was there something about judgment and stuff like that?"

Jordan handed the Bible to his seatmate, then turned again

to Sally. "Whenever one of my teachers was asked a question about anything," he said, "he would respond by saying, 'Well, first of all, there's the ambiguity of it.'"

Sally stared at him. "What does that mean?"

"It means I really don't know what to say to you. If I did, I'd say it."

"Thank you for your cooperation."

"Of course."

A few minutes later on the flight deck Sally handed Foster's card to Captain Medeiros. "He's very sharp. He was in the john when you turned on the seat belt sign."

"A preacher," mused Medeiros. "Could be our boy. Does his voice sound like what we heard?"

"I couldn't tell. If he had a southern accent, he's lost it."

Garrett spoke up. "He could have done it. You say he's black? He's got my vote."

"Did you check the head?" asked the captain.

"Not yet," said Sally. "I came right here."

"Notice anything about him? His clothes? What about his hand luggage?"

"He has only a briefcase with him. When the lady next to him asked for a Bible, he opened it up, but all I could see was papers."

"And he said and did nothing that would make you think he might be a hijacker?"

"Not so far."

Captain Medeiros frowned and fingered his necktie. "Take a look around that lavatory, and tell the girls to let me know the minute this person leaves his seat. We're going to have to have a little talk with him."

Sally handed Medeiros a sheet of notepaper.

"What's this?"

"I thought you'd like to get the message straight. One of the passengers wrote out the words for you." She reentered the cabin, leaving the captain staring at the paper in front of him.

6

*F*or Charlotte Embree, who liked to think of herself as the distinguished founder and president of Victorian Tearooms Limited, Flight 803 had deteriorated into a nonevent. Had it not been for her desire to square accounts with her brother Irwin, she never would have consented to fly to Los Angeles to address the National Association of American Executives. But Irwin's plant was also in Los Angeles, her Learjet was in the shop, and on short notice Intercontinental—with shocking disregard of her stockholder status—could come up with nothing better than the present crummy flight.

Charlotte glared at the narrow leg space in front of her as she bent over to grope for some loose pages of the rough draft of her forthcoming speech. After the aircraft emerged from its plummet, the speech had been scattered over a number of seats. With the seat belt sign finally turned off, Charlotte's two companions, Ralph Epstein and Alison Pitt-Barr, were combing the area (frequently on all-fours) trying to find the missing pages.

For several minutes Charlotte had been jamming her thumb on the call button, determined to elicit some kind of official response to her plight, but her appeals went unheeded. Now, as Kristen moved swiftly down the aisle with a load of used sick bags, Charlotte adopted the voice of a stentor: "Young lady, I have been ringing the call bell for a quarter of an hour!"

Kristen paused to scrutinize her. She took in the square face, the flat nose that curiously came to a point, the designer-label traveling suit of Chanel knit, the manicured hands devoid of jewelry except for a three-carat diamond in a solitaire setting, the handsomely-attended hair brushed with gray. Obviously the woman was no person to offend or ignore; she reflected that indeterminate middle-age that only money and careful grooming can protect. But there was something more that Kristen noticed—a strange fire that glowed in her eyes and gave her a flinty look.

"Can I get you something?" asked the flight attendant.

Charlotte responded by speaking so her voice carried to both smoking and nonsmoking sections. "I wish to speak to the captain!"

She was acting like Margaret Dumont in a Marx Brothers comedy, but Kristen was equal to the occasion. "I'm very sorry, I'm afraid the captain is unavailable."

"I know how busy he is. I happen to be a stockholder in this airline, and I am acquainted with your president. Please tell him that I wish to speak with him. Now!"

Attracted by the conversation, Sally came down the aisle and joined them. "I'm sorry," she said, "it's been a real difficult flight and the captain asked not to be bothered. I'm sure you'll understand."

Charlotte sat up straight. "Young lady, I want you to know I am not a bother. Now, you tell him to get back here."

Before the plane left New York, Sally had received a print-out of V.I.P.'s aboard the flight. One of the names, she recalled, was connected with the airline. "You're Miss Embree, aren't you?"

If Charlotte was inwardly gratified, she refused to show it. Ralph Epstein, who had taken his seat on the aisle next to Charlotte, explained, "I guess you know Miss Embree is the founder of Victorian Tearooms. . . ."

Sally had already taken in Epstein. He was impeccably groomed in a Brooks Brothers outfit with buttoned-down shirt. Even his acrobatics while retrieving the scattered pages failed to shake his cool reserve or ruffle his aristocratically waving locks. He couldn't have been more than thirty-five, and he did not wear a wedding band. Hoping for good things, Sally asked him, "Can I get you some champagne?"

"You can get me you-know-who," butted in Charlotte, thereby nipping what looked like a promising acquaintanceship. After Sally left, Charlotte sat breathing heavily, her dissatisfaction unappeased. "Where's Alison?" she demanded. "She's got to put these pages together."

"Up front, I believe, talking with some youngster," said Epstein.

"I wish to get out," Charlotte informed him, and she made her way down the aisle with solid tread.

The truth was, Alison Pitt-Barr had found her element, cheering up a wan and airsick seven-year-old boy. The child's indisposition she had taken care of by making appropriate squeals, while pretending to sew up the fingers of her left hand with an imaginary needle held in her right.

The boy was charmed. "Do it again!" he said, but at that moment Charlotte Embree made her appearance.

"Alison," she ordered, "come back and straighten out those papers; I can't do it."

Alison patted the lad on the cheek and stood up. "Be back after a wee bit. Cheerio."

"Do you have children?" asked the boy's mother, sitting beside him.

Alison hesitated. "I—" She adjusted her tam, smoothed her tweed skirt, and followed Charlotte back to their row.

"Absolutely the worst piece of flying I ever saw," Charlotte declared as they resumed their seats. "Believe me, Harold Fairbank is going to hear about this one!"

"What did you think of that announcement that came over?" inquired Ralph.

"I didn't think anything of it."

"I'd like to know how the schlocks piped it in."

"What if they didn't?" Alison's comment caused the others to stare at her curiously. Brought up in a Church of Scotland orphanage, Alison was in some way a relic of nineteenth-century Aberdeen. Her grandfather, she had been told, was Frazer of Tain, the young preacher who led the great revival at Campbeltown. Both her parents had been swept away in a midcentury flu epidemic, and she had come to America as a teenager after being "discovered" by a touring Rhode Island dowager. Alison's duties as a domestic servant were interrupted by the attentions of the dowager's husband, whereupon she packed her suitcase for Manhattan and found employment as a waitress in Charlotte's first tearoom. She attended night school and eventually was brought into the office. For the past ten years she had served as Charlotte's confidential secretary, which made her (among other things) the butt of Charlotte's heavy humor.

Alison finished sorting the pages of Charlotte's speech and inserted them in a folder, after which she picked up a copy of the *New York Times.*

"Where did you get that newspaper?" demanded Charlotte. "I didn't see you buy it."

"It was blowing around. You could say I liberated it," said Alison, calmly adjusting her shell-rimmed glasses.

"You see what we're reduced to," said Charlotte to Epstein. "My secretary is now a petty thief. If we'd booked first-class on another flight, they'd have given us all papers."

"I'll settle for your private jet," purred Ralph.

"In the hangar. They'll have it out next week. So here we are on the Goodyear Blimp. Perfectly ridiculous."

"I'd say we are very well indeed. We're alive," said Alison.

Charlotte turned to her. "Be sure you get us first-class return reservations on another airline. One that doesn't serve chicken and rice."

"You think we're going to make it back?" Epstein's voice had a touch of irony. "The threat of—let's say divine wrath hasn't affected your plans?"

"Nothing will change my plans," said Charlotte, pressing her lips together. "Neither heaven nor hell nor the Second Coming."

"Not even if it's coming in a couple of days, darling?" teased Epstein.

"Nothing is coming in a couple of days," retorted Charlotte. Alison remained silent.

"What would Jesus Christ come back for?" Epstein wanted to know. "He's been here once."

"He may be coming for me," said Alison.

"Please don't get her started," said Charlotte irritably. "Alison doesn't get religious very often, but when she does, her opinions are like Scotch tape—she sticks them on everything. Let's run through this once more, Ralph. Alison can look for Jesus out the window."

7

"You know, Captain," First Officer Garrett was saying, "our passengers are going to sing all over the place when they hit the ground."

"Let 'em."

"And you've got the media monitoring the ATC frequencies. Shouldn't we be talking with Operations?"

"Already done it," said Medeiros. "PR will take care of the media. I can handle the FAA."

Garrett watched a 747 passing them up, heading west. "What about the intrusion on the P.A.?"

"What about it?"

"I just wondered if you notified—"

"It's some kooky stuff some twerp said he heard. He may have heard it for all I know. So what?"

"Everybody heard it," Garrett reminded him.

"Sure. You hear it every day. The world is full of crazy people, talking about the end of the world."

"You didn't read what Sally brought in," said Barney Bricklebine. "It said something else."

"Like what?" demanded Medeiros.

"Something about coming into the ark. Sounded like a boat party."

Perhaps it was the emotional strain they had been under. Perhaps it was the engineer's pixilated reply. Whatever the cause, Medeiros and Garrett burst into unrestrained laughter.

At that moment the call bell chimed and Sally asked to come in. Once admitted, she wasted no time. "Got another one, Captain. Says she knows the airline president and owns stock in the company. Wants to see you."

Removing his headset momentarily and smoothing his hair, Medeiros turned to Sally. "You tell that broad I wouldn't go back there if the President of the United States was asking for me. There's nothing any passenger has to say that can't wait till we're on the ground."

"Explain it's an emergency," added Garrett.

"She thinks she's the emergency!" replied Sally.

Medeiros studied Garrett for a moment. "You go back and while you're there, check that head," he ordered, replacing his headset. "What we've got here, apparently, is a little electronic dipsy-doo, and we'll just have to stonewall everybody till we find out more. Don't worry about your passengers, they're going to talk anyway. But tell your girls to clam up. If people ask questions, they're to say it's still under investigation. O.K.?"

"O.K."

Meanwhile, Garrett had slipped into his jacket, donned his cap, and was patting Bricklebine on the shoulder. "If there's a party, old buddy, count me in." Then running his fingers over his silky mustache, he stepped into the cabin, where his appearance was greeted with a burst of applause.

Moving slowly along the aisle, First Officer Garrett was the picture of command authority. His regular features, easy posture, and friendly manner seemed to invite comments from the passengers. To inquiries about the aircraft he responded lightly and pleasantly, yet seriously enough so that the ordeal in the mountains seemed almost to have been some kind of proving test they had to go through together. Technical questions he answered with impressive jargon that was quite incomprehensible to the passengers, yet everyone nodded as if they understood. Oddly enough, no one asked about the voice.

By the time he reached row 18, Garrett had established his image and was prepared to meet with aplomb whatever challenge the lady stockholder wished to present. He spotted Charlotte in the middle seat, flanked by her two companions. Alison, in the window seat, had folded the *Times* into small sections and was perusing it commuter-style. Epstein, looking bland, was watching the first officer.

As Garrett paused, Charlotte put down the speech she had been studying and removed the tiny gold reading glasses from her nose. She informed the copilot that a hitch in her private transportation had forced her party to book with Intercontinental; that while she was a stockholder in the company, she never traveled commercial except in emergencies. She did see Harold Fairbank, the president, socially a few times a year.

At this statement Alison lowered her newspaper and stared at her employer, small lines of skepticism firming her jaw. Charlotte was obviously on the attack. She had the gold-braided officer on the defensive and was reveling in it. As for Garrett, he was inwardly cursing the fate that had saddled him with this cheap prima donna who enjoyed sticking needles into people.

Charlotte took a gold pen from her handbag and asked Garrett his name, which she wrote on the back of her speech folder. Epstein threw the copilot a glance that locked the two in a mutual male assistance league.

"I'm sorry to say this," Charlotte was intoning, "but I don't feel your crew has handled this plane in a way that properly safeguards the interests of the passengers. We have been bounced and jostled and batted around like Ping-Pong balls."

Garrett answered coolly, "Madam, this aircraft took a direct hit by lightning. We do not accept responsibility for acts of God."

"Don't give me your acts of God," Charlotte fired back. "I'm talking about that squawking voice you turned on back there during that terrible dive we took. If this was some kind of stunt, I will personally take pleasure in reporting it to the proper source."

Garrett examined her keenly before answering. "Madam, the weather ahead looks good. We are due to arrive in Los Angeles in sixty-five minutes. Is there anything else?"

"Excellent work, Captain," said Epstein approvingly.

"Cheers!" added Alison.

Charlotte's face remained granite. Smiling, Garrett touched his cap. "We appreciate your interest," he said, and moved down the aisle to where the Reverend Jordan Foster was sitting.

"How are you?" First Officer Garrett's approach was supremely correct as he took in the tailored suit, the expensive blue tie, and the monogrammed shirt. Jordan Foster, immediately on guard at sight of the uniform, acknowledged the greeting with a nod.

"They tell me, Reverend," Garrett continued, "that you loaned your Bible to one of the passengers. We appreciate that."

"Quite all right."

Garrett wished he could see inside the man's head. What business did he have that brought him aboard this flight? What did he know about the voice? "The flight attendant showed me your card. I believe you pastor a church in Southern California."

"That's right."

"Do you make this trip often?"

Jordan Foster was not about to divulge anything. "You never know."

The copilot was irritated. With all the security checks at the airport, the man could not possibly have sneaked aboard with the kind of sophisticated electronic equipment needed to reproduce a voice. Yet unquestionably this holy joe knew something. What was he doing in the toilet?

At this point Sally joined the pair. "The lady who was sitting next to you is returning your Bible and wants to thank you."

"My pleasure." Foster took the Bible and held it in his hand while he fixed his eyes on Garrett. "Did you want something, Captain?"

It was obvious to the copilot that the man was baiting him. "We were wondering if you knew anything about that freak transmission during the turbulence. I understand you were in the lavatory at the time."

Jordan Foster's suspicions were confirmed. "I think, Captain," he said, an edge in his voice, "if you ask this lady who works for you, you'll find that I was sitting right here all the time with my belt fastened. Otherwise I might have gone through your roof."

First Officer Garrett made no further attempt at cordiality. Ignoring Foster, he walked stiffly to the end of the aisle. There he opened the lavatory door, checked it visually for two minutes—including the ceiling—and closed the door. He then strode silently and rapidly back to the flight deck.

8

"*F*unny," said Alison Pitt-Barr as she lowered her copy of the *New York Times,* "I don't recall your being so thick with the president of this airline."

"There's a lot you don't know about me, Miss Brigadoon," flashed back Charlotte, adding, "and a lot you know I wish you didn't." She turned to Ralph Epstein. "Let me take a look at those proxy forms."

Epstein produced a small key and unlocked a section of his briefcase, from which he extracted a folder. "It's a risk," he said. "Cousins have been known to leave town."

Charlotte riffled through the forms. "Risk was exactly what I avoided. If I'd told them we were coming, it would have taken only one call to tip off Irwin."

"What options are open if they refuse?"

Charlotte burst out with harsh laughter. "Refuse? You don't know our family. They're not stupid. They can add."

"I've never advised trading away good money for bad," said Epstein. "I can't see—"

"No, you can't see," mimicked Charlotte, toying with a diamond earring. "You didn't watch a business your father gave forty years to, disintegrate while your brother had his head in the liquor cabinet." She pushed the lean-back button on her seat. "Two weeks before Father died, Irwin got him down to the office and made him change his will. Get the picture? I was just opening my first tearoom in Providence. In the middle of a divorce, desperately needing funding, and getting frost from the banks." Charlotte closed her eyes and tasted the resentment that rose like bile to her mouth. "And then ripped off by my blood brother, whose monthly booze bill alone would have carried us."

Alison had heard it all before. Epstein broke the silence

with, "At this moment I can say I'm glad I'm your lawyer and not your brother." Charlotte, eyes closed, did not react. He went on, "Try putting it into perspective. You're president of a highly successful franchise operation. You own all the keys. You're traded on the American stock exchange. It's only ninety days since your last split. You're on your way to Los Angeles to address people who have paid 500 dollars a head to hear how you did it. You're sure to pick up a few more franchises. And you want to spend your time messing in a funky little family disagreement!"

Charlotte shook her head, her eyes still closed. "You don't understand."

"Who cares? But what if the cousins don't understand?"

Charlotte opened her eyes. "I'm not worried about their signatures. They'll think they're picking up Krugerrand gold."

"But why get mad in the first place?"

"I'm not getting mad," replied Charlotte coolly, "I'm getting even. I want to see Irwin's face when I tell him he's fired."

Ralph looked at his slim platinum wristwatch and began to laugh. "I just thought—your brother won't be in his office until Monday, and by that time we all may be gone bye-bye."

"Bingo," said Alison.

"Baloney!" Charlotte sat up straight. "God wouldn't pull something like that on me. I've waited too long. How long will it take to transfer the stock—a week?"

"Depends." Ralph gave Alison a surreptitious wink. "I don't think Alison believes we have a week."

"Alison doesn't know what she believes," was Charlotte's response. "She's half Scotch and half plutowater."

"Oh, now, wait a minute," said Ralph with detached amusement. "We're none of us immortal, Charlotte. We all have to go some time."

But Charlotte ignored Ralph's reflections on eternity. "The Scots really are crazy, you know," she continued. "When I can't sleep I read Boswell's *Life of Samuel Johnson*. It seems in England oats is a grain they give to horses, but in Scotland it supports the people."

Alison rattled her newspaper. "The English could use some horse sense," she observed.

"I've got to remember that," Ralph chuckled. "In England the horses have all the brains. And speaking of horses—I'd like to see some of the countryside while I'm out here. Take a few days off."

"Once you've cleaned this up, your time is your own," said Charlotte. "You were going to look up that franchise in Malibu. But all I want is for you to hand me the controlling interest in Embree Drywall Incorporated, so I can say, 'Good-bye, Mr. President.' "

"Double, double, toil and trouble," muttered Alison.

"What did you say?" Epstein leaned forward and looked at her, laughing.

"Fire burn and caldron bubble."

Charlotte gave a disgusted snort. "Don't listen to her, she thinks she's Lady Macbeth." Examining her diamond-studded watch, she asked, "How much time before we land?"

9

"If it was some kid playing a joke, how could he make the plane drop the way it did?" Colleen Phillips in row 9 was talking to the distinguished-looking man seated beside her. He was Dr. Raymond Llewellyn Phillips, nuclear physicist, president-elect of the Pacific Institute of Technology and Science. They were on their way to inauguration ceremonies at the Azusa, California, campus.

Pulling at his patrician nose, Raymond Phillips looked at his wife and smiled. "It was a matter of timing. He was lucky."

"And you think God had nothing to do with it."

"I don't think, Colly. I know."

"How can you be so sure?" Colleen's face was troubled. It was a pretty face—or had been. Life had left deep marks under the gray-green eyes that makeup never could obliterate.

Dr. Phillips took a deep breath. "First of all," he said in the pedantic twang he used in the lecture hall, "there's the matter of congruity. Let's assume that some intelligence in outer space wished to transmit a message to this planet about—oh, about an impending shower of asteroids. Would it be sent to a collection of casual passengers on a domestic commercial airliner?"

"But this message wasn't like that."

"The point holds. Why would anyone send it to *us*?"

"I have no idea. All I know is, we heard it."

"The military has receptors all over this continent. Don't you think they would pick it up?"

"They could have."

"I get it." Dr. Phillips' lean face crinkled in amusement. "This was a message that should have gone to the Pope, or to some evangelical coalition, and we got it instead!"

Dr. Phillips enjoyed baiting his wife. Reducing her to tears was to him one of life's innocent pleasures. The deeper she went into antinuclear activities and (more recently) religion, the more opportunities she afforded him for his favorite indoor sport. And Colleen was always obliging.

"Did you think we were going to die?" she asked after a while.

Phillips looked at her with calm amusement. "The thought of death never bothers me. I say if the sky falls, let it fall."

Colleen picked up the book in her lap. "I know how you think. But you didn't always feel that way."

"It happens all the time. Dying is a process. That's all."

Colleen read aloud from her book.

"Tomorrow we shall meet, Death and I—
And he shall thrust his sword
Into one who is wide awake."

Her husband tapped the book. "Did Hammerskjöld write that?" She nodded. "He should have stuck to politics."

Colleen looked out the window. "It's ironic in a way," she said.

"What's ironic?"

"I mean if it's true. Here you come out and take this great position and then God steps in and says, 'Scrub everything!' "

Phillips slapped his knee irritably. "I told you it was a hoax. It couldn't be anything else."

"Why?"

"Because the only alternative is that a supernatural intrusion occurred. And that makes no sense whatever."

"Why doesn't it make sense? I really want to know." Colleen felt her pulse quickening.

"Because to accept that, the law of uniformity would have to be suspended."

"We split the atom, didn't we? And they said that couldn't be done."

Dr. Phillips pursed his lips. "Splitting the atom, Colly, was achieved by experimentation based on established scientific criteria." Taking a champagne glass from Sally, he explained to her, "My wife does not drink." He then asked Colleen, "Would you like a Coke?" When she demurred, he continued, "The whole principle of causality is at stake, don't you see? The voice was carried on sound waves from a specific source of energy. That's all there was to it."

Colleen tilted her pretty Irish nose. "I know your theories of mechanistic determinism, Raymond. But at thirty thousand feet or so I'm not finding you omniscient. And I have met a few God-fearing scientists."

"Cranks and enthusiasts, I imagine," hemmed Raymond.

"That doesn't reflect on them, love. It reflects on you." As Raymond lapsed into silence, Colleen persisted. "Suppose it wasn't any trick or fluke. What could have caused it?"

Raymond raised a hand in annoyance. "I really have no opinion. I'm occupied with other matters."

"I know. You're expecting trouble at the school." Colleen had seen a letter or two.

"Possibly." Raymond was annoyed that the subject had come up.

"Who is this Professor Alcorn they keep talking about?"

"He's the provost. The academic senate's overwhelming choice for president. A no-nuke—like you."

"Which is why the trustees picked you instead?"

"They picked me," replied Raymond testily, "because I was qualified."

"And—available. But now we're hearing about something else that may happen on Sunday."

"Sunday afternoon," said Phillips, sipping his champagne, "I expect to be in the amphitheater in Azusa, in robe, hood, and mortar board, being inducted into the presidency of the Pacific Institute of Technology and Science. And I expect you to be there, too."

"It will be a pleasure," said Colleen, standing up and smiling, "unless my other commitments interfere."

Dr. Phillips appeared mildly irked. "Just what do you mean by that remark?"

Colleen picked up her purse and moved past him into the aisle. "I don't know, love," she said. "I just may be going on a boat ride!"

10

As she made her way toward the rear lavatories, Colleen's eyes took in a curious cross-section of air travelers under stress. Some passengers carried on as if nothing had happened. A business man held his slightly banged-up attaché case on his knees while he studied production charts. A bald elderly man slept with his mouth open. A plump lady sipped champagne and scanned an in-flight magazine. Across the aisle from her a large gentleman sat rubbing his nose. A teenager who was one of the few interested in the movie now studied a sci-fi paperback that had fallen in his lap.

But the rest of the passengers were in varying states of agitation. Some of their talk was in loud and excited tones, and a few had turned around and were kneeling on their seats to converse with those in the row behind. Call bells seemed to be ringing every few seconds. Kristen was administering oxygen to a middle-aged Salvation Army officer who was apparently suffering from an asthma attack.

A mother of three was holding her fretting infant and trying to quiet her five-year-old son, who was whistling shrilly while his older sister lay with her head in the aisle and uttered animal calls. A solitaire player slapped his cards on his tray-table with unusual vigor, while next to him a woman was whispering and fingering her rosary beads. A blue-haired woman wept silently and continuously, dabbing at her eyes and nose. Snatches of conversation came to Colleen as she passed along the aisle:

"I wish I'd got to Spain. . . ."

". . . and I always make the crust the day before. . . ."

"I hope it's true. I'll take my chances with my Maker. In nine days I've got a fifty thousand dollar note coming due."

"By the actuarial tables I've got another fifteen years. . . ."

". . . of course I was just a little girl. . . ."

". . . and you let that policy lapse. . . ."

"I'm going back by the bus. . . ."

". . . she died right in my arms. . . ."

"The way I look at it, there must be some kind of continuation of life, don't you think. . . ?"

". . . then they fired the minister and that turned me off. . . ."

A grizzled rancher type was leaning back and singing softly,

> "I am going, said the hobo,
>   to a land so fair and bright,
> where handouts grow on bushes
>   and you sleep out every night."

In the seat adjoining the rancher a woman waited for him to stop singing, then asked him, "What's a five-letter word for junk?"

Near the rear of the plane Colleen found a line of people apparently waiting to use the lavatories. Minutes passed with no sign of activity, whereupon Colleen asked Maybelle Lewis, who was just ahead of her, "Is there some problem?"

Maybelle cuddled Henriette in the crook of her arm. "I'd say we're a whole lineup of problems!"

"Can't anything be done?"

"One of the doors has been locked for a long time. They say a girl's in there."

"Maybe we ought to help her."

Ralph Epstein, standing behind Colleen, chose that moment to remark, "Man has been defined as an ingenious system of internal plumbing. I suppose that would apply equally to woman?"

Maybelle turned, a droll expression in her blue eyes. "We've got a different set of drains."

Ralph began laughing. "Did you say drains or brains?"

"Both."

The grizzled rancher was now standing behind Epstein and singing softly:

"The dying hobo's head sank back
as he sang his last refrain;
his partner grabbed his shoes and socks
and caught the eastbound train."

For the first time, as he sat staring at his champagne glass, Raymond Phillips, Sc.D., LL.D., began to face head-on the matter of his future relationship with his wife of twenty-four years. Certain developments in her behavior raised the question as to whether she was not unfitted for the role of wife of the president of a renowned institution. True, she was a lady of grace and distinction, and in the past had proved to be an excellent hostess. She had many influential friends, and was a gifted speaker. But on the negative side, she was a reformed alcoholic.

Phillips wondered why the drinking business had not surfaced during the committee's investigation into his background.

Possibly Colleen's personal history had been skipped because he was a compromise candidate and had appeared late in the selection process. She had been dried out for more than three years, and the matter had been discreetly handled; it was a well-kept secret.

Two years ago, however, she had become involved in the antinuclear movement, which took so much time that it had been months since she had accompanied him to a scientific convention. Instead she had been attending environmental lectures and participating in peaceful marches and demonstrations, carrying signs and learning activist songs. She had avoided having such groups in her home, but had made no effort to hide her sympathies.

Lately Colleen had added to Raymond's list of her undesirable traits by becoming interested in religious groups. She was attending something called the Village Church, and had joined a weekly Bible study class. Phillips, a one-time seminary student who had long since parted company with the church, looked upon her growing spiritual activities with high disfavor.

The latest discussion over the voice in the airplane pointed up to him how far apart they really were as husband and wife. If there was one single group of people he despised above others, it was those who ranted about the end of the world. He remembered with avid distaste a particular seminary professor who never seemed to tire of talking up "prophecy." And now here it was again, thrust upon him by some nitwit through a fluke transmission. . . .

11

"Row 16, I think. He's got the window seat on the right as you go back, you can't miss him." Maybelle Lewis was visiting with Colleen Phillips as they stood in line for the lavatories. "They tested him out as a genius. He's only fifteen."

"Really!"

"Oh, yes. He skipped some grades. But I'll tell you, he's a handful to his parents. You never know what's coming out of that brain. His principal said he's living in the twenty-first century."

"How interesting"—not that it was to Colleen.

"But I know that kid, and I made a deal with him."

"Oh?"

"I told him if he behaved himself this summer and stayed away from the City Hall computers, I'd take him to visit a school in L.A. where he thinks he wants to go."

"Which one?"

"It's called Pacific Tech, I think."

"That's incredible! Pacific Institute of Technology and Science? We're on our way out there. My husband is the new president."

"Of Pacific Tech?" Maybelle's eyes and smile widened. "Isn't that something! Funny things happen on planes."

"On this plane, anyway," laughed Colleen. Since not many people carry dolls with them to the restroom, Colleen felt a further comment was necessary. "That's a beautiful doll you're holding."

Maybelle nodded. "She's a rare one. This type doesn't come on the market very often, but she's the reason for this trip. A dealer in Burbank is interested in her. Her name's Henriette, and she's a Jumeau." Aging fingers fondled the lace. Colleen took a closer look at the doll's delicately modeled bisque features and antique brocade clothing.

"She's exquisite. I don't know much about dolls."

"I've got over a thousand in my collection," said Maybelle happily. "We have a very active doll club in Schenectady. There's some kind of doll convention going on at this hotel in L.A. and that's where I'm meeting the interested party."

"What hotel?"

"The Bonaventure."

"Oh . . . well, I hope I meet your grandson sometime."

"Yes, perhaps—you don't suppose, Mrs. Phillips, I could bring Reginald where your sitting just to say hello to your husband. . . ?"

Jack Denlinger, a burly carnival operator, had joined the slowly moving line. Encouraged by the champagne, he began stabbing his finger toward the rear of the plane and singing a line from "Chloe":

> *"Through the black of night,*
> *I gotta go where you are. . . ."*

Denlinger followed it with a whistle. "Stewardess, you got a little problem here, dearie." Sally Carstairs paused, champagne bottle in hand, and looked back. "We got a gridlock in the number one head." Laughter followed.

"They're certainly taking their time," said Maybelle.

Sally handed her bottle to Kristen, but before she could move past the line, the door to the number one lavatory opened. Out stepped Mary Zlibin, a girl in her late teens, to be greeted with applause and cheers from those waiting in line. The girl's makeup failed to hide her blotchy complexion. The flesh around one eye was particularly tender. She wore black satin pegleg pants and a T-shirt that blazoned the words, SATISFACTION GUARANTEED. Her feet were encased in open-toed shoes with four-inch heels. Oblivious to the banter, she slipped past the line toward her seat. Sally stood by her row, holding her coat. "I'm moving you forward," she said.

"Whuffor?" Mary had just popped the last of her "reds."

"The captain wants you as comfortable as possible. Just take any empty seat."

Mary shrugged, clutched the coat, and walked forward to a row whose window seat was occupied by the blond young man wearing the blue-and-yellow sports jacket. He was reading a rather thick book. After sitting quietly in the aisle seat for a few minutes, Mary reached in her purse and took out a cigarette and a lighter. Then she opened a crumpled letter she had read many times. "Come and stay as long as you like," it read. "I love you." It was signed, "Stella."

The young man was speaking: "This is a nonsmoking section. Sorry." Mary inhaled deeply and blew the smoke at him. Then she snuffed out her cigarette. The young man had laid down his book and was staring at her with cold, ice-blue eyes. "Something still wrong back there?"

She turned and faced him. He was clearly upper middle class, outside her environment. Not that she hadn't met his type during her few weeks in New York, but the contact had been more commercial than social. Curly hair, aquiline nose, athletic physique—at one time she might have been romantically inclined. But that was before life had turned rancid and left her streetwise and atavistic. "Somebody upchucked on the seat."

The young man resumed his reading without comment. A snob, Mary decided. Thinks I'm trash. I'll give him a bad time. "What are you reading?" she demanded.

The young man shifted his legs. "Lucretius."

"What's that?"

"Philosophy." Then condescendingly, "Very dull."

Mary paused briefly. "What happens when you die?"

The tone went from smugness to exasperation. "Who knows?"

"You know where Ojai is?"

The young man gave up and closed his book. "It's a place outside L.A."

"How far?"

"Fifty—sixty miles, maybe."

Another pause. Then, "I wanna know what happens when you die."

The young man's nostrils flared as he sighed through his nose. "Depends on where you're coming from, I suppose. Were you expecting to die back there?"

"Uh huh."

"How are you going?"

"Huh?"

"To Ojai."

Mary shrugged. "Cab, I guess."

"Cab?" The young man sounded disdainful. "You mean a taxi? Nobody takes a taxi out there; it would bankrupt you. I think there's a Greyhound."

Mary ignored him and closed her eyes. The young man

subjected her to further scrutiny. Obviously she was a mess, probably a whore; yet despite her complexion, something about her sparkled. The nose was quite piquant, and one eye, at least, had a spontaneous look about it. The other showed the effects of a powerful blow, well-aimed. She was probably spaced out. Needed a bath. But with different clothes and some attention to skin and hair, he could see her in the pledge line at Chi Omega. She stirred, and a deep bruise appeared on her upper arm. He looked at his watch. In another hour he would never see her again. Thank God for that! Somebody had sure worked her over. He wondered what she was doing on the plane. Why all the talk about dying? Was she carrying a bomb?

"So that book doesn't say what happens when you die?" Mary's eyes were open.

The young man laughed briefly. "Lucretius? He says nothing happens. Less than nothing."

"D'you believe that?"

It was the young man's turn to shrug, but as he did so he winced and rubbed his shoulder. Turning to the window, he gaped at the red mountains of Arizona far below. Talk about filthy luck! His mother's death had forced him to fly east and miss the Stanford matches. U.C.L.A. had lost. Now, thanks to the flying briefcase that zapped him during the thunderstorm, he was nicely banged up for U.S.C. He could feel his shoulder stiffening.

Mary was speaking again. "That voice back there."

"What about it?"

"It was some knucklehead talking about the end of the world."

"Yeah. Forget it. It was a put-on."

"How did they work it?"

"Easy. Somebody planted a mike."

"Really? You're off the wall, son." The young man raised his eyebrows as she continued. "I can see the mike thing, and I'm not buying religion, but no kook could make that lightning hit us. You better pull up your socks. Somethin's goin' on."

The young man looked amused. "Coincidence."

"Yeah. Big coincidence." But Mary ignored his efforts to

resume his reading. "I'm not ready to die. I want to kick a few people in the groin first. What's your name?"

"Arvie. Why?"

"I'm Mary Zlibin. Arvie what?"

"Erickson." He regretted it the minute he said it.

"Do you go along with that book of yours?"

He looked at her disgustedly. "Look, I'm on my way back from my mother's funeral. Do you mind?"

"I'm sorry."

But Arvie's peace of mind was shattered, and as he reopened the book, the hexameters of Lucretius got no further than the retina of his eyes. What was she after? Was this a crude solicitation? Why the hang-up about death? Did she actually believe that stupid voice?

"On the right side," announced Officer Garrett, "we are approaching the Grand Canyon."

"For the last time," said Arvie, "don't pay any attention to what you heard back there. Somebody rigged it up."

"Did you hurt your shoulder?"

"An attaché case hit it."

Apropos of nothing, Mary said, "I used to go to Sunday school at First Baptist, Fergus Falls."

But Arvie had retreated into silence.

12

The huge foreign-looking man in row 27 had been squirming restlessly ever since the commotion surrounding the lightning strike. The phlegmatic behavior he had displayed from the time of boarding, staring inertly at the seat ahead of him, was no more. His face, which earlier resembled nothing so much as the Eigerwand in the Bernese Alps, had become contorted. He wiped his forehead and the back of his neck with a soiled handkerchief, caressed a mole over his brow, and fished out and put on a pair of tinted glasses. Then, after solemnly picking his teeth with a celluloid toothpick, he removed his passport from an inside pocket.

The document—for all the world as if it were true—disclosed that his name was Vasily N. Mechikoff and that he was born in 1949 in Erevan in the Georgian U.S.S.R. Thumbing idly through the little red book, Mechikoff saw that it was stamped with a B-1 United States visa. He examined several items tucked between the pages. One was the snapshot of a smiling young girl in a swing, which occupied his attention for some time. He then studied an official card on which was typed the name of Yakob Malof, the consulate attaché in San Francisco, who, so the card stated, would be meeting him at LAX.

Opening a folded slip of paper, Vasily read a brief note in his mother's shaky hand which ended with the words, "Natasha and I pray for you." His shoulders moved; something was obviously unsettling him.

If the cause of Vasily's inner agitation was homesickness— for his mother in Georgia, his wife and child in Leningrad—it had been exacerbated by the strange voice heard during the storm. He understood perfectly the words, having learned English well at the University of Tiflis. And while his mind totally rejected what he had heard, something deeper in his psyche was responding to it. He very much wanted to account for the phenomenon. Other passengers, he noted, seemed to shrug it off, but his training demanded that he not only take cognizance of the weird statement, but try to make sense of it.

To Vasily it was ludicrous to think that God existed, or that if He did, He would choose such a medium as an airplane to communicate with human beings. It had to be a joke. (He understood that Americans were obsessed with jokes.) For six years of his own childhood, until his father died, Vasily had been exposed to a peculiarly Slavic form of Christianity known in the rural districts of Soviet Georgia as "the Russian Molokan Church of Spiritual Jumpers." His father had been a collective farmer and an elder in the church.

The shock of his father's death during a kulak purge made it easy for Vasily to doubt the benevolence of a Supreme Being.

Later he joined the Young Communist League and embraced its ideology. His brilliant school record led to his being accepted for advanced technical training. As the Marxist indoctrination proceeded, his hostile attitude toward religion hardened.

Now as he sat aboard Flight 803, on special technological assignment to the West Coast, memories of his mother's teachings came back to Vasily and mingled with the accents of the strange voice. His mind kept reverting to the cadences of impending judgment. He took out his notebook and wrote the words of the message in Russian.

It was at that point in the journey that the fifteen-year-old boy in the window seat of row 16 spoke to him.

"Are you the Russian ambassador?"

Vasily Mechikoff turned and looked curiously at the boy. He saw a face dotted with a few pimples and weak eyes shielded by large, thick prescription lenses. Two or three black hairs had sprouted on the boy's upper lip. He was rather less than average height. In his lap he held a blue flight bag with the lettering, "Schroon Lake Bible Camp."

"No," Vasily replied, puffing out his lips for emphasis.

The boy was not daunted. "I saw your passport. Are you with the KGB?"

Vasily extracted a card from his pocket. As he did so, the boy, who seemed to be in his middle teens, added, "You're either a spy or a double agent. I won't tell anyone!"

Vasily handed him the card. It read, "V. N. Mechikoff. Amtorg Trading Company." He said kindly, "I'm a businessman."

After studying the card, the boy looked up. "I'll bet you're into data processing." When there was no response he added, "Do you sell computers?"

"I don't sell anyth—." Mechikoff sensed an opening and shifted gears. "What do you know about computers, young man?"

"I know a lot. I cracked the ARPANET network. And I copied game cartridges from Atari. Made up my own Pac-Man."

Vasily himself was well-known in some circles in the Soviet Union as a systems analyst specializing in international computer developments. He had read about the American "microkids" and their astonishing ventures into the computer industry. Putting aside his sentimental unprofitable reflections, he asked the boy, "Where do you go to school?"

"In Schenectady, New York. My dad's an engineer with General Electric, but I know more than he does about computers."

"I see. Schenec—"

"It's upstate. My grandmother's taking me to California. She thinks she can get me into Pacific Tech next year."

"Ah. The Pacific Institute of Technology and Science." Reginald gave a low whistle. "Boy, you *must* be a spy!"

"I am a businessman."

The boy would not be put off. "I read yesterday that you can pick up our telephone conversations from anywhere by microwave at your embassy in Washington. Is that right?"

Mechikoff shook his head. "I've never been to Washington. Let's talk about you."

The boy gave him a long squint. "You're tryin' to recruit me, ain't you? Suppose I turn you in. I bet they'd swap you for somebody big!"

"You are a very bright young man," said Mechikoff.

"My I.Q.'s 154," Reginald acknowledged. "I've formed my own computer company, and this fall I'm going to start selling graphic programs and computer games. A magazine has already written me up." He paused. "Did you hear what came over the loudspeaker back there in the storm?"

The huge Russian jaw trembled ever so slightly. "Tell me what it said."

"Well—" replied the youth, but at that instant he looked up and discovered his grandmother, Maybelle Lewis, standing in the aisle and clutching Henriette.

"Isn't it time, Reginald, you returned to your seat? I have a surprise for you. Some very important people want to meet you."

"Certainly, Grandma," said Reginald, displaying accommodation that was totally out of keeping with his character. Zipping shut his flight bag, he patted it and gave Vasily a knowing look. Then he squeezed past him and said to Maybelle, "I've got a surprise for you, too!"

13

D r. Raymond Phillips' face was a study in controlled irritation as he looked up at his wife, standing in the aisle. "You expect me to talk to some kid? Don't be an ass."

"I thought you'd be diverted. He's a pure scientific product, a clone of Einstein, one of your brain-children. You'll get a good look at the world of the future you're building."

"How'd you meet him?"

"He's with his grandmother. She says he's a genius and he wants to enroll next year at Pacific Tech."

"Please, Colly, I'm into these papers. . . ."

"You're not that busy," was the cool reply. "For all you know, this Mrs. Lewis may be rich. You could snare an endowment. Just tell them how he can go about signing up for next year."

"We don't take many freshmen. The standards are very high."

"Tell them that. They're staying at our hotel—you could even invite them to the reception tomorrow afternoon."

Raymond put down the brochure he had been reading. "Colly, you just don't go dragging strangers to something like that. You know better, or you ought to. The mayor's going to be there."

"So?"

Raymond fingered his mustache. "Where is this kid?"

Colleen returned in a moment with an eager Maybelle and a reluctant Reginald, and introduced them. Raymond nodded unsmilingly as he scrutinized Reginald closely. Breaking into Maybelle's pleasantries, he demanded, "What's your I.Q.?"

"Depends on which battery of tests you're working with," replied Reginald. "I'm in genius category in all of them."

"He's bright," added Maybelle with a tinkling laugh, "but I can't say he gets it from me."

Dr. Phillips gave a grunt and addressed the boy. "Suppose I bought a car for eleven thousand dollars and sold it for a thousand more than I lost on the deal. How much did I sell it for?"

"Six thousand dollars."

The president-elect picked an in-flight magazine out of the seat pocket and gazed at the cover. If he was startled, he did not show it. "What's your specialty?"

"Computer technology. I'm forming my own company."

"We'll see that you get some literature. I'm afraid the entrance examinations for freshmen students are rather formidable. The class is quite small." He nodded to Maybelle and resumed his perusal of the magazine. Maybelle left with Reginald, and Colleen followed them to their seats.

"Didn't you tell me you were staying at the Bonaventure Hotel?"

"Why, yes."

"We would like to invite you both to a civic reception they are giving my husband tomorrow afternoon."

"That's very kind of you."

"Come to the Balboa Room about 3 o'clock. We'll see that you meet some people from the school. I'll tell them to be watching for you."

14

Reginald St. Columba Tibbets was not happy about the new president of Pacific Tech. The man was obviously a "stiff." But so jubilant was the youth over the electronic masterstroke he had brought off during the storm that he pushed all thoughts of future schooling to the back of his mind. Meanwhile, Maybelle was sitting beside him, volubly emphasizing his good fortune and extolling a number of virtues that Reginald did not and (she feared) never would possess. But as wisdom continued to flow from his grandmother's lips, all Reginald could think was, "If she only knew! If she only knew!"

The idea had first occurred to him one Sunday morning six months earlier during an interminable sermon on the Second Coming of Christ. As the minister recapitulated the warnings and prophecies in the Bible, droning on in an unpleasant nasal inflection, Reginald glanced around at the congregation. He was struck with the thought, "They don't really believe this. Some of them are half asleep and the rest are thinking about something else." The more he reflected on it, the more the question arose in his mind, "What if they did?"

Reginald knew that if there was any one cardinal doctrine of faith emphasized by the pulpit week after week, it was that Jesus Christ was coming back, soon, to judge the earth. But what occupied the boy's finely tuned mind on successive Sunday mornings was, how could he test this conviction? How could he be sure that for people like his parents, the "end times" they talked about were nothing more than a religious fairy tale? And that led to the deeper question as to whether there was any truth in it at all. Just because everyone expected it to happen, did that mean it would? Science seemed to know nothing about Jesus coming back.

Reginald's parents attended an independent Bible church in Schenectady. They had placed their sons on the cradle role as soon as they were born, and had taken them to Sunday school faithfully. As they became aware of Reginald's precocity, they began praying long and earnestly over him. He was provided with numberless opportunities to give his life to Jesus. But unlike his younger brother Dick, Reginald had stubbornly maintained his independence of mind. He went to church with the family, but stayed neutral. As his grandmother put it, the boy was "a country mile from the kingdom."

When Dick went forward to commit his life during an

outdoor evangelistic rally in nearby Albany, Reginald thrilled his parents by joining his brother—but it was not with godly intent. Reginald merely wished to investigate the complex system of ground cables hooking up the sound console and the television cameras.

The idea of a controlled experiment was reinforced by the words of the monkey demon. Reginald did not like to dwell on his unhappy experience with PCP, but the chattering monster would not be silenced. *We know. The demons know. Angels don't, but we do!* And then that tantalizing word, *Pick a date!* As if it knew that he was already toying with the question, *if Christians really believed Christ was coming back right away, what would they do?*

Less than a week after that episode, Reginald was making plans. First he would put together some kind of doomsday pronouncement. Then he would get on the air waves with a simulated broadcast and observe the behavioral reactions of people. To prepare the message, he began to read through the Bible slowly and carefully; he wanted just the right wording. Drafts were written and discarded; the preparation of a supernatural communication became for him almost an obsession. He had been told to pick a date, and pick a date he would.

Once the final wording was decided upon, Reginald began some electronic experiments, using different filters to distort his voice on the tape recorder. Then, when his grandmother proposed taking him to California, things began to crystallize. The time had come to try out his plan in a bold and unique way, with a limited audience and under controlled conditions.

As the image of an airplane broadcast developed, Reginald began to investigate telephone apparatus. He paid surreptitious after-school visits to the Schenectady Municipal Airport, where he learned they would probably be flying in a Boeing 727. He was even able to slip aboard an empty parked plane and examine the public address handsets at front and rear.

Back in his lab, with all kinds of computer equipment at hand, Reginald set to work. The project called for the construction of a handset with a modified microphone cartridge, to which was added a small FM receiver on a couple of frequency-controlled integrated chips. This receiver contained a push-talk circuit which could key the integrated P.A. circuit and feed the audio into the system, with the microphone cord serving as the antenna.

In the flight bag which never left his lap, Reginald carried two portable tape recorders, one of which he had hollowed out himself to make into a 40-megahertz FM transmitter. This was the instrument that carried his message about "executing judgment and justice on the earth." The riskiest part of his game plan was unplugging Sally Carstairs' station microphone and inserting his own handmade mike. He accomplished this by sneaking his grandmother's boarding pass out of her ticket. When they boarded the plane, Maybelle was held up by Sally at the entrance. Reginald went ahead, quickly exchanged the microphones, and then gallantly produced his grandmother's boarding pass, to her great annoyance and relief.

The security check at the gate had proved no problem at all. The women inspectors who opened his flight bag looked briefly and perfunctorily at the telephone handset, earphones, microphones, tape recorders, and decoy learning tapes in Spanish and French. Since they were searching for firearms and found none, they waved him through.

The microphone he had substituted at Sally's station held a concealed cartridge that permitted normal usage and, when activated, would also convey a message. Some three hours after Flight 803 left Kennedy Airport, when the plane took a lightning hit, Reginald sensed that the psychological moment for his experiment had arrived. He had taken the precaution of moving away from Maybelle to an empty window seat. Then, opening his flight bag, he pressed the switch activating the transmitter's oscillator just before the aircraft went into its plunge. Confusion on the flight deck over the disconnected generator kept the flight engineer, Bricklebine, from investigating the intrusion and pulling the main circuit breaker.

For Reginald two immediate benefits resulted from the broadcast. The first was his immense gratification that the electronic skulduggery had worked: he had triumphantly invaded the airplane's communication system. The second was the startling effect the pronouncement had on the Russian passenger—a man who, Reginald was convinced, was one of his country's most dangerous enemies. This effect alone was worth the risk. It was a hazardous game, but Reginald was in no mood to quit.

15

*L*imping its way through the skies with two engines at twenty-four thousand feet, the Boeing 727 roared over the Grand Canyon and headed for the Colorado River. As the weather improved and the scenery became visible, faces were pressed against windows, looking for landmarks. Watches were set back to Pacific time. Already the lightning strike was proving a boring topic of conversation. Privately most passengers thanked their stars, crossed their fingers, and hoped for a safe landing. As for the voice, it was almost forgotten in the heady promise of life and love that awaited them.

As the flight attendants began gathering up the headsets, the calm was interrupted by musical sounds coming from three young people wearing T-shirts that proclaimed their allegiance to Calvary Bible College of Arcadia, California. "It won't be long," they sang, "till we'll be going home." The song was about heaven, but most who heard it thought it was about Los Angeles. A warm patter of applause greeted the melody's close, and one of the students promptly reached into the baggage closet for his guitar.

Within minutes raucous noises began to reverberate from the other end of the cabin. Jack Denlinger, who had been absorbing an abnormal quantity of champagne, swayed to his feet. Coat off and tie askew, he moved into the aisle, glass in hand, and declared loudly, "Now hear this! All human life will be totally discombobulated soon as I finish this drink!" His performance evoked an instant response from nearby passengers.

"Lay it on, pal!" said Nick Gavrilovich, the solitaire player. "Hallelujah!" shouted someone else.

Sally and Kristen tried good-naturedly to remove the glass from Denlinger's hand and to encourage him into his seat, but he proved difficult to budge. Holding his glass above his head, he burst again into song:

> *"The bells of hell go ting-a-ling-a-ling*
> *for you but not for me.*
> *For me the angels sing-a-ling-a-ling*
> *for me but not for thee!"*

For Charlotte Embree the eruption of the second sound was too much. Ordering Ralph Epstein to allow her past, she clambered into the aisle and stood with arms akimbo, muttering and glowering first at one scene, then at the other. Alison slipped out behind her and joined the group gathered about the young singers, drawn to the music as a butterfly to a field of poppies.

Now Charlotte was bellowing, "How do you expect us to hold a business conference with this floor show going on?"

None of the flight attendants responded, but from across the aisle came an unexpected response: "BILGEWATER!" The speaker was Nick Gavrilovich. This sixtyish, black-haired, tattooed individual had been working his lips as he played his cards. When Charlotte turned to see who dared to challenge her, he told her, "Take it easy, lady, they're not hurtin' anything."

Charlotte gave him one of her looks of high disdain. "That's what you think!"

Nick proceeded to slam down his cards one by one. "Aw, for cat's sake," he said, "sit down and tie a can on it!"

At that point an announcement came over the public address system that put an end to both words and music.

16

"Last chance. Ain't you drinkin', Colonel?" asked Gus Krieger in seat 13A after his champagne glass had been filled for the third time.

The paunchy Salvation Army officer in 13C opened his eyes, removed his glasses, and smiled as he gave a negative response. "I'm Commissioner Hilliard. Forgive me, I'm afraid I've not been very companionable on this trip. You saw my little bout with asthma." He spoke with a British colonial accent that stamped him as many years out of Sussex.

"Sorry about that," said Krieger.

Sally's voice came over the intercom. "Ladies and gentlemen, we have started our gradual descent into the Los Angeles area. We ask that all tray-tables be put away and all seats returned to their original locked position in preparation for landing. And please notice that the captain has turned on the seat belt sign. Thank you."

"Well, Colonel, what's your official opinion about that bump we took back there?" asked Krieger.

Commissioner Hilliard replaced his glasses and peered at the hard-lined and badly bruised face of his seatmate. "I suppose it was a bolt of lightning, but I really can't say. I'm from India, and I'm not used to traveling in your American planes. Mind you, we took a bit of a drop, didn't we?"

"A bit of a drop? Man, didn't you hear that voice?"

"Oh, yes, rather. I did hear something. I expect I'll be discussing it with my colleagues tomorrow."

"O.K., Colonel—"

"Commissioner, if you don't mind."

"C'mishner, right. Here's what you tell 'em tomorrow," said Krieger, holding up his glass. "The whole cotton-pickin' show ends sometime after Sunday afternoon. Got it? And I'll tell you somethin' else: I'm ready to go."

"Eh?" Hilliard adjusted his hearing aid.

"Look at me," continued Krieger. "Born under Capricorn. Jinxed by a crooked finger. See that?" He held it up. "I was born with it. See what happened to that mirror in the can? Know what day it is? Friday the thirteenth. Know what seat this is? Story of my life. Look at this horoscope I picked up at the airport. Read it! I mean, I'm pegged out. Ready to go. Wrap it up. Boom!"

"I don't believe I'm quite following you," said Commissioner Hilliard.

"O.K., Colonel, here I am on my way to jump off the Catalina ferry and drown myself, and now we hear this bird saying somebody else is doing it for me. Way to go! Better drink up, Colonel."

"Yes, well, thank you, but no, thank you. I used to—uh—be quite fond of sherry before I joined the colors, matter of fact. But I do believe we're coming in, aren't we, Mr.—er—"

"Krieger. Call me Gus."

"Oh, yes. Gus. Interesting. Named for Saint Augustin, I presume."

"Huh?"

"Gus, I've written a little message on hope that you might like to read. I always carry a few in my pocket. You never know." Commissioner Hilliard handed Gus a tract, which the latter examined while draining his glass.

"You wrote this?"

"Oh, many years ago. But I like to think it still has something to contribute, you might say."

"Thanks, pal. I'll read it later," said Gus, stuffing it into his shirt pocket.

Sally came by and picked up Krieger's glass. "We'll be on the ground in four minutes." Looking at Commissioner Hilliard she asked, "Are you all right, sir?"

"Oh, yes, fine, thank you." He turned to Gus. "It's been very nice chatting with you, Augustin. I do hope our paths cross again."

"Who knows, Colonel?" replied Krieger. "But if they do, I'll lay ten to one you won't be wearin' that monkey suit."

17

As the wheels of Intercontinental Airlines Flight 803 brushed, then settled smoothly on runway two-five right at Los Angeles International Airport, applause broke out among the passengers, along with cheering and expressions of relief. Emergency vehicles were now racing alongside the aircraft. Despite Sally's pleadings, most people were on their feet, impatient to vacate their abode in the sky and to start a less harrowing chapter in their lives.

Standing in the aisle, Arvie Erickson found himself directly behind Jordan Foster. He noted the clerical collar and was prompted to ask, "Did you get the message, Reverend?"

Foster turned around, surprised. "Are you kidding? You a brother?"

"Afraid not. I almost became one back there."

Foster took a tract from an inside pocket and handed it to Arvie. "Here," he said dryly, "this might unkink your thoughts."

"Thanks." Arvie tucked it away. "I'll smoke it later."

Sally Carstairs felt as if she could sleep for a week. She stood inside the forward exit saying good-bye as the passengers filed out, using her nose to stifle her yawns. Several stopped to express their thanks to the crew, others to indulge in broad humor. Giggling helped shake the drowsiness. Seeing Jordan Foster approaching, Sally was suddenly wide awake. She signaled the airline security officer on the jetway, and when Foster stepped out of the aircraft he found himself discreetly flanked by two airport policemen. While Sally watched, they invited him to accompany them to a room for questioning. Foster balked and demanded that the security officer show his credentials. Sally went back to the business of polite and smiling farewells, unaware that in the interval her station telephone had been unscrewed and a cartridge removed by the callow genius from Schenectady.

In the crowded baggage area Arvie Erickson spotted Mary waiting at the carousel, and moved casually alongside.

Mary was quickly aware of him. "Finish your book?"

"If you're stuck I'll run you out to Ojai."

"Don't trouble yourself."

"You're the one in trouble. I just thought . . ."

"You think too much, butcher boy." She turned and saw watching her a squat, burly man in open shirt and wrinkled trousers. "And you're too late." She reached for her bag, which was what the burly one was waiting for. He pushed between them.

"Mary?"

She tried to ignore him, but the man jerked the bag out of her hand, grasped her elbow, and hustled her toward the exit door. Arvie watched, frozen, as they moved outside toward a waiting Lincoln Continental, where the man squeezed in beside Mary on the front seat.

As the driver sped away, Arvie continued to stare until he heard a familiar voice behind him. "Nice friends you pick up!"

He turned to face his chief sexual interest of the moment, Brenda Cosgrove, president of Chi Omega sorority. She was wearing Gucci shoes and a stunning beige pantsuit, and kissed him on the cheek, adding, "Such popularity must be deserved."

"They put her in my row," said Arvie airily. "You can't believe what happened on that miserable flight."

"I heard people talking. What was it?"

"We were hit by lightning. I got it in the shoulder."

"Your friend looks as though she were hit by something."

Trying to divert the conversation, Arvie said, "I was kind of expecting some of the team or the guys from the house."

"Coach called me yesterday. Said he thought with the funeral, you'd had enough bad news without hearing all about Stanford. I had a date, but I said I'd meet you."

"You're very kind."

"How bad are you hurt?"

"Don't know yet."

"Think you're up to dinner and a piano recital?"

The prospect was appalling. Arvie struggled with his suit bag and finally asked, "Gerald Pomeroy?"

Brenda nodded. "I promised I'd go. I know you like Chinese food."

"I'm a mess."

"It's a private party. You can bring your bag and change if you want. I mean, if you feel like it. Here, let me help you. . . ."

A sorority sister was waiting in a Porsche as Arvie and Brenda emerged from the baggage claim. They were followed by Gus Krieger, who came through the door in company with a short-haired man who escorted him to an unmarked Ford. Except for a two-way radio, nothing suggested a government vehicle.

A sleek limousine drove up and a chauffeur leaped out to open doors for Charlotte Embree and Ralph Epstein. Alison waited to see that the baggage was safely stowed, then joined them.

An Oldsmobile bearing diplomatic license plates arrived next for Vasily Mechikoff, who had trouble squeezing his frame into the backseat. He was followed by a man who clutched a black briefcase in a tight grip. After they were seated, a third figure emerged from the crowd on the sidewalk and joined the driver in the front seat.

A Cadillac from the Pacific Institute of Technology and Science, driven by a young man in uniform, pulled up, and doors were opened for Dr. and Mrs. Raymond Phillips. But before the car could drive off, it was surrounded by a dozen placard-waving students chanting, "WE WANT ALCORN! WE WANT ALCORN!" The driver nervously threaded his way through the throng.

Finally, a gasping Volkswagen van arrived from Calvary Bible College, and the three musicians piled in with their luggage and instruments. As the van departed for Arcadia, its rear bumper announced to the public, "IN CASE OF RAPTURE, THIS CAR WILL BE UNMANNED!"

18

Airport police escorted the Reverend Jordan Foster into the gate area and toward a small office normally used by an airline ticket agent. As they crossed the waiting room, a slim young woman wearing dark glasses rose to her feet. Foster was barely able to look in her direction before disappearing through the door.

He was presented to a Mr. Pfaff, seated at a desk, who explained he was the F.B.I. resident agent at LAX. Foster was invited to empty his pockets on the desk and to sit in a straight-backed chair. Standing around the desk were another F.B.I. agent, the airline security officer, and a policeman. The interrogation began on a note of restrained hostility. Foster was asked for his driver's license, which he took from his wallet on the desk.

"May I inquire why you were traveling on this flight?"

Jordan Foster was all too familiar with the kind of authority he was now facing. He had no doubt that he was being marked as a scapegoat for the strange occurrences on Flight 803. What infuriated him was that he felt he had been singled out without any basis, not because he was a minister, but because he was black.

"I was on a business trip."

"What are your New York connections?"

Jordan widened his eyes. "Connections?"

"Were you on church business?"

"Of course."

"In New York?"

"That happens to be our church headquarters."

"I see. Traveling alone?" Foster nodded. "Mr. Foster, the pilot reports that some kind of religious message was picked up by the passengers on the flight. Did you have anything to do with it?"

"Nothing."

"You didn't say anything or reproduce anything between New York and here that fit the description?"

"I heard what the others heard."

"And what was that?"

"What they told you."

Pfaff showed signs of impatience. "Why did you go into the toilet after the seat belt sign was flashed?"

The corners of Foster's mouth twitched. "Because I had to. That's usually the—"

"Did you bring any electronic equipment on board with you?"

"Of course not."

"Did you contact any electronic firms in New York?"

"Why should I?"

"Mr. Foster," said Pfaff, adopting a more conciliatory tone, "no charges are pending against you. We are simply investigating an unusual audio reception on your flight. Perhaps it would help if you detailed for us your movements in the New York area."

"You think I might be a hijacker?" demanded Foster.

"We are authorized to investigate crimes aboard aircraft," said Pfaff elliptically.

Among the belongings Foster had taken out of his pockets was an envelope. He now picked it up from the desk and silently handed it to Pfaff. It bore the postmark Washington, D.C. and the imprint, "The White House." Pfaff opened the envelope and read the letter quickly.

"You attended this meeting?"

"I did."

Pfaff swung around, held the letter to the window, and examined its watermark. The American eagle showed plainly. He returned the letter to the desk, pushed back his chair, and said, "No further questions at this time. We know where to get in touch with you."

"Any further questions," said Foster coldly, rising and taking his belongings from the desk, "are referred to my attorney." He paused in the open doorway. "I wish you well in your attempt to unscrew the inscrutable."

19

"All I know," said Roger Gillespie of the F.B.I. as he and his passenger, Gus Krieger, crossed the Sepulveda underpass, "is that you were involved in a heist, and became an informant."

"I *was* an informant. Now I'm nothin'. What's that sign mean?" Gus pointed with a toothpick to a flashing neon at the corner of Century Boulevard and La Cienega which read, "COME TO THE ARK."

"Just pushing a place outside the city. Why?"

"Forget it. What time you got?"

"Five thirty. I was saying you were an escort on that shipment of plutonium to the Middle East. . . ."

"You got it all on tape back there." Krieger turned the digits on his watch. "This was not my caper, see? I was just helping out a guy I knew in upstate New York."

"Attica?" asked Gillespie, but Krieger ignored him. The agent continued, "How much was involved?"

Krieger spread his hands. "Who knows? All I saw were some lead containers." He fished out a cigarette. "This whole thing was flaky from the start. I was just excess baggage."

"Who worked you over?"

Krieger touched the welt on his cheekbone. "As if you didn't know."

"The office says there's a contract out on you."

"I know." Gus snapped his fingers. "My life ain't worth that. And you know something, mister? I don't care. They conned me, and I went to your boys, and I'd do it again, only next time I'd do it somewhere else."

Gillespie stopped his car on Figueroa Street in front of the Bonaventure Hotel. "Mr. Krieger," he said, "the government

appreciates your cooperation in this investigation. It's not finished yet, but you have your immunity. If you want, we'll program you with a fresh identity."

"I'll get out here," said Gus.

"The agent supervisor asked me to give you this." Gillespie
handed him an envelope. Krieger took it, looked inside, and
pocketed it without comment. "You have relatives out here?"
Gus shook his head. "We can put a man in the next room." Gus
opened the door. "Nothing more I can do?"

"Nothing."

"Here's my card anyway."

Krieger took it in his thumb and forefinger and shook it at
the agent. "Look, just forget about me. I'm free as a bird and
don't owe nothing to nobody."

"Just be careful," said the agent.

"Oh, I ain't bumping myself off," said Krieger, misunder-
standing him, "not now. And I ain't playin' hardball. The way I
see it, the score is even. Tell 'em that from here on out it's all fun
and games."

"See you," said Gillespie.

"Yeah," said Krieger, dropping the card in the gutter. As the
agent pulled away he muttered, "In hell."

20

Seated in the yellow Opel GT, Sally Carstairs let the breeze
from the ocean blow through her rich auburn hair as her
friend Diane drove them east on Los Angeles' Century Boulevard. Diane was talking about the captivating plans for the
evening.

Diane had looked forward to this reunion for weeks. She
and Sally had attended the same high school in South Dakota.
After her divorce, Diane moved from Rapid City to Los Angeles,
where she had acquired a boyfriend and a handsome position
with a Malibu decorating firm. Sally had been out once to see

her. Sally was not that fond of Diane, whose lank hair and willowy figure contrasted oddly with Sally's compact frame. Diane moved with the swingers, and Sally found party life uncongenial with the discipline of a flying career—at least, uncongenial to her stomach. Gin-fizzes and coke-sniffing tended to fight Intercontinental departure schedules. And Sally liked her job.

As they moved onto the San Diego Freeway Sally noticed the multicolored sign, "COME TO THE ARK" at the corner of Century and La Cienega. "Isn't that sign new?"

"What sign? I'm watching traffic."

"Back there. 'Come to the Ark.' I don't remember seeing it my last time out."

"It's a new superamusement park near Ojai."

As they drove along the ocean shoreline Sally let Diane chatter away, but when they approached Malibu, Sally spoke up: "I have a funny kind of request to make, Di. Do you suppose they have a public library in Malibu?"

"A library? What do you want a library for?"

"There's a book I want to look up."

"What's the name of it?"

"I dunno . . . it's a book on fashion design. Somebody told me about it."

"Do you know the author?"

"I think so." Sally was feeling less comfortable by the minute.

"I'll take you to a bookstore I know. They ought to have it. But we won't have much time."

"It's got to be the library."

Diane took out her annoyance on the accelerator. "Why, for heaven's sake? We can go tomorrow."

"They won't be open tomorrow."

"But you've got to unpack and press your clothes. The fellows will be picking us up at 8 o'clock, They've got reservations and it's a big deal. I mean, if it's something that means a lot to you—"

"It means a lot to me."

"A book on fashion design and you don't even know what it is?"

"I'm sorry."

Diane stopped at a filling station telephone booth. Half an hour later she was sitting in her car, tapping the steering wheel with her fingers and listening to "your fifty-thousand-watt news voice for southern California." Meanwhile, Sally was standing before the reference desk in the Malibu Public Library, facing a rather shriveled, pleasant-faced lady with white hair. The nameplate read, "Mrs. Van Roux."

"May I help you?"

"I have just a minute," said Sally, "but I'd like to see what you have on heaven."

"Heaven. Yes, of course. We've not much, I'm afraid, but it would be in our nonfiction stacks, about 230."

In five minutes Sally was back. "I couldn't seem to find anything except a lot of theological arguing."

"I was afraid of that," said Mrs. Van Roux. "Just step over here. I've located a few lines in the encyclopedia."

Putting on her glasses, Sally read:

"HEAVEN, the expanse of space surrounding the earth, especially that which seems to be over the earth like a great arch or vault or inverted bowl (the firmament); the place above and around us where the sun, moon and stars appear; the sky; the region of the clouds and winds and flying birds. Cf. ether . . ."

Sally closed the book and returned to the reference desk. "This isn't helping me much."

"Oh?" Mrs. Van Roux expressed surprise. "You asked for heaven, didn't you? I thought I found the right place."

"If that's the right place, I've got the wrong place. What else might you have?"

"Dear me. Well, let's see. Do you want a Catholic or a Protestant book?"

" 'Do I want—' Heaven's just one place, isn't it?"

Mrs. Van Roux blushed. "I really couldn't say. I'm Episcopal myself."

"And where does that put you, if I may ask?"

Mrs. Van Roux's hand went to her throat. "It's really a matter of interpretation, isn't it?"

Sally looked at her wristwatch. "I think what I want is not an interpretation but a prospectus. A kind of tour guide. I want to know what it's like. You've got somebody who's totally ignorant on the subject. I'd like to know whether heaven is blue or pink or green, whether it has furniture and shops and transportation and running water."

"Is this for a paper you're doing?" inquired Mrs. Van Roux.

"Paper my eyeball!" exploded Sally.

"Shhh."

"Isn't there a book somewhere on 'Heaven and How to Get There?' "

"If there is, I've not heard of it. You might look over our shelf of new books. Or you could try the microfilm reader. We're just a branch; it may be somewhere else in the county."

"How long would it take to get such a book?"

"A week to a month, if it's in our system. I can check *Books in Print*."

At this point Diane marched into the library and made straight for Sally. "*What* is going on?" she demanded.

"Shhh," said Mrs. Van Roux.

"We're way late," insisted Diane. "Can't this blasted book wait till Monday?"

"You're going to have to keep your voice down," said Mrs. Van Roux.

"I'm sorry, Di," said Sally, "this is more important than your date tonight."

"What do you mean? We've had this set up for a month. And Jerry hates to be kept waiting."

"Why don't you go on?" urged Sally. "I'll get a cab."

"Listen, I quit work early to meet your plane, and fought all that traffic, and now you—"

"Shhh," said Mrs. Van Roux.

Sally decided to be difficult. "What's so momentous about this date anyway?"

"Momentous? You're out to lunch, woman—"

Mrs. Van Roux reached for the telephone. "Just let me try something. Father Jessup happens to be on our library board. He's the rector at St. James, and maybe he can help us out."

"Help us out!" yelled Diane. "We don't need a rector; we need a kidnaper to get this woman over to my place!"

A tall, bespectacled gentleman emerged from an inner office and spoke to Diane. "I'm sorry, I'm going to ask you to leave the building. You are disturbing people. Will you come this way?"

Diane stared at him defiantly, then turned on Sally. "If Jerry backs out of that condo deal because of you—"

But while her indignant friend was being escorted out, Sally was listening to Mrs. Van Roux, who was saying, "I suggest you look at our subject catalogue under 'H' while I'm on the telephone." The subject catalogue turned up nothing, but when Sally returned to the reference desk, the librarian's countenance was serene.

"Father Jessup says he will be speaking on this very subject at Vespers next Sunday, and you're invited. We serve coffee and refreshments afterward."

"What time is Vespers?" asked Sally, looking again at her watch.

"Five o'clock."

"That may be too late."

"I beg your pardon?"

"I said it may be too late. I mean—oh, forget it!"

Diane made a reappearance. "What's the holdup this time?" she demanded in a stage whisper.

"Shhh," said Mrs. Van Roux.

"I'm coming," said Sally.

"Father suggested you might look in the closing chapters of Revelation," said Mrs. Van Roux.

"Where's that?"

"In the Bible."

"The Bible?" Diane was once more in full voice. "I thought you wanted something on clothing design!"

"I'm going to ask you to leave again," said the bespectacled gentleman. "And this time—"

"Who wrote it?" asked Sally, ignoring them.

"Revelation?" Mrs. Van Roux was by now considerably agitated. "Why, St. John, I'm sure."

"St. John? That's not Pope John?"

Mrs. Van Roux glanced at the large clock on the wall as Diane made her second exit under constraint. "I'm sorry, we're closing now. You may have time to check the Bibles in section 220 if you hurry."

"I have a Bible at home," said Sally, apropos of nothing at all. "Look at the table of contents. . . ."

"All right," said Sally to Diane as she got in the car, "let's try the bookstore."

21

The two Russians got out of the Oldsmobile limousine at Pershing Square, a tiny green oasis in the smoggy heart of downtown Los Angeles. "We shall walk," said Malof, the consular attaché from San Francisco. "Slivkov will take your luggage to the hotel and book you in." After the car drove off he added, "He is a Ukrainian. I never trust Ukrainians."

For several minutes they strolled among the Angelenos who were sitting, eating, sleeping, talking, listening to music, and jogging in the afternoon haze. When they reached a less populated area of the park, Malof broke the silence. "You are a systems analyst with Amtorg, on assignment to the scientific and technical branch in New York."

"Yes, comrade."

"Tomorrow you will be attending the convention. Here is your room key and your registration, and a full list of delegates with their connections. You are to seek out and meet certain people whose names are checked. The consul general is particularly interested in the electronics and high-technology men who will be attending from San Jose."

Vasily Mechikoff sighed heavily.

"You will make purposeful acquaintances with all of these, size them up, and report to me fully."

"Yes, comrade."

"If they invite you to visit their laboratories, you will accept, but you will take no notes and make no effort to recruit. You will be affable, curious, and knowledgeable. Is that clear?"

"It is clear. I am glad, comrade. I qualify better as a software technician than as a recruiter."

"You leave that to us."

"But when they learn I am from the Soviet Union—?"

"You will learn how capitalism works in imperialist countries," said Malof patiently. "These people are the true enemies of the revolution. They are not military or government; they are what they call big business. They run half the world. But if they think money is to be made by dealing with us, they will deal. Your assignment is to provide us with profiles of the men who are developing and manufacturing this software. The productive contacts you make will be screened later."

"Yes, comrade."

"Now tell me about your flight from New York."

Vasily first described two passengers, one he understood was about to become president of the Pacific Institute of Technology in Azusa, the other a woman who would be speaking at this convention. Malof nodded approvingly. Vasily then told of the storm they encountered, the damage to the plane, and the mysterious announcement that followed the lightning strike. Malof showed interest and asked a number of questions.

"I confess I do not understand the American behavior," Vasily concluded. "Was it a joke, comrade?"

Malof studied a flight of Navy F-14's overhead, zooming toward Miramar Air Base to the south. "In politics," he said, "there are no jokes."

"Then what do you think?"

"I do not think, comrade. Your report will be transmitted

and I shall await instructions. Just where did this storm occur?"

"Over the mountains. Colorado, I think they said."

"Ah, yes. Colorado. This is very significant."

That night, after Malof had relayed his coded information to the San Francisco consulate, a telex went out from the consulate to Moscow.

22

At 7 o'clock Charlotte was talking on the golden telephone in the Huntington Suite, which comprised the penthouse at the top of the Bonaventure's green tower. Alison, who had been in Charlotte's bedroom opening suitcases and hanging up clothes, came into the luxurious sitting room to answer a knock at the door. Two maintenance men in white coveralls entered, struggling with a massive antique desk. Alison pushed aside a small table to make room while Charlotte gestured to have the desk placed before the curved glass wall that overlooked several roof gardens in metropolitan Los Angeles.

Charlotte put down the phone and examined the desk critically as the men wheeled in a large office chair. "I told your manager I was not going to sit at that scrawny glass-and-chrome thing you call a desk, not for fourteen hundred dollars a day." She rubbed the surface of the new desk with her hand. "Could stand some refinishing."

"It was last used when this was the Presidential Suite," offered one of the men as he wielded a dust cloth.

"Probably English, late eighteenth century," said Charlotte. "Anyway, it's not Grand Rapids. Which President was it that used it?"

"I'm told it was Gerald Ford."

"You can tell your manager if he's interested in cutting down on storage, I might like to purchase it."

The men kept dusting and polishing the desk until Charlotte gestured to Alison, who found her purse and came up with a gratuity. After that they departed speedily. Alison then placed a briefcase on the antique desk, stripped the cellophane from a massive basket of fruit on a side table, and flopped onto a deep sofa with an apple.

Charlotte stared at her. It seemed her secretary was acting a bit out of character. "Do you intend to have a menu sent up?"

"It's on its way," replied Alison.

Charlotte had stopped frequenting hotel dining rooms years before, not because she was instantly recognizable, but because the food and service, she found, seldom matched the size of the menu. Charlotte's culinary standards were higher than most chefs' hats. Room service was equally up for judgment before her; but it seemed that if one could sit at table in a dressing gown and not be surrounded by strangers, much could be excused.

On her part Alison, by adroit use of the Scottish burr, could order and get the breakfast menu for dinner no matter where they were. Charlotte subscribed to the belief that eggs in their simplest form narrowed the margin for error, especially when one was away from home.

Thus it transpired that while Sally Carstairs and her friend Diane were throwing themselves into evening attire in a Malibu condominium, and Mary Zlibin was facing the perils of Sunset Strip, Charlotte Embree and Alison Pitt-Barr were sitting down to a cheese omelette. Alison did the serving at a table on wheels with a pink linen tablecloth, set up near the empty fireplace in the sitting room.

Alison had just poured the tea when the telephone rang. She stepped to the desk and heard Ralph Epstein's voice on the line. "I have contacted one of the cousins and am on my way out to see her. Tell Charlotte the proxies look as if they're in the bag."

"Does that mean they're agreeable to signing?" asked Alison sharply.

"Agreeable? This one sounds ecstatic!"

Alison relayed the news to Charlotte, who lifted her wineglass in a gesture of triumph.

After the two occupants of the Huntington Suite finished their meal, Charlotte took her coffee cup and moved to the desk, which by now was furnished with a brass tole lamp. She was soon immersed in the papers before her, while Alison sat quietly at the little table, studying her employer. The events of the day seemed to have left no mark on the woman. If a global countdown were indeed in progress, Charlotte seemed totally unaware of it. For her, life moved as it had always moved, centripetally.

Alison drained her cup, then rearranged the dishes in order to lower the sides of the table and push it into the hall. She then telephoned room service and turned to Charlotte. "The chef wishes you to know that he gave special attention to your omelette. He hopes it was pleasurable."

"You tell the chef," said Charlotte without looking up, "that a cheese omelette does not have to be distinctively pleasurable, but that a chef should know the difference between Gruyère in the French manner and some processed wonder that tastes like Kraft American."

But before she had finished, Alison affirmed her employer's sincere gratitude and hung up.

The assistant manager, Mr. Battersby, made a brief appearance in the penthouse to ascertain that "everything is all right" and was given brisk instructions for breakfast, after which he made a polite and rapid exit.

With the city skyline a dusty silhouette, and the lighted towers of the Bonaventure taking form in the advancing darkness, Alison picked up her tote bag.

"Don't go," said Charlotte.

"What?" Alison was startled.

"Why don't you stay out here? I won't bother you. You can read or watch television."

Something, mused Alison, is bothering her. Dutifully she took her tote bag to the sofa where, after switching on a lamp, she sank into a relaxed after-dinner mood. From the bag she extracted Samuel Rutherford's *Letters* and the copy of the *New York Times* she had picked up on the airplane. Turning to an inside page of the newspaper, she began to peruse it lazily, but within a few minutes she was sitting up straight, reading aloud to Charlotte a news story with an overseas dateline.

"Listen to this: 'The librarian of the Free University of Amsterdam today announced the discovery of a reputed fragment of the long-sought Gospel of the Hebrews, containing a previously unrecorded saying of Jesus that he intended to announce in advance his return to earth.'"

"Let me see that," ordered Charlotte. Alison obediently handed her the section of the *Times*. She read, " 'The quotation from the noncanonical gospel was found in a rare first edition of the Medulla Sacrae Theologiae—' " Charlotte stumbled, then read with increasing speed. " '—published in Holland by a seventeenth-century English controversialist named William Ames. . . .' " Charlotte handed back the paper to Alison with sublime disinterest. "Here."

Alison took it back. "You missed the best part," she said, moving nearer the window to get a better light. "Something about Jesus telling His disciples—here it is—'before the Son of Man cometh . . . is it not written in the Testament of Daniel that His appearing for His church shall be portended to an assemblage chosen of the Father's own pleasure?' " Alison began pacing the room. "Did you hear that? It ties in perfectly with what the voice on the plane said. And it came out the same day! It's incredible!" Her face was flushed with excitement.

"If you've had your fun," murmured Charlotte, marking up her rough draft with her gold pen, "I'll get back to work."

But the import of the newspaper account was coming home to Alison. Her Scottish reserve, which usually kept her from letting herself go in the presence of her employer, was proving unable to control her feelings. Whatever this meant, it was giving rise to thoughts too big for the room she was in.

"If you don't mind," said Alison, collecting her things, "I'll see you in the morning."

Charlotte did not bother to look up.

"I've got a dog on my hands."

Diane read Tony's note, scrawled on a paper napkin, with a sense of utter frustration. They were seated at the Paddington Station, a posh seaside restaurant, and for the past half hour, in spite of several rounds of drinks, the conversation had sagged. The party started late, and by the time the food arrived, no one was in a mood of high elation. On the contrary, the jokes were taking on an increasingly hostile edge.

That Sally was the villain of the piece everyone understood, including Sally. It was unfortunate, however, that the bearded gentlemen escorts, Jerry and Tony, chose to devote the entire evening to extolling their prowess at running wild rivers, since the only river with which Sally was acquainted was a trickle called Bull Creek in the plains of Dakota.

Eventually the party moved to the Riviera Club, where Diane had a chance to speak her mind in the powder room. "I don't know what's eating you, but this is my party, and so far it's a lemon squash."

"I'm sorry, Di—"

"Don't give me that. You've been spooked ever since I picked you up. Here's this guy, on his way to the top in western wear, and you act as though he was the Night Stalker."

"He's O.K., I guess. I just feel as if I've been capsized in the Colorado River."

"Well, he told me he'd been oversold on you."

They returned to find Tony and Jerry arguing about the skills of Idaho river men as opposed to their California counterparts. The issue was left dangling as the couples engaged in some desultory dancing. They returned to their table to look at their watches and consider the prospects for the rest of the evening.

"I'm off for Atlanta tomorrow," said Jerry. "Meetin' some guys and we're takin' on the Chattahoochee. Some Class V stuff. They claim it beats anything in the West."

This led to a machismo-style discussion of rubber rafts, kayaks, dories, and other means of river transportation. Finally Tony glanced at Sally. "How about dropping over to my place?"

Sally returned his look, deadpan. "So I can have breakfast in bed?"

The issue being joined, Tony leaned back and surveyed her. "What you got against sex?"

"Nothing, really."

A pregnant silence followed, until Sally broke it with a query: "Is there sex in heaven?"

Jerry started to laugh. Tony was baffled. Diane looked as if she had been handed a fish.

"I don't know about heaven," said Jerry, "but hell has a reputation as a pretty sexy place. Why don't you just go to hell and find out?"

"That's what's bugging you," said Diane. "You've been going to church!"

Sally shook her head. "Nope. Haven't been to church in three years."

"We can have church here!" announced Jerry. "Let's have some more drinks. Di, you can be the reverend. Come on, get in the spirit. Preach it up, sister!"

"I'll be the rabbi," said Tony, warming to the idea.

"You mean the deacon." Jerry handed him a saucer. "Here, take the collection. Now you folks realize these telecasts cost a lot of money. But for everyone who writes in, we will send you free and postage-paid this beautiful quart bottle of Stolichnaya vodka, direct from the cellars of the Lubiyanka prison. . . ."

Tony began to sing "When the Saints Go Marching In."

Whereupon Sally (who was not ready either to ride with Jerry or sleep with Tony) marched out, leaving Diane to pronounce the benediction.

24

"Come in, come in!" said Dean Mallory, his face rosy with hospitality as he opened the door of his on-campus home to the three Calvary Bible College students, fresh from Flight 803. "Glad you telephoned. How's it feel to go big-time on television?"

The hearty greeting drew snickers of embarrassment from his guests. They were well aware that the dean was camouflaging his real feelings. Since they first invaded the campus three weeks ago, they had been making raucous notes in the pastoral symphony of Bible school life and putting burrs under the dean's saddle. So different was their lifestyle that they had become known to faculty and administrative personnel as "objects of prayerful concern."

That the trio was in school at all was due to the questionable enthusiasm of a wealthy pizza manufacturer who sat on Calvary's board of trustees. This zealous gentleman had offered musical scholarships to half a dozen rock groups that hung around the local church he attended. The church itself, an enormous complex known as Restoration Chapel, drew some ten thousand people through its doors each week—most of them young.

As it turned out, the only musical group that Calvary College's board of admissions would accept was the most popular of them all, known as "The Lofters." And even in their case some academic scruples had to be overcome. Two of the Lofters were high school dropouts, and their entrance examination scores were such that they qualified only as probationers.

The Lofters, who arrived that night at the dean's house, were made up of Rick Ramsey, guitar and electric bass; Linda McDowell, guitar; and Rennie Lopez, trap case, snare, and high hat. Together they put out a sensational sound that was becoming known in the world of Christian rock. They had cut their first record, and were fresh from an exciting appearance on the

CBN Christian television network at its headquarters in Virginia. They were nineteen years old, and for each only two things seemed to matter in life: music and Jesus.

Linda was an adopted child, part Cherokee Indian, with an astonishing voice that ranged from low and mellow to the high screech of punk rock. Her hair, once dark and glossy, was now wild and gnarly and showed a streak of bleached blonde. Her parents had moved west from Bartlesville, Oklahoma, precipitating a domestic crisis. But before Linda made up her mind to split, a neighbor girl took her to Restoration Chapel and she was saved.

Less than a week later she met Rennie, the son of undocumented Mexican aliens who had moved north from Guadalajara before he was born. Rennie's musical career began at age two when he started beating a suitcase with the end of a stick. One Sunday when he was seventeen some rock musicians from Restoration Chapel spoke to his soul on the beach at Santa Monica when the surfing was poor and he was recovering from a bad trip. Linda was in the group. She and Rennie quickly became friends, and his conversion followed during a concert on a glorious Sunday night at the Chapel.

Rick, the leader of the trio, was a Methodist minister's son who could play any instrument, but who had been turned off by his father's explosive temper at the age of twelve. He disappeared for the better part of a year, then returned and completed high school, during which time he took up a number of radical causes. Tall, brilliant, and sullen, Rick stayed completely aloof from church until one night when he wandered into a rock concert at a downtown theater in Los Angeles. The performers were from Restoration Chapel. Afterward a young man appeared on stage in dress pants, white shirt, and black string tie that contrasted oddly with his partial Mohawk haircut. He gave a Christian testimony, and as a result Rick Ramsey (much to his own amazement) was saved. He began attending services at the Chapel, moved into a church-sponsored commune, and quickly became a popular writer of contemporary Christian rock. Whether old beat, new wave, rockabilly, punk, or hymns of worship, Rick had a pure touch.

Life on campus, however, was fast approaching the proportions of a debacle, and it was only the prospect of the immediate end of the world that sent the Lofters to the house of Dean Mallory. Linda opened the conversation lamely by asking, "Did you watch the show?"

"Watch it?" exclaimed the dean. "The whole student body watched it! We thought it was great. . . . Well, sit down. You must be tired from the trip."

"We only got in three hours ago," said Rick.

"What can I do for you?"

Rick proceeded to relate to the dean their experience on Flight 803, beginning with the storm, the lightning strike, and the mysterious voice. Dean Mallory's face became grave. After the other two had added their impressions, he ran his hand over the top of his sparse hair.

"Have you talked to anyone about this?"

"We decided to ask you about it first," said Linda.

"Anyone at all?" The dean looked at her sternly.

"I did call home and talked to Mom," Linda admitted.

"What did she say?"

"She didn't believe it. Thought it was some kind of gag."

Mallory's eyes rested on Rennie. "My folks are on a fishing boat," he said hastily.

"What about yours?" Dean Mallory inquired of Rick.

"They don't believe in the Second Coming," Rick answered quietly. "There'd be no point."

"Your pastor . . ." suggested the dean.

"We did try Restoration Chapel," said Linda slightly embarrassed. "I think the pastor's off speaking somewhere."

"We want to know what *you* think," said Rennie bluntly.

"What I think isn't important," said the dean. "We need to catch the mind of Christ—to find out what God thinks."

"Do you think it was from God?" asked Rick.

Dean Mallory cleaned his spectacles. "If you ask me whether it could come from God, I would say yes. God can speak anywhere. But if you ask me whether what you heard on that airplane was actually the voice of Deity—" He reached for his Bible on a lamp table. "—I would have to say no way!"

"Then if we go around telling people we heard God speak," said Linda, "we're—"

"—false prophets," finished Rick.

"Perhaps," replied the dean, "but why don't we wait and see? The Bible says to test the spirits. Time will tell. Meanwhile . . ."

"Yeah, *meanwhile!*" said Rick, a note of bitterness in his voice. "Meanwhile the word doesn't get out and everybody dies with their blood on our hands."

"Look at this campus!" Linda jumped to her feet. "These kids don't care about anything here except getting a degree. I've talked to plenty of them. Jesus isn't running their lives. They're not studying the Bible. They're not in the library. There are no gospel teams going out. There are no all-night prayer meetings. Who wants Jesus to come back? Nobody!"

"Sit down, Linda," said the dean. "So you think the end is coming in two days?"

"We don't know, sir," said Rennie. "We came to ask you."

"People come into my office every day and tell me what God said to them," replied Mallory.

"So it's a question of truth, isn't it?" said Rick.

"Yes it is," said the dean, "and I just thought of something. President Silverthorne has called a special meeting of the Bible faculty tomorrow afternoon to take up the matter of cults beginning to appear on campus. I'll be chairing it. I want you three to come to that meeting and tell the professors just what you've been telling me. If they give their approval—if they accept your interpretation of what you heard—"

"The Bible faculty?" echoed Rick in astonishment. "They wouldn't give us the time of day."

"That gives us only one day to warn people," said Rennie.

"I don't see the point," said Linda.

"That's it." Dean Mallory rose, signifying that the discussion was at an end. "I'll see you in the faculty room of the administration building at 1 o'clock. Now let's pray. . . ."

"See anything exciting, Grandma?" Reginald Tibbets was squatting on the carpet of Room 809 in the Bonaventure's Green Tower, with parts of the hotel's television set scattered about him. Open at his side was his flight bag, into which he dipped for tools as he industriously attacked the set's forest of connections.

Oblivious to his activity, Maybelle stood by the large convex window studying the panorama beneath her. "I'm wondering if I shouldn't try to sell my whole doll collection to this man tomorrow."

Reginald looked up, astonished. "You wouldn't do that, Grandma!"

"I'm just cogitating. It's been quite a day. Suppose that airplane had crashed into a mountain this afternoon."

"It didn't. So what the heck?"

"I'm not thinking about myself, but about you."

"What about me?"

"I'm not sure you're ready to go." Maybelle turned away from the view and looked at him. "Reginald, what in heaven's name are you doing to that television?"

"Don't worry, Grandma. Just getting your picture a little sharper."

"I give up!" Maybelle took her purse from the bed, opened a notebook, and seated herself in the small room's only chair where she began writing.

Reginald continued his tinkering. "You're thinking about going to heaven. I'm thinkin' about som'pn to eat!"

"I suppose you are."

"We could get room service."

"No, it's always too slow. We'll go down—after you get that thing back together."

"It's ready now!" Reginald closed up the back, put away his tools, and flipped the switch. A bright picture snapped on. "How about that?"

Late that evening Reginald lay in bed, pajama-clad with arms behind his head, chattering away as his grandmother went through her preparations for retiring. "You know, Grandma, I've never stayed in a hotel before, but I can tell you in the future it's all going to be different. There's going to be a computer in every room, so we can play games off floppy discs on the TV."

Maybelle emerged from the bathroom, rubbing skin cream on her face. "And you're just the boy to do it."

"Why not? And I'd change the food processing too, so you won't have to wait an hour in a restaurant downstairs to be served."

"How would you change it?"

"I'd set up a microwave oven in all the rooms, so all you'd have to do is select something from the menu and press a button. You insert a packet of space food and in one minute you'd have your meal, just like that, drinks, silverware, even music."

"And when will all this take place?"

"You wait. They'll have robots cleaning the tub and sweeping the carpet and making the beds—everything."

Maybelle sighed. "Right now, Reginald, I'm afraid I'm not quite up to it. But tomorrow I'm taking you to a skin doctor."

Reginald was off on a fresh tack. "Grandma, do we have to go to that stupid reception? I saw an arcade down the street, and I want to check out some computer centers if they're open. And then Sunday I'd like to go out to that place they call 'The Ark.'"

Maybelle sat down on the edge of her bed. "Reginald, I need to talk to you. You understand that on this trip you're in my charge, and you're not going to be able to handle me the way you handle your parents. They tell me they can't keep up with you. But I can, budzo!"

"Grandma—"

"Listen to me! I know you think I'm a funny old lady who talks to dolls, but something happened today and I'm not sure you're aware of how serious it is."

"You don't mean—"

"I mean that message that came over the P.A. during the

storm. You don't believe what it said, but I do. And I've been taking inventory." She rose up and drew the curtains.

Reginald shivered. "You mean about the ark and all that stuff?"

"That's just what I mean. There isn't much time left, and what there is, I'm giving to you. I love you, boy. You're so bright, and have such tremendous gifts, and you're not using them. You're just throwing them away, and it's like a toothache with me. Only it's in my heart—I can't get away from it. I just want to help you, and one way for sure will be to go to that reception."

Reginald blinked his eyes. "O.K., Grandma. I'll go."

Maybelle kissed his cheek. "I just pray that someday you will ask your computer, 'Tell me something about God,' and the computer will blink and rattle and flash the words, 'He made me!' Then perhaps you'll understand."

She turned out the light and slipped into her bed.

Reginald lay awake, studying the cracks of light through the curtains. *I underestimated her,* he decided. *I guess you can't judge somebody just because they like dolls. But this is a real drag. Talk about confusion! I never guessed Grandma would go for it. Now if I tell her who it was faked it, she'll freak out and won't forgive me. . . .*

Events having taken a turn that he could no longer control, Reginald let his mind revert to the exploits of the day. When the plane landed at LAX without screaming fire trucks or foam on the runway, he was disappointed. On the other hand, the sensational success of his penetrating the audio circuit, plus his flushing out a Soviet spy, made it the most triumphant day he could remember. Score one for the monkey demon!

How much of it could he share with his brother Dick on the phone tomorrow? Maybe he would wait and write it all up in a piece for *Popular Science* or the *Washington Post*.

For a second or two he wondered if God knew about this business. Did He mind pranks? It wasn't any big deal, really. Reginald didn't mean anything by it, and it sure didn't hurt anybody. The demon business, of course, was probably just baloney. . . .

The spy! He wondered what frequency the Russians used for their transmissions. If there was a Soviet consulate in L.A., maybe he could cut in. He really did shake up that guy Mechikoff. That was fun.

The reception. It would be dullsville, but he guessed he'd have to go. Maybe he wouldn't sign up for Pacific Tech after all—the new president was a jerk. But he'd take his flight bag along tomorrow and maybe have some fun.

The end of the world, the end of the world—and dear old Grandma believed it. Perhaps he'd have to blow his cover after all. Wait till Monday. Reginald yawned; he was becoming drowsy. Someday, when he grew up, he would build the world's greatest transmitter and it would all be his, and he would contact some space people and get them to beat the Russians, and then maybe they would work out some new games with him. . . .

26

As he signed for his dinner at the Bonaventure's Sidewalk Cafe, Gus Krieger looked at his watch, realizing he had been doing so oftener than usual. Minutes later he presented himself at the bar of the revolving cocktail lounge on the 34th floor of the Orange Tower, and ordered a Scotch and soda. Lighting a cigarette, he said to the bartender, "Well, the word's out. The place is gonna blow up day after tomorrow."

A scowl greeted him. "Don't talk like that around here, man. This place is crawling with security."

"I don't mean this place. I mean the whole world."

The bartender's face relaxed. "Oh, yeah? You one of them? I thought the guy said it was yesterday."

"You think I'm mouthing off. We're in double overtime, buddy."

"How about that?" The bartender winked at a female customer. "And me stuck with a seven-point spread Monday night."

"Who's playin'?"

"Rams at Houston."

Krieger pushed his glass for a refill. "Can't win 'em all."

"Good time to go to the moon, baby," said the bartender.

"Huh?"

"I say maybe it's a good time to bug out."

"Yeah."

"Where you gonna hide?"

"Me?"

"Yeah."

"Well, I was gonna take a boat to Catalina. Now I think I'll just go upstairs, if you can fix me up with some company."

"Any preference?"

"Just somp'n nice."

The bartender wrote a telephone number on a pad of paper and tore off the sheet. "Try this."

"Thanks." Gus slipped him a five-dollar bill.

"*Toujours gai*," said the bartender.

"Whazzat mean?"

"It means if you're on your way to hell, enjoy the ride!"

Back in his room at 7:43, Gus dialed the number, then ordered drinks from room service. After replacing the receiver, he picked up a Gideon Bible from the bed table and thumbed it, wondering if he could find something about the end of the world. Then he remembered the tract the old Salvation Army bird had given him on the plane, and took it out of his shirt pocket.

At 8:12 room service arrived. Gus gave up attempting to read and turned on the television. At 8:18 he fell asleep.

27

Major Sebastian McCorkle brought his Salvation Army van to a halt in the public parking ramp across the street from the Bonaventure Hotel, and gave a final briefing to his crew. "Remember your instructions: this is a surprise appearance. You're to follow me through the lobby to the Green Tower and wait at the elevator until I join you. Then we go up and assemble outside the commissioner's door. And the instant it's opened, we march in."

"Are you sure of the room number?" inquired Mrs. McCorkle, a suspicious edge to her voice.

"I'm double-checking on the house phone, while you wait."

The other three in the party, Gary, Frances, and Clarence, lifted out their instruments and proceeded across Figueroa Boulevard into the hotel, where they took the escalator down into the stunning lobby court. Walking single-file behind the McCorkles, they paraded past the scalloped fountains to the Green Tower, making such a striking appearance in their colorful uniforms that it seemed as if Virtue itself was on the march. So much attention came their way, in fact, that two visitors in the lobby court walked up to Frances and handed her some conscience bills.

While they waited, the major was connected with the commissioner's room. McCorkle identified himself, inquired if he could come up, and asked for the room number. "I've gone and mislaid my glasses, old chap," said Commissioner Hilliard, "but I do believe it's 1106. Yes, I'm quite certain that's the number. I'll be looking for you."

The party of five then entered the elevator, and the major touched the floor button. Once assembled in the hallway outside room 1106, they arranged their instruments and waited for McCorkle to give the downbeat. He knocked and, as the door opened, brought down his hand.

"Come in, baby!" said Gus Krieger, swinging the door wide

with a grin, but his words went unheard. He was fairly knocked off his feet by Major McCorkle and the Congress Hall Salvation Army band, consisting of tuba, cornet, alto, trombone, and bass drum, blaring out the bars of Sir Arthur Sullivan's "Onward Christian Soldiers" as they filed into the little room.

Eyeing the bottles on the bed table, Major McCorkle quickly deduced that the commissioner was taking medication. The open Bible on the bed, together with Commissioner Hilliard's tract on "Hope" next to it, gave reassurance. Sullivan's air being rounded off, the band moved spiritedly into "God Save the Queen."

Gus Krieger made no effort to stop the music. He stood in a daze and finally sat down on the bed. "I can't believe it," he said.

Mrs. McCorkle paused by the bed table, cornet in hand, her nostrils twitching slightly. "There's been a mistake," she said.

"What room is this?" asked her husband.

Gus looked blank. Mrs. McCorkle glanced at the telephone. "1106. Isn't that what the operator told you?" Without waiting for a reply, she picked up the receiver and punched 0. "Please connect me with Commissioner Hilliard." A minute later she replaced the receiver and looked at her husband through narrow lids. "I thought so. His room is 1206."

"Please excuse us, sir," said Major McCorkle, removing his cap and wiping the perspiration from his fringe of hair. "We missed our floor. We're terribly sorry."

"Wait," said Krieger in a choking voice, spreading his hands on his knees. "Do you have a minute?" The group stood with instruments raised, poised for departure. "Everything has gone wrong," said Gus in a trembling voice. "Friday the thirteenth. I—I'm—" He threw himself facedown on the bed, his shoulders shaking. In a muffled voice he cried out, "God hates me. Everybody hates me. They're going to kill me! I'm going to die!"

"No!" cried Frances, the alto player, tossing her instrument on the bed and kneeling down. She reached for Gus' hand. "God loves you!"

"We'd better be getting upstairs," ventured Mrs. McCorkle.

"Put down your gear, everyone," ordered Major McCorkle. Turning to his wife, he said, "Dial 1206 and tell the Commis-

sioner we were planning a surprise reception, but something
happened. We have to deal with a seeker here in the hotel and
will be a few minutes late." He sat on the bed beside Gus and
placed his hand on his shoulder. "Would you like us to pray for
you, brother?" he asked.

Frances interrupted her praying and lifted her head. Krieger
sat up and reached for his drink on the bed table. Taking a large
swallow, he said, "See, I was on this plane today, and this voice
came on."

"What shall we call you?" asked McCorkle.

"Gus."

"Well, Gus, I'm Major McCorkle, and this is my wife, and
these are some Christian folks—Frances and Gary and Clarence.
And we're going to lift you up to the Lord in prayer right now,
O.K.?" The major gently removed the glass from Gus' hand and
set it on the bed table.

"Look, Major," said Gus, "don't waste your time. You got
business someplace else. Don't mess with me."

"I wasn't aware," said Major McCorkle gently, "that God
played favorites. But where did you get that tract?"

"A guy on the plane gimme it. The colonel."

McCorkle picked it up. " 'Hope, by Peter Hilliard.' You
must have been on the same plane." He turned to Gus. "Did you
speak with him?"

Gus rolled his head from side to side. "You don't get it. I'm
in another world from you. I thought I could get away from it,
but it's no use. They're gonna get me." He buried his head again
in the bedspread. The major nodded to Frances, who knelt
again and began to pray fervently.

A knock came at the door, and Gary opened it to admit a
security guard. "I'm going to have to ask you to take your
instruments and leave at once," he said. "We can't tolerate this
kind of music; it's disturbing our guests."

The praying ceased, and Major McCorkle gave eloquent
assurances that the music was finished forthwith and would be
heard no more. The guard, who seemed to be impressed more
by the uniforms than by the spoken words, relented and left
after issuing a modified warning.

Frances resumed her praying in a hushed voice, and Gus seemed to be listening in a receptive frame when after a few minutes another knock came at the door. Gary answered it and found a blonde young woman in a low-cut blouse staring at him, cigarette in hand. "Is this 1106?" she inquired.

"Yes, it is. Come in," said Gary.

Frances, kneeling with her eyes closed, now called out, "Thank You, Lord, here comes another!"

The woman peered past Gary at the praying group. "Come in with those spooks? Yuk!" She turned and walked rapidly around the bend to the elevator. Major McCorkle signaled to Gary to close the door.

For a long time the praying went on. Soon Gus himself was praying, pouring out his misery, and the atmosphere became electric. Questions were put and answers were given. Tears were shed. Great decisions were being weighed. A soul hung in the balance. A change was taking place in the moral order of the universe.

At 9:38 P.M., to his utter amazement, Commissioner Peter Hilliard in room 1206 was introduced to a new recruit in the Army of the Lord. The new believer turned out to be none other than his seatmate in row 13 on Flight 803 that very afternoon. "And to think," the commissioner remarked to Mrs. McCorkle, "that my little tract was so greatly used. It's very moving!"

28

"Don't you think Gerry's an exciting young artist?" asked Brenda Cosgrove as she tooled her Porsche along Santa Monica Boulevard after the recital.

"Uh huh." Arvie Erickson was noncommittal.

"Oh, I think he's marvelous. So dramatic! Such power in his fingers. I get goosebumps everytime he goes into the *Polonaise in A*. He makes it sound like a Polish insurrection."

"Yeah."

"And that studio of his. Talk about exotic!" Brenda's laugh had a liquid sound. "I drank too much. Shouldn't be driving now. What did you think of it?"

"It was O.K."

"You sound exhausted, poor dear. Maybe I shouldn't have asked you to go, but you seemed to enjoy it."

"The music was fine; it was just my shoulder."

"Well, for pete's sake take care of it. You've got U.S.C. coming up."

"That's not what's really bothering me."

"Well, what is?" She caught her breath. "I know. That little whoozit that was on the plane with you."

Arvie looked out the side window in disgust. "You really want to know?"

"I'm listening." Her voice had gone dead.

"No. Forget it."

Brenda lit a cigarette. "If that's the way you want it."

Arvie lowered the window. "When I saw you," he said, "wearing my pin and sitting there in Gerald Pomeroy's studio after the recital, drinking his gin and kissing knees with him under the table, I thought, Shakespeare had a word for suckers like me. I've always been a team player. I put a premium on loyalty."

"You're kidding!"

"Not tonight. I'm just a cheap escort service."

Brenda pulled the Porsche off the boulevard, parked under a street light, turned the key, and locked the doors. "Been doing a little snooping, haven't you?"

"You can't help matching levels of behavior."

She gave a quick laugh. "Oh, can't you? That little slut I watched you trying to make out with at the airport—how do you think that made me feel?"

Arvie's voice shook with anger. "That slut, as you called her, was asking me what happens when you die."

"What was her problem?"

"I told you about the broadcast we heard on the plane during the storm. That's what we were talking about."

"You mean the end of the world and all that weird guff?" When Arvie remained silent, Brenda continued, "I don't intend to choose any man's friends for him, Arvie, but I happen to be very particular about mine. To me Gerry Pomeroy is a really neat guy who is making a contribution. It's my guess that in the next five years the world will be hearing from him."

"Whereas an ordinary tennis player like me is—"

"A jock." She did not smile.

"A jock. Right. I get the message." Arvie nodded.

"But it's still a high-class sport, in spite of the jocks in it. And nobody has to stay a jock. Gerald is a fine tennis player, not as good as you, and I might add, not as good-looking. But he isn't hiding behind a façade like you. Gerald's a down-to-earth human being. I'm not in love with him. I just admire him. He's made something of himself, and he's enriched my life."

"Well, good old Gerry!"

"You're not jealous. Your pride's been hurt, that's all. And it's such a waste." Brenda tamped out her cigarette nervously.

"That's right, pride. I'm proud of you. And I want to keep it that way. And when I see you and that guy—"

"Diddle, diddle, diddle. Isn't there anything else to talk about? I'm sorry, but I'm studying Bernard Shaw this semester. He says that most people just sit around all their lives and look bewildered because nothing makes sense to them, but the true joy in life comes from being used for a mighty purpose, when we identify ourselves with a force that the whole universe is behind. I'm not quoting him exactly, but that's the—"

"What's this mighty purpose we're supposed to have? Music?"

"I don't know. He says you'll find it in *The Pilgrim's Progress,* which I haven't read."

"Neither have I."

"I guess I still love you," Brenda went on, "but I'm finding it hard, Arvie, to love somebody who thinks he's so superior to everybody else. I guess the dinosaurs felt that way once."

"First I'm a jock, now I'm a dinosaur."

The ride was finished in silence and when they arrived at the Alpha Chi house, the fraternity pin was returned.

TWO

SATURDAY

At 5:05 A.M. the telephone rang in room 905 of Bonaventure Hotel's Orange Tower. Yakob Malof, the Soviet consular attaché who shared the room with Vasily Mechikoff, was sleeping by the telephone and took the call. It was, as he expected, from the consulate in San Francisco; but not as he expected, it came in open code: "They called from the garage; your car is ready."

Putting on his clothes and a topcoat, Malof proceeded to the hotel lobby and walked across the street to the parking ramp. There he placed a call in a coin telephone box to San Francisco. From his coat pocket he took out a copy of Mikhail Artsybashev's novel, *The Breaking Point,* and a note pad. When the voice on the line said, "With reference to your letter of the twenty-fourth," Malof turned obediently to page 24.

By dint of considerable eyestrain, Malof was able to underline certain words in the pages of the novel. The San Francisco contact rang off after repeating a rubric familiar to Malof, and adding the word "Mechikoff." Going back to his hotel room, Malof spent the next half hour piecing together the message. He was to establish daily surveillance of Vasily's movements, while encouraging him to investigate further the mysterious message heard in the storm. An imminent major propaganda attempt was expected from Washington, aimed at convincing the masses that a preemptive nuclear strike was essential to survival. The plane on which Mechikoff traveled may have been a spy plane similar to the Korean jumbo jet shot down over Sakhalin. The message may have concealed in code projected unfriendly troop movements in Lebanon or Central America.

Malof stood up, stretched, and stared out the window at the smoggy light of dawn creeping over the City of Angels. On the Harbor Freeway the huge trucks were rolling with a steady hum while the rest of the city turned over for a few more desperate minutes of sleep. He studied the skyscrapers sur- rounding the hotel—arrogant monsters of steel and reinforced concrete that made up the bastion of dying capitalism. Evidently Los Angeles, like San Francisco, was a stinking residuum of decadence. And these people were planning a preemptive nucle- ar strike? Where were the underground shelters? The civil de- fense warnings?

And yet, Moscow's intelligence was invariably correct. The message had been heard over Colorado, and Colorado was the headquarters of NORAD, where there was a mole in place. Malof scratched himself and looked at the still-sleeping figure in the next bed. He lit an American cigarette. So Mechikoff was suspect. Hah! Who wasn't?

2

As he walked through the campus to his 8 o'clock anthropolo- gy class, Arvie Erickson, captain of the U.C.L.A. tennis team, was in a distinctly dismal frame of mind. He reflected on the fact that on the previous evening a fortune cookie proverb had informed him, "Something has just taken place that will affect the rest of your life." But what it was—Brenda, Mary, the death of his mother—and how it would affect him, did not appear. That it was bad news seemed certain.

During the class hour Professor Warrenton took Arvie's mind off his troubles temporarily by detailing the nature of the elaborate term paper he desired from his students. "I'm sure this subject has never been assigned before in the history of this undergraduate institution," he said blandly, "so you won't be able to buy it on the local market. I am asking you for five thousand words on the subject of apocalyptic literature. You will describe and evaluate the relevant ancient writings of the

Greek, Assyrian, Babylonian, Egyptian, and Roman cultures, together with the Biblical pseudepigrapha and the books of Daniel and Revelation. Against the background of this material you will interpret the apocalyptic visions of Jakob Boehme, William Blake, and Teilhard de Chardin."

As he listened, Arvie removed from his pocket the tract Jordan Foster had given him: "THE END OF THE WORLD: WHAT THE BIBLE TEACHES." He skimmed the first few words: "You hear them everywhere, voices announcing that the end has come, or is coming. . . ." He slipped it back into his pocket.

Reporting to the athletic department after class, Arvie received a gloomy welcome that was not lightened by an examination of his injured shoulder. X-rays and a few volleys in the driving court confirmed the trainer's prognosis: he was out of the U.S.C. matches and probably through for the season. More X-rays and a taping session followed. By the time he arrived at the main library that afternoon, Arvie learned that every copy of Frazer's *Golden Bough* had been checked out, and there was not enough on the shelves for his research. What he needed first of all, he decided, was a Bible.

Finding the campus bookstore closed, Arvie returned to the fraternity house and located a religious bookstore in the Yellow Pages. Half an hour later he was driving west on Sunset Boulevard in his three-year-old Camaro with a new twenty-dollar Bible in a bright orange jacket by his side when he spotted Mary. She was standing on the corner of Larrabee Street, wearing a halter-top and wet-look pants, and carrying what appeared to be a dummy bag of groceries. Arvie swung around the block, not sure why he was taken with a strange excitement. She was clearly a tart. What was appealing about soiled and damaged goods? Yet he felt drawn, perhaps by the exotic nature of the encounter. Here was life on a different planet from tennis courts and sorority parties. He decided to play it for what it was worth, with gloves on.

"Want a lift?" He reached over and opened the door. Mary stopped in her tracks as she recognized him. "Hop in."

"Let's see your money."

"What?"

"The color of your cash."

"All I've got is traveler's checks."

"Pull around the corner and sign them."

"I've got a Bible!" He grinned as he held it up. "I thought maybe you wanted to talk." He noticed that both of Mary's eyes were now black, and the backs of her hands were swollen. She seemed to speak with difficulty.

"You want fun, you pay. You want to talk, you pay."

"Get in." Mary obeyed, but only after hesitating and looking around warily. She put the sack between her feet as Arvie drove around the corner onto Larrabee Street and stopped. "Did they beat you up?" he asked, leaving the engine running.

By now Mary realized her mistake. "You're no good," she said. "You're wasting my time." She reached for the door handle, but Arvie quickly went into drive and headed down the street. Mary broke into a stream of profanity.

"Don't you try to get out," Arvie warned. "I'll turn you in."

"Turn me in!" she yelled scornfully. "They'd have me out with one phone call. You don't know what you're into, Bud. They'll wipe you out. I'm being watched. You're costing them money by the minute. You're stealing. Kidnapping. God, I wish I was dead!" Mary sank back on the seat and Arvie let go of the wrist he had been holding. Keeping his foot on the throttle, he swung back onto Sunset. After a while she asked, "Are we being tailed?"

"No."

"Lucky for you. But they'll find you. These people have connections."

"You know what you can do with your connections."

"Heavy, man," Mary mocked. "You're a fool, trying to play hero. 'White slave rescued from life of shame!' Baloney."

"Was I a hero at the airport?" retorted Arvie.

"You'd have had a knife in your guts. Why did you pick me up?"

"I want to know why you asked me what happens when you die."

"Because my life is sheep-dip. I've got nothing to live for."

"What about your folks?"

"What about them?"

"Don't they worry about you?"

"Worry? What a laugh! All they ever did was push me around and beat me up. My father started playing games in bed with me when I was three years old. When I ran away and the pigs brought me back, you know what Mom said? 'Take her back, we don't want her.' Don't talk to me about folks."

"Maybe there's some way to turn things around," said Arvie.

"Nobody cares about me. I'm destroyed. Where we going, creep? Let me out."

"We're going to my fraternity house."

Mary lit a long, slim cigarette with the car lighter. "I know I'm going to hell," she said, "so when makes no difference to me. But I'm warning you, they'll ream you for this. They'll gun your car off a cliff with you in the trunk. In pieces."

"That's better than Lucretius and his vultures."

As the Camaro put distance between Mary and her turf, she began to relax slightly. "So I'm to sleep with the boys tonight, is that it?"

"You'll sleep in my room. My buddy and I'll be on the sun deck."

"You think I got AIDS?"

Arvie let it pass. "Nobody's going to bother you. We have what we call little sisters boarding at the house. They're girl students. I'll get them to look after whatever you need."

"Like angel dust?" Again Arvie pretended not to hear. "Don't make me your project, turkey," Mary went on, "it won't work. They'll have me back in a couple of days and you'll be in over your head."

Arvie smiled. "Tomorrow morning you and I will cruise out to Ojai to see your aunt."

"Oh, goody. What about tonight? Do we have sex or Bible verses?"

"You heard what I said."

"Boy, you're great. You take away my business, my customers, my protection, and then you brush me off. Thanks a million."

The instant the Camaro stopped in front of the Alpha Chi house, Mary leaped from the car and dashed down the sidewalk. Arvie sprinted after her and caught her by the arm, after which he marched her into the house and pushed her into an overstuffed leather chair. She sat catching her breath while three little sisters gathered around, drawn by the excitement.

"What's going on?" demanded one of the girls.

"This creep tried to rape me!" shrieked Mary.

"That's a lot of bull," Arvie assured the onlookers. "This kid was trying to escape from the mob and they caught her and beat her up."

"Where'd you find her?" asked Arvie's roommate, the fraternity president.

"On the plane from New York. Then tonight she was working the Strip."

"What'd you bring her here for?"

"I'm taking her out to her aunt's place tomorrow. Do you mind if she bunks in our room?"

"Tell him to bug off," shouted Mary.

"She can have the room," said the president. "Did you call her aunt?"

"She won't give me the number."

"I just want to be let go," said Mary, trying to get out of the chair as several hands held her back.

"If Arvie says you're going to your aunt's, that's where you're going," said the president. "Now, you're safe here, understand?"

"He just wants some free nookie," sneered Mary. The onlookers laughed in derision.

"Will you walk up to the room?" asked one of the little sisters, "or do you want to be carried?"

A gong sounded. "Clean her up a little and bring her to dinner," said the president. Two good-sized sisters dragged Mary out of her chair and forced her up the stairs, Mary commenting on their efforts in the language of the day. Dinnertime conversation at the table was slightly strained as many of the pledges had never seen a woman of ill repute except on television.

As they left the dining room, Arvie asked the sisters to

remain with Mary while he went to the library. This request was acceded to by everyone except Mary, who informed him he could bite the wall.

3

At 8:13 A.M. Gus Krieger was awakened out of a delectable dream. He was playing with his five-year-old daughter on the floor of their Miami apartment. Julie, the daughter, had received a miniature Noah's Ark for Christmas and was busy lining up tiny animals to go in two-by-two. But now the ark appeared to Gus to be life-size, and Julie was beckoning him to follow her as she walked up the gangway into the vessel. Gus attemped to follow his daughter, but a gate appeared before him, blocking his way. Julie was on the other side, and she came back to the gate calling, "Daddy! Daddy!" She was crying. Then an enormous elephant lumbered out of the ark and, putting his trunk over the gate, lifted Gus clear of it. He placed Gus and Julie on his back, and they went happily into the ark where a telephone was ringing. . . .

Gus answered it too late; the connection was dead. He shook the dream from his head and went into the bathroom. It had been two years since Julie's molested body was found by searchers near a schoolyard. When he finished shaving and was under the shower Gus heard a persistent knocking at the door of his room. Wrapping a towel around himself, he stepped to the door and took off the chain latch.

A dull-eyed young bellman stood in the hallway holding an envelope. "Two gentlemen in the lobby court asked me to give you this," he said.

"How did they find my room?" demanded Gus. "Did you tell them?"

The eyes of Arturo, the bellman, snapped wide with fear.

"The hotel don't give out room numbers," he said hastily. "They just said give it to the gentleman in 1106."

"You lie through your teeth," said Gus, snatching the envelope.

Arturo backed away. "They said they would like you to join them for breakfast under the umbrellas in the lobby court."

Gus ignored him, shut and bolted the door, and ripped open the envelope. He looked inside and found nothing; the envelope was empty. But on the thick carpet at his bare feet lay a dime that had fallen out. Gus stopped and picked it up. The message was clear: his life was worth ten cents.

He returned to the bathroom and nervously finished toweling. Who had tracked him? Where could he hide? How could he get out of this? Again it was the familiar role: he was the hunted, the prey. Where to go? "God, what next," he muttered, reaching for his trousers with a trembling hand.

That word! *God.* Suddenly it seemed important, as if he had used it some other way. Yes, last night! Scenes came floating back on his memory—music, people in uniform, hands being laid on him; and in it all something coming from his own heart, asking for help. God! *He had called on God!* It was a prayer. And now he had spoken the same word.

As Gus stepped out of the bathroom he noticed a copy of the *War Cry* magazine on the bed, a memento from Frances. "Jesus Christ!" he blurted as an idea flashed through his mind. The colonel! One flight up! He grabbed the magazine and stared at the cover, then threw it down. As he slipped into his clothes and glanced at the mirror, he became aware of what he had said, and a half-smile formed on his lips. Incredible as it would seem, maybe Jesus Christ had something going for him. Maybe.

From his open suitcase Gus removed a black wig and mustache which he added to his appearance. Then, clutching the case, he stepped into the circular hallway, carefully closed the door, and made a quick search for the stairwell. From the elevator door he could see clear to the base of the vaulted atrium lobby. As he looked down he noticed two men standing near the fountain, talking with the young bellman.

Gus turned and continued his search for the stairwell. Locating it at last, he bounded up one flight and walked around to room 1206, the domain of Commissioner Hilliard. A "Do Not Disturb" sign hung on the doorknob. Gus began pounding on the paneling, while a dozen ideas occurred to him. "After I shake these torpedoes, there'll be somebody else; they never quit. Some kid will fish me out of the harbor. But maybe I'm not ready to kick in after all. If that voice on the plane was dead on, then . . . but so what? I wouldn't mind going to heaven with Frances. . . ."

4

"When I was a bairn, I spak like a bairn, I esteemed things like a bairn, I thocht like a bairn; but noo, bein a man, I hae putten-awa bairn-like things."

Alison Pitt-Barr was reading aloud a chapter from her "Braid Scots" New Testament. She liked to think that she read it every morning, but it was a custom honored more in the breach than the observance. True to habit, she had risen early. After neatly spreading her elegant bed, she ordered room service, showered, dressed, and then enjoyed a breakfast of tea, toast, and oatmeal. Her reading finished, she flipped on the television and went into the bathroom to brush her teeth.

Within seconds Alison was standing in front of her set, toothbrush in hand, staring at the anchor man who was smilingly announcing another "exclusive" for his channel's news team. It seemed that an early edition of the *Los Angeles Times* had reported that an Intercontinental flight from New York had encountered a lightning storm over Colorado, during which the B-27 aircraft had been struck and damaged, and the passengers allegedly heard a "mysterious message from God."

"News 32" had located one of the passengers on that flight, and viewers were urged to stay tuned as the interview would be "coming up right after this message." Alison drew a chair to the television set. The anchorman announced that sitting beside him was the Reverend Jordan Foster, who had just returned to Los Angeles from a White House conference on prison work, and who would be videotaped in a panel discussion on recidivism later this morning on this same channel. Reverend Foster was a passenger on Flight 803 and had heard the "mysterious message from God." He kindly consented to be interviewed on this news program.

The placidly smiling Jordan Foster came into camera range. "Reverend Foster," his host adressed him, "do you think God ever talks to people?"

If Foster was startled, he did not show it. "Of course He does. Why shouldn't He? Communication was God's idea in the first place."

"Yes, but would He talk in a particular language like ours, do you think? Or would He perhaps use symbols?"

"In the Bible He uses both language and symbols—manna, rainbow. He's God. He can use anything."

"But you definitely think God uses human speech to communicate today?" The anchorman drove home his point. "Then was it God who spoke to the people on your airplane? And if it wasn't, where did the voice come from?"

Jordan Foster grinned. "Some people thought I did it."

"So they're still investigating?"

"I believe so. But they may be wasting their time."

"Why?"

"Because," said Jordan, looking straight at the camera, "if it was from God, it came from nowhere."

"But it had to come from somewhere. People heard it."

"Sir," replied Foster gravely, "I heard it too. I'm just saying that if the voice came from God, it came from nowhere, because that's where God came from."

The anchorman attempted a diversion. "Did you talk to any—?"

"It's very clear," said Jordan, ignoring him, "that God came from nowhere because there was nowhere for Him to come from."

The anchorman decided the best way out was to assume

that his leg was being pulled. "All right, Reverend," he chuckled, "you say God came from nowhere. Then how was the universe formed?"

Jordan Foster glanced at the ceiling. "In Africa they say, 'No rain, no mushrooms. No God, no world.' "

"And what do you say?"

"I say that God reached out where there was nowhere to reach, and caught something where there was nothing to catch, and hung something on nothing, and told it to stay there."

Alison could hear laughter in the studio, in which the anchorman joined self-consciously. "Well, you've cleared up just about everything this morning. . . ."

Captain Frank Medeiros was enjoying buckwheat cakes with his sleek young wife in their opulent La Habra home when the telephone rang. On the line was Roark Maddox, the man who was supposed to be sponsoring Frank for the post of assistant director of operations.

"Better turn on Channel 32, Captain."

"What's up?"

"One of your passengers is talking about what happened on your flight yesterday."

Medeiros switched on his set and flipped to Channel 32. "I gave Operations a full report on it," he said.

"I've seen that." The voice was flat. "It's not what this man's talking about."

Recognizing Jordan Foster's face, Medeiros told Maddox, "The man is an eccentric. I said in my report that we took a lightning hit over Colorado and lost some altitude. No injuries."

"Did you report hearing an intrusion on the P.A.?"

"I saw no reason to. We're investigating."

"F.A.A. has requested an irregularity report. It will be due at 10 A.M. tomorrow."

"I'll get on it."

"Let me see a copy."

"Yes, sir."

The pilot cradled the receiver with misgivings. Something in the pit of his stomach told him that the luck that had carried him nearly to the top of his profession was petering out; that his last hurrah on Intercontinental Airlines was developing into a career crisis. All those thousands of flying hours could become sawdust. The plum he had sought so long could go for grabs. He knew of two other officers with equally impressive performance records who were pressing for the job.

Medeiros turned up the volume as Jordan Foster was talking: "God reached out where there was nowhere to reach, and caught something when there was nothing to catch. . . ." Angrily Medeiros switched off his set. Ordering his wife to cancel a golf date, he picked up his briefcase and walked to the garage, where he backed his Corvette out of the driveway and headed for Los Angeles International Airport.

The anchorman held up a newspaper clipping. "One other question, Reverend. Did you ever hear of the Testament of Daniel?"

"No, sir. . . ."

The interview was over. Alison wrote on her notepad the name, "Jordan Foster. Rose of Sharon Church." In the Yellow Pages she easily located the church address and copied it, after which she returned to the bathroom and finished brushing her teeth.

5

At nine o'clock Saturday morning Alison Pitt-Barr, moving swiftly and with determination, paid a visit to the travel office on the fourth level of the Bonaventure shopping gallery. There she obtained a map of Los Angeles, then returned to her room and tried to reach the Reverend Jordan Foster by telephone.

While thus engaged, Alison was summoned to the sitting room by Charlotte, who handed her a sheaf of handwritten pages torn from a yellow pad. "I spent three hours writing this last night and this morning," Charlotte told her. "It's everything I know about the history of Embree Drywall. I want it typed up and a copy run off. Send the original to Sarah in New York by registered mail before noon. I've added a note to Sarah telling her to mail copies to the board to let them now what we're doing. The audits and appraisals will come later. Wait a minute!" she ordered as Alison edged toward the door. "I'm not through with you yet. When Ralph brings the proxies, I want them statted and put in the same package, with instructions to Sarah to put them in the safe. Now, have you got it straight?"

"I have that," said Alison. "Will there be anything else?"

Charlotte waved her away, and Alison returned to her room, where she continued her efforts to reach Jordan Foster.

The day had started badly for Colleen and Raymond Phillips. First there was the breakfast. A truckers' strike had eliminated the eggs, the Bonaventure toast was on the cold side, and the prunes left something to be desired. Finishing his coffee with a look of distaste, Raymond wiped his mustache with a linen napkin and brushed some lint from his blazer.

Colleen interpreted his silence as a bad omen. "Something troubling you?"

Raymond waved his hand impatiently. "I was just reviewing our years."

Colleen could feel the muscles shift almost involuntarily across her face. He always said that she revealed too much, too soon, and at the most inappropriate moments. "Our years?"

"A sort of time capsule."

"What—"

"Two people can cease to be of value to each other in a relationship, Colly," added Raymond. The words hung between them, carved in stone, taking on dimension and substance. The barrier was up.

The woman behind the coffee cup contemplated the presence of the new atmosphere. "Am I supposed to go with you on the tour this morning?" she asked, trying to divert the conversation.

Raymond rose from the table and studied himself in the mirror. He liked the streak of gray over his temples. "I've been trying to decide what you are, Mrs. Phillips. I'd say you're a flawed diamond. You hold a Phi Beta Kappa key, you're widely read, you're traveled, your art background is impeccable. Turning your back on alcohol—so far, at least—is all to your credit. But joining the antinukes was a mistake; and when you walked the plank for Jesus, you destroyed something between us. I used to wonder sometimes what it was like being a martyr. Now I know—I'm married to one."

Colleen carried the breakfast tray to the corridor and came back. "For twenty-four years," she said icily, "I have been faithful to you, Raymond, and to this thing we've called a marriage. You talk about my 'background'! You didn't mention that I've borne your children and supported your work and put up with your midlife excursions into other people's bedrooms and taken you back—twice. Now it seems to me that if I wish to believe in God, that's my affair."

"God—God—God. I'm up to here with the subject. Colly, you ought to read some history. Get into Durkheim. He'll set you right. There isn't any Supreme Being and never was. What you've got is a tribal deity, a disappearing idol, hanging over from the ancient Middle East. Archaeological rubbish!"

"It's apparent," said Colleen quietly, "that your quarrel isn't with me."

"And now you've got Jesus coming back," Raymond went on, riffling through the papers in his briefcase and snapping it shut. "And all this praying." He straightened up. "It was a character in Dickens, wasn't it, who beat his wife because she was always praying for him? Anyway, I have a suggestion."

Colleen felt the blood draining from her face.

"You can see, I'll need you here for two or three weeks to

get through this inauguration business. After that I propose that you plan a trip east, with say western Europe thrown in. When you come back, I'll fly east and we'll work out a settlement. I'm not a monster, Colly. You'll be taken care of."

"A charming prospect. Who says daydreams aren't productive?" Colleen's words were spirited, but her tone was hollow.

"There's no reason why we can't be friends even if we aren't congenial," replied Raymond. "I'm sure the children would prefer it that way. And yes, you will be going with me on the tour this morning."

"I'm ready," said Colleen.

6

When Commissioner Peter Hilliard stepped out of his room in the Bonaventure Hotel he was accompanied by another man. This odd-looking personage sported a black mustache and was attired in an ill-fitting set of India whites and a white Salvation Army cap that sat high on his bushy hair. It was the new Gus Krieger hidden behind spectacles and carrying a stack of *War Cry* magazines.

Commissioner Hilliard was equally loaded down, and after the Green Tower elevator descended to the lobby court the pair walked around the fountain area, handing magazines to everyone in sight, including the desk clerks and the bellmen gathered at the concierge desk. During this operation Gus left the lobby court to the commissioner and dispersed most of his copies on empty tables in the adjoining Sidewalk Cafe.

When Major McCorkle arrived in his van at the Figueroa Street entrance to the hotel, he found the commissioner engaged in a strenuous altercation with a security guard who seemed eager to eject him from the premises.

"The management does not permit any solicitation or distribution of any kind," the guard was saying. "Out you go, buddy."

"Young man," expostulated the commissioner, "I have given out the *War Cry* in prisons and palaces and hotels and bars too, all my life, since before you were born, and have always been kindly received. I will be very happy to talk to your manager."

Gus, noting the disturbance from a distance, ducked into the elevator waiting area and sent his remaining copies up thirty-two floors of the Orange Tower in an empty lift.

Major McCorkle managed to pacify the commissioner, and then drove his two passengers to divisional headquarters. First he stopped at the Congress Hall and obtained a set of coveralls for Gus so that Commissioner Hilliard could reclaim his summer uniform.

As they waited for the major in the van, Hilliard could not resist imparting advice. "Augustin," he said, "you have taken a great step forward. Life will be different for you now. When the going is difficult, you will get help."

"Them magazines of yours nearly done me in, Colonel," replied Gus.

Ignoring him, the commissioner continued, "Remember that adversities are part of life. Will I see you in church tomorrow?"

Gus smiled. "You're the boss."

"Good. Now, I'll just take my glasses and hat if you don't mind. And—oh, yes." Hilliard reached in his breast pocket and drew out a shiny steel cross made of two odd-shaped nails which hung on a chain. "I brought this from India, Augustin. I told the bishop who gave it to me that I would present it to the next person I led to Christ."

Gus examined the cross and stuffed it in his pocket. "Much obliged."

Major McCorkle returned to the van with the divisional commander, who took Hilliard in tow, and McCorkle drove to the Salvation Army's Seventh Street store, where Gus was outfitted with work pants and shirt, dress pants and jacket, sweater, shirt and tie, socks and underwear. Gus was then escorted upstairs, still wearing his wig and mustache, and introduced to the intake supervisor of the adult rehabilitation center, Lieutenant Slocombe.

The interview that followed was not an unqualified success.

Lieutenant Slocombe had been briefed about Krieger's connection with the visiting commissioner from India; but when she sought to reconstruct the details of Gus' contacts with local personnel, she found him bewildered.

"You'll have to ask the major, ma'am," said Gus. "Whatever he says, I'll go along with."

"You're to be enrolled as an Adherent," said the lieutenant, reaching for a yellow form. "Are you detoxed?"

"Huh?"

"Sober?"

"Well, I could use one. Got a bar?"

"Married or divorced?"

"Just on the lam."

"Date and place of birth?"

"The FBI's got all that stuff."

"We need it here, Mr. Krieger."

"What is this place?" asked Gus curiously, looking around.

"This is the guidance service. We're to help you establish your identity as a person."

Gus narrowed his eyelids. "No identity! Got it? I'm lookin' for cover."

The lieutenant returned to her typewriter. "If you wish to become involved in our total therapy program, you will need to sign up for a minimum of ninety days."

Gus shook his head. "Tomorrow."

"I beg your pardon?"

"It's all over tomorrow."

Lieutenant Slocombe let it pass. "We are assigning you a bed in Dormitory Four. If you have valuables, they can be checked. I need your occupation."

"Self-employed."

"Doing what, Mr. Krieger?"

"Bankruptcy proceedings."

"Do you have a home address?"

"I moved."

The typewriter clicked. "We're listing you as transient, but that can change."

"The major said I was a pilgrim."

"Of course. Now, sir, we plan to enroll you in our program of vocational, psychological, and religious therapy, designed to restore you to full membership in society. You will attend a Bible class tomorrow afternoon."

"O.K."

"And church services in Congress Hall at 11 o'clock tomorrow morning. A van will pick you up."

"O.K." Gus stood up.

"Mr. Krieger," asked Lieutenant Slocombe, "are you baldheaded?"

"Why?"

"If not, I suggest you remove the wig before church tomorrow morning."

Gus twirled his false mustache and walked out without replying.

While he was being billeted in his new quarters, Krieger's pursuers at the Bonaventure were becoming restless. Their stakeout was proving unproductive. The bellman, Arturo, told them that Gus had not checked out and had not been seen in the atrium lobby. After waiting an hour, the two agents of retribution took the Green Tower elevator to the eleventh floor, where they palmed a chambermaid with a ten-dollar bill. She led them nervously to room 1106 and inserted her key in the lock, calling out "Maid!" But the pair behind her pushed her aside and burst open the door. One of them made for the bathroom, where he found the water still running in the basin.

"He took off fast!"

"Look at this," said his colleague, picking a copy of the *War Cry* off the bed. "Remember them two guys passing out magazines in the lobby?"

"Yeah. The sucker with the mustache. Let's go!" He looked at the maid crouching terrified by the window. "This bum left without payin' his bill," he told her. "Now, was that bein' a good citizen?"

7

Parking his car at Los Angeles International Airport, Captain Frank Medeiros walked into the Intercontinental Operations office and obtained a computer routing sheet that enabled him to locate his aircraft of the day before. Without divulging his intentions to anyone, the pilot found the aircraft, side number 717, parked at Gate I-18 for repairs. The plane was empty, and a portable ramp stood alongside.

Climbing aboard quickly, Medeiros used his key to enter the cockpit. Inside he flipped two switches that started up the auxiliary power unit. The natural starting place for his search was the cockpit voice recorder. Normally the recorder only reproduced the last ten minutes of cockpit conversation, but when he saw the weather system ahead, Medeiros had pulled the circuit breaker, so that the tape recorded the entire episode. This, then, was what he wanted to hear and what had brought him back to the airport on an off-day. He felt it would provide the data he needed for his irregularity report.

It provided nothing.

Plugging in the headset, Medeiros listened to the replay, and as the flight deck conversation came through, his pulse rate climbed: "What's in it for us? . . . I hear we're opening up Tonopah . . . I'm puttin' in for early retirement. . . ." There followed the seat belt announcement and conversation with Denver and then a loud "pop" accompanied by a change of tone in the engine whine. Medeiros heard himself calling out to Bricklebine; Garrett was swearing; Denver was silent. More seconds passed. Chills began to ripple down Frank Medeiros' back as he rewound the tape and played it again. *No voice!* What everybody on the plane had heard, the cockpit voice recorder did not register.

Removing his headset, Medeiros took a Phillips screwdriver

and loosened the overhead panels above the flight deck. Using a flashlight, he inspected every inch of the space.

Nothing.

The time had come for less effort and more thought. Exactly what was involved in this situation? The actual content of the message that came over Friday afternoon, Medeiros dismissed as irrelevant. Growing up in a Portuguese community in Gustine, California, he broke early with the culture. For a few years he was forced to attend Mass with his parents, but as soon as he was old enough to get away, he spent his Sundays rabbit hunting or swimming in the San Joaquin River. Once he visited a revival tent in Los Baños and watched an itinerant evangelist illustrate his points by throwing chairs off the platform. After he joined the Air Force, Medeiros quickly learned that religion had little to do with aerial navigation. More productive were superconducting magnets and high-powered microwave tubes and the meat and potatoes of technology.

In the present instance the issue was not the content, but the source of the message. If Jordan Foster had to be eliminated—and Medeiros had not quite yielded up his suspicions—then where did it orginate? After Flight 803 landed at LAX, the captain had walked through the cabin, searching for a hidden sound box or microphone or anything of a similar nature. He spent a good bit of time in the rear toilets. Now he concluded his search had been too cursory.

Perspiring freely, the captain replaced the panels and shut off the auxiliary power unit. He then carefully checked all the intercom phones. Uttering a malediction on aircraft 717, he set out on a systematic search of the main cabin. Row by row he stretched and bent, looking under life jackets, in overhead racks, in galley cupboards, in waste receptacles, feeling in every crevice and cranny and shelf for a little device that would answer all questions and take care of all "irregularities."

Fingers and flashlight turned up nothing.

Captain Medeiros' shoulders slumped a bit as he descended the portable ramp and reentered the terminal. He would have to wait until Monday before a crew could be called in to "sweep" the aircraft for bugs.

As he drove his Corvette out of the parking lot, Frank

Medeiros found himself bemused by the irony of his plight. A lifetime of brilliant achievement in aeronautic engineering left him shafted by some religious crank who had cut in on his frequency. But who could have done it? And why? And how could the voice have been synchronized with the lightning strike? And if it was a tape, why didn't the recorder pick it up?

He stared at the bumper sticker on the rear of the van ahead of him. It read, "IF YOU LOVE BUDDHA, SQUAT." He need- ed a drink. Somewhere there had to be an explanation to this business, and he was going to find it.

8

A shapely olive-skinned young woman wearing dark glasses (the same person he had seen at the airport) was waiting for Jordan Foster in a Malibu Classic outside the television studio.

"No covey of cops meeting you this time?"

Jordan laughed. "I'm free at last!"

"*You* may be. But after watching your act, I guess I'm disoriented."

He laughed again. "That makes two of us." He squeezed her arm. "Thanks for waiting."

Once in the car, Jordan headed south to the two-story wooden house that served as the Rose of Sharon parsonage. The front lawn showed signs of neglect. He got out, leaving the engine running.

"Coming over?" asked Paula Marie, slipping behind the wheel. "You talked about getting acquainted."

"I hope so. I'll call you after I find out what's going on."

Foster's next stop was the Beth Eden retirement home in south-central Los Angeles, where his mother had been a resi- dent for several years. For Jordan to visit Mother Foster was to take a radical step; it was like invading enemy territory, and he avoided it as much as possible. He usually limited his contacts to greeting her on Sunday morning and helping her board the bus after the service. During his last visit to the home some weeks earlier, Arlowene Foster's remarks had left her son vexed and uncomfortable. And since his estranged wife Vivian also called on her, Jordan ran the risk of an embarrassing encounter. In fact, there were any number of excuses he could think of that would keep him from the retirement home toward which he was heading.

Now, however, a crisis had blown up in his church, and he needed support. Arlowene was considered a saint by his flock, and since his leadership was being challenged and a confrontation was brewing over his behavior, he decided he would try to mend this particular fence. If anyone could quiet criticism and override opposition just by force of personality, it was his mother. She was always talking about miracles, and in view of the charges being leveled against him, a miracle was just what he needed.

Parking his car, Jordan strode up the walk to the double-entrance doors of the fifty-year-old structure that housed the retirement home. Once inside, he caught the faint antiseptic odor that hung in the airless corridors. As he approached the information desk, one of the nurse's aides began to laugh. "Didn't I see you on television a few minutes ago?"

He smiled. "I don't know. Did you?"

"I sure did. You were talking with somebody about how the world was going to end. You're Reverend—"

"Jordan Foster. I'll have to admit it."

"Foster," the girl repeated. "We have a Mrs. Foster living here."

"I know. She's my mother."

"Oh, I'm sorry, I'm new. Would you like me to take you to her room?"

"Please."

They walked the corridor together, the heels of the pastor's fancy boots clicking on the linoleum that was still wet from a cleaning woman's mop. "I'm always reading about Jesus coming back," said the nurse's aide. "Once I wrote a story about it. . . ."

Jordan Foster entered the room to find a wrinkled, gray-haired woman sitting in a rocking chair, reading her Bible. He bent swiftly and kissed her forehead. She raised a gnarled hand and removed her glasses. "My stars, Jordan! Bless the Lord, I'm so glad to see you. Been on a trip, aincha. Pull that chair over here so 's I can see you by a better light. My, you lookin' fine."

"Mama, how you been?"

"Been good, all 'cept this arthritis. Had to miss church last Sunday. Here, help me up." She limped out of the room and returned with a tray containing mugs and a coffeepot.

"Let me take that pot," said Jordan, getting up.

"You sit there, you'll burn yourself," said his mother. "I'll just set it here and you can pour it." A plain pine table served as her one piece of furniture for the purpose.

"What would you say, Mama," began Jordan as he poured the coffee, "if I told you that yesterday on that airplane from New York I heard a voice talking about the end of the world?"

"I'd say it was about time." Mother Foster winced as she adjusted a knitted gray shawl about her shoulders. "My right arm's gettin' worse."

"It happened sometime yesterday afternoon," said Jordan. "We were in this storm, and dropping and bouncing all over the place, when this voice came on."

"What'd it say?"

"I can't remember exactly, but everybody was supposed to come into the ark, because in two days judgment would be executed."

Mother Foster shook her head. "I think you got the wrong voice, son." She put on her glasses and peered at him.

Jordan grinned. "I knew right away it was a fake. I just wondered, Mom, what you'd think about it."

"You know Jesus ain't tellin' nobody about His plans. And there ain't no judgment without Him."

"Right on, Mama."

"I'll tell you somep'n else. He ain't comin' back 'thout me bein' invited to go with Him."

"The cops thought it was me talking on the loudspeaker."

Mother Foster put down her cup. "What you tellin' me all this for?"

"Didn't you tell me once that God spoke to you?"

"Talks to me all the time. Has since I was a little girl."

"How can you tell?"

"How can I tell when I hear God's voice? Tell me, sonny, can you hear my voice?"

"Sure, Mom."

"How d'you know it's me?"

"I see you talking."

"What about on the phone?"

"I could hear you anywhere and I'd say, 'That's Mama.' "

"That's the way I hear God, boy."

Jordan scratched his head. "He doesn't talk to me that way."

"No, an' you ain't shoutin' 'Glory!' But I got my heavenly bags all packed and ready." When Jordan chuckled, she snapped at him. "What you laughin' at?"

"You. It's hard to explain."

She limped around, tidying and picking up papers. "You don't have to 'splain nothin' to me. I go to your church. I know what's goin' on over there."

The time had come. Jordan's tone now became abject. "Mama, maybe you can help me."

She limped to her chair and sat down. "You're a man now, Jordan. You get yourself in trouble, you get yourself out." He sat quietly as she went on, "When they called you to that church, I was proud of you, real proud. The whole family was. But for a long time I've known that you and the Lord was barely hangin' on. You been in bed with the world."

"You got no right to say that," he protested. "All I did was preach the gospel. Then we started that halfway house, and next thing you know they're calling me from Washington, wanting to put me on a Presidential commission."

"I ain't talkin' about no Presidential commission—I'm talkin' about you, boy. When I see you runnin' around tryin' to act like Martin Luther King—"

"You're hittin' below the belt."

"Don't get me wrong, son. You ought to follow Dr. King. He was a great man, but he was God's man. He never made a move until God moved first."

"I'm just trying to serve the Lord. Can I help it if that takes me to the White House?"

Arlowene reached out her arm, then drew it back in pain. "Hand me my Bible, son. I want to look up somep'n." She riffled some pages, then studied a passage. After a pause she closed the book and said, "You don't have to play the game no more, Jordan. You home free. All you got to do is be God's man for the time left."

Jordan was stunned. "What are you talking about?"

"That voice you heard. I didn't believe it, but I do now." Arlowene had taken off her glasses, but now she put them on again. "Listen to this. Revelation 22:20—'Surely I come quickly!' "

"I told you it was a caper some guy rigged up."

"That's what you told me. But I'm tellin' you that you heard it straight, and it didn't come from no White House. Two days, you said."

"That was yesterday. But—" Jordan's tone became anxious. "I told you, Mama, I need help."

"You need *God*."

"Yeah. Not much of that at Bible school. Only now—"

"I know, I been listening to you. You sure run off on a siding somewhere."

Jordan caved in. "O.K., tell me about God."

Mother Foster settled back in her chair. "If a man's close to God, if God's got a grip on him, he can't be close to the world. I reckoned you'd find that out."

"Go on." Jordan poured some fresh coffee.

"The name of the Lord is a strong tower, an' the righteous can run and hide in it and be safe. But when a preacher's spendin' all his time makin' noises in the world, he can't be filled with the Spirit of God."

"You're saying I'm not close to God?"

"I'm saying you're a disappointed man, Jordan. You tryin' to go big time, an' all you done is bust up your family and bring reproach to God's house. Lucy tells me they're changin' the locks on the doors just to keep you out."

"And you really think the Lord's coming?" Jordan wondered whether this was a first sign of Alzheimer's disease.

"I've had that feelin' for a month. I'm an old woman, Jordan. I seen a lot of pain, a lot of heartache. An' I done a lot of prayin' for you in this room. So much of my joy an' my hope in this life is wrapped up in you, boy. I remember the day you left for Bible school, you were so full of Jesus they couldn't hardly get a baseball glove on you. But then they went to work on your mind and let your soul go. I still say you're a good man."

"Thank you, Mama."

"God don't want to hurt your pride, son."

"No, Mama."

"He wants to kill it."

Jordan smiled ruefully. "How about that!"

"Do you pray, boy?"

"Oh, I pray. I haven't slammed the door on God. I just think most people use religion to get one-up on other people."

"I want you to start pleading the promises of God. Ask Him to do what He says He'll do, then back away so's He can do it."

"Yes, ma'am." Foster stood up and looked at his wristwatch. "It's about your lunch time, right?"

"Sit down," ordered Mother Foster. "I ain't finished." He sat down. "What you goin' to do about that church?"

"I'm going to tell them I'm sorry—" His voice broke.

She leaned forward. "Jordan, kneel down." He did so, and she laid her hand upon her son's head. "Listen to me. God is going to squeeze all that hot air out of you so He can pour His Spirit into you. Understand? He's gonna teach you how to straighten out your life and love everybody. Even your wife. And when a hand is laid on your head just like this, you'll know it has come to pass."

A numinous shudder went through Jordan as he rose to his feet. Wiping his eyes, he kissed his mother, thanked her for the coffee and the blessing, and left. Once outside and in his car, he paused a moment before turning the key in the ignition. Where did things stand? What had changed? Nothing. And yet at that instant he had an overpowering feeling that something remarkable, something supernatural was about to take place, and that for once he was on the right side.

9

"Look, Colly," said Raymond, turning around in the blue Buick sedan, "Colorado Boulevard—the street of the Rose Parade. Too bad you'll miss it." His voice sounded as if they were the best of friends, but his smile had an edge to it.

"Oh?" asked Dr. McMurtrie, the scholarly vice president who was driving them to the Azusa campus.

"She'll be in Europe," explained the president-elect.

"We may have kind of a parade today," observed McMurtrie wryly, "but there'll be no roses."

Colleen spoke from the backseat. "I'm afraid I don't understand, Doctor."

"People don't want our jet propulsion laboratory turned over to the Pentagon. It's generating some controversy. Most of the faculty want it kept for pure research in space—and so do the students."

"Then why do it?"

Raymond snorted at Colleen's question, but the vice president was gentler. "There's the matter of funding. Right now there's no federal money available for space probe work. We have to stay alive."

"And that's not all," said Phillips grimly.

"Oh? I suppose you mean the election." McMurtrie pulled onto the Pasadena Freeway, heading east. "You've probably heard, Mrs. Phillips, that some of our faculty are claiming that your husband's election was rigged."

"I thought it was all settled."

"Not quite. They're petitioning for a new election."

"Welcome to the land of COBOL and FORTRAN, Mr. President," said a bearded young man with a Magyar nose as he greeted the official tour party at the entrance to a low, cryptlike stone building. This was the massive structure known around the world as the Pacific Institute's Division of Technological Research or "think tank."

President-elect Phillips turned to the others in the group, which included a student security guard, the chairman of the board of trustees, two vice presidents, the president of the academic senate, the director of the research division, the director of the jet propulsion laboratory, and Colleen. "This, gentlemen, I couldn't wait to see," announced Phillips in a tone of dignified and subdued excitement. "I have great plans for this building. Unfortunately, when I was here before it was closed."

"One of those things, Mr. President," apologized the director of research. "A student broke under stress and ran amok. We were operating again in two days."

"It's really a peek into the future," said Phillips, ostentatiously taking Colleen's arm. "Lead on, sir," he told the bearded one, who informed them his name was Zoltan. Except for one or two persons lounging at desks, the windowless building was empty of personnel, it being Saturday morning. Zoltan led the party through room after room filled with computers, word processors, printers, modems, storage blocks, read assorters, memory banks, and linkage equipment.

Making sure Colleen was watching, Phillips pointed to a device over the door of one room. "Cameras?" he inquired with a professional air.

"Yes, Mr. President," said Zoltan smoothly, "we have cameras everywhere."

"Occasionally secrets are developed here that commercial researchers would like very much to exploit," commented the director of the research division. "We're always checking for unauthorized personnel."

"Unfortunately you can't stop bribery," remarked Phillips. Then he asked, "Is there much head-hunting?"—using the jargon pointedly.

"We've lost a few of our younger faculty to the corporations," admitted the research director. "We have to keep our telephone books locked up. But it's hard to protect your staff, sir, when big money is floating around."

They passed some rooms with more comfortable furniture. "Advance development work is usually done by groups of faculty and graduate students," Zoltan said, "but sometimes a program analyst or researcher wants to explore a line of thought by himself." He pointed to a series of small rooms, each locked. "These are the isolation chambers," he said, "the real 'think tanks.' No rocks to examine, no test tubes, no telescopes."

"No interruptions," added the research director.

"What do they think about?" asked the senate president dubiously, his field being the history of Greek civilization.

"Not about Aristotle's categories," laughed one of the vice presidents.

"Among other things, about the future," said the director of research. "What will be the requirements of the earth's population thirty years from now? Suppose there are space colonies—what will life be like there? What genetic modifications will be required? What fuels will people be using? What machines will they need? And where will the energy come from? All this requires basic research before programs can be instituted."

Phillips sensed the need to reassert control of the tour party. "You see, gentlemen," he said with a touch of pomposity, "coming into this building for me is like coming home. In fact (with a sidelong glance at Colleen) I expect it *will* be my home. One of the strong reasons why I accepted the call to your presidency was my growing conviction that this division must be expanded into a great projective research center. I can see it providing accurate forecasts in a dozen fields for scientists and government commissions all over the world. There is a sense of destiny about this place. I feel it!"

"Over here is my cubicle," said Zoltan in a flat voice, as they passed a central section. "I'm a publications specialist."

By now they were aware of a gradual buildup of noise coming from the front entrance. Automobile horns were sounding, and shouts were turning into something that sounded like a rhythmic chant. The security guard had been conversing on his walkie-talkie; now he returned and whispered to Zoltan. The rest of the group crowded around them.

"It's a small demonstration," Zoltan announced. "The police are asking us to remain inside."

"Would some of the people who work here be among those out there?" asked Colleen shrewdly.

"A few," conceded the research director.

"More than a few," said Dr. McMurtrie.

"Some of the people on our research staff are—let us say—politically motivated," explained the research director.

"I wish it were that simple," said McMurtrie. "President Phillips no doubt is aware that the whole research industry is high in personal and emotional problems."

"They're shouting my name," said Phillips, ignoring the discussion. "I would like to go out and speak to them."

"Sorry, sir," said the security guard, "we've been asked to keep the group here."

"I'm going," said Phillips, striding toward the front door. "Don't try to stop me." He pushed it open and stepped outside, to be greeted by a score or more of students who had gathered at the entrance. Several of them were carrying placards, announcing their opposition to war or calling for the election of Professor Alcorn.

"I am Raymond Phillips," he said. "What can I do for you?"

"Go back where you belong," shouted a balding student. "We want Alcorn." Loud cheers echoed his statement.

"Your election was phony," said a student with a bushy red beard. "We demand that you resign."

"I can't resign," quipped Phillips coolly. "I haven't been installed yet."

"You want us to build bombs and kill people," shouted a female student who wore designer Levis and a T-shirt emblazoned with the initials, "P.I.T.S."

"You are mistaken," retorted Phillips.

"We're for peace," said the balding student. "We didn't come here to make Star-Wars weapons for the Pentagon."

"Suppose," said Dr. Phillips, "you all come to my office on

Monday and we'll set up a forum to discuss this and any other issues you might bring up."

"What about the jet lab?" asked the red-bearded one. "Will you keep it a peace lab?"

Dr. McMurtrie, who with the others had come outside, now stepped to the side of Phillips. "The school has concluded no final arrangements with the Defense Department," he said. "Let me assure you we are still in the consulting stage."

"We don't trust you," said the girl in the P.I.T.S. shirt.

"May I suggest," responded McMurtrie, "that you accept President Phillips' generous offer for Monday? I'm sure many of you have heavy weekend study assignments. There's no point in further discussion."

"No! No! No!" shouted the students. A heavy-set football letterman spoke up: "We want your promise that this school will not become part of the war machine!"

Colleen Phillips, who had been standing with the others in the tour group, now walked forward to face the students. She raised her hand for silence. "I am Mrs. Raymond Phillips," she said in a high, clear voice. Her startled husband's mouth puckered as if he had just eaten a green persimmon; he seemed to sink into his collar. "I'm with you!" she announced to the students, who responded with scattered applause and the waving of placards. "I don't want to see this beautiful campus—or any campus, for that matter—become a staging area for mass murder. I'd sooner see it blown up and floating in the ionosphere." The applause turned to cheers.

"I think, however," Colleen continued, "that you are not being fair to my husband. We have just arrived from the East. Your president-elect has given out no interviews to the media. He has chosen not to say publicly what he believes or does not believe. He has deliberately waited until he could address you, the faculty and students who have invited him here. If I understand American sportsmanship, we should let him deliver his inaugural message tomorrow. After that you will have a right to judge both him and the future of this campus. Thank you very much. God bless you."

Cheers went up from a few students, and some of the placards were lowered. Not all were happy, however. The heavyset student objected, "It'll be too late then. We want his word now!"

"What about you?" asked the P.I.T.S. girl. "Will you picket the school if the Pentagon takes over?"

"An 'if' question deserves an 'if' answer," said Colleen easily. " 'If' I'm here."

By this time the students had begun discussion with each other, and it was obvious the confrontation had come to an end. Members of the tour party gathered around Colleen to congratulate her, but found several female students ahead of them. Dr. McMurtrie sought out the president-elect. "What a jewel," he murmured, "and what an asset she must be to you. I had no idea—"

Raymond, stunned and disconcerted, waited by himself until he could take Colleen by the elbow and steer her toward the waiting Buick.

10

Dressed for lunch in a knit that shouted "French," Charlotte waited with Alison for the Green Tower elevator to reach the thirty-second floor. As the lift paused at that level a rumpled-looking man in his middle forties emerged, wearing a convention badge. "Charlotte!" he exclaimed.

Both women appeared startled, but Charlotte recovered quickly. "Why, hello, Irwin," she said smoothly, nudging Alison past her brother into the cage. "I didn't expect to see you."

"I was just coming up to give you an official family welcome," he said, smiling.

"Oh?"

Alison's shrewd eye looked over her boss' brother, about whom she had heard much, none of it favorable. Irwin was slightly taller than Charlotte and had the same square build around the shoulders. There was a resemblance, too, about the eyes; but how much of Charlotte, Alison wondered, was in him?

"Look, sister, I'm free for lunch—why don't you join me?"

Right enough, thought Alison, he's making contact early. Aye, but he has his chores cut out before Charlotte will ever treat him like a brother.

They paused at floor 10, where a man in T-shirt and running pants came aboard. He had been jogging in place while waiting in the hall, and now began flexing his knees and arms in the elevator. "Lobby, please," he puffed.

"Yes, I believe I will," said Charlotte with sudden purpose "Alison will excuse us, won't you, Alison? This is my secretary, Miss Pitt-Barr. My brother, Mr. Embree."

Alison nodded and murmured, "Pleased, I'm sure."

"You're holding up the package, since we haven't heard from Ralph," Charlotte reminded her. "Aren't you?"

"Right." Alison had difficulty concealing her elation.

When the elevator reached the lobby floor, the runner darted out. Alison followed him with her eyes, then shrugged her shoulders and jogged out through the lobby herself. She made her way to a telephone, then went out onto Figueroa Street where a taxi was waiting.

"I didn't know you were part of this group," said Charlotte after she and her brother Irwin had been properly seated in a nook of Beaudry's exclusive restaurant off the lobby court. "I thought these were all top executives."

Irwin smiled at the cut. He had, in fact, a perpetual smile, not because things were that good, but because he was a solo drinker, and was always a dram or two up on the world. His quiet habit kept his jowls puffy and his eyes moist, giving him the look of a compassionate beagle. A lighted cigarette on which he never drew was usually dangling from his mouth, causing a perpetual squint in the left eye as he bent his neck to avoid the smoke.

122 / The Doomsday Connection

"I admit I don't look the part," he said (a fact obvious from his tailoring), "but here I am!"

"Is the drywall business still paying your salary?" Charlotte asked, eyeing the ashes on his lapel.

"Oh, sure." Irwin blew off some more ashes and drew a letter from his pocket. "Before I forget, I was coming to see you and give you this letter. In it I've tried to explain some things. Take it along and read it later."

"I'll read it now," said Charlotte, putting down her fork and opening the letter with her knife. She skimmed through four paragraphs, then put it down and reached for her wine glass. "Very interesting."

"I thought it might help straighten things out," smiled Irwin.

"It's a little late," she replied. Should she add something? It was such a delicious moment. The impulse was there. The cousins' portion of the firm was all but in her pocket. If there had been any hitch, Ralph would have telephoned. She decided to do what she had contemplated doing a thousand times: drop the forge on her brother. "You might be interested to learn that I am now the principal stockholder of Embree Drywall."

The smile disappeared and Irwin's face turned a sickly white. "When did you work that?"

"My lawyer picked up the proxy certificates last night. They will give me controlling interest, and after the board meets I will be serving you with one month's notice. Your services will no longer be required by our company."

"But you can't—"

"Oh yes I can," said Charlotte, attacking her salad. "You'll get your severance pay and a retirement settlement."

Irwin lit another cigarette and left his expensive luncheon plate untouched. "How long has all this been going on?"

"Ever since you pulled that on me."

He ignored the wine and drank from his water glass. "What do you intend to do?"

"First I'll be sending in a team of managers to take over and put the plant on a cost-efficient basis. We use some drywall in our expansion work. Then after I study the flow charts, I may put it on the market."

"They told me you'd grown hard, Charlotte, and you slice off heads without a trace of gore. . . ."

"Is that so?" Charlotte sipped her wine.

"I told you in my letter I plan to make things right. Full restitution for anything you feel—"

"Forget it. You'll be needing restitution more than I will."

"Blanche says she'd like to see you."

Charlotte sniffed. "We're flying back tomorrow evening."

Irwin removed his cigarette. "Don't you think, Sis, that we're just a little old to be perpetuating a family feud like this, for God's sake. . . ."

"I'm not interested."

"You weren't like this when we were kids. I know you, Charlotte. You're not this way underneath."

Charlotte slipped the letter into her purse. "Samuel Johnson said that no man is a hypocrite in his pleasures. This is my pleasure, Irwin. Thank you for the lunch." And sliding out of her seat, she walked into the lobby court.

11

"Rick says he's not comin'," announced Rennie Lopez as he met Linda outside Calvary Bible College's faculty board room.

"How come?"

"Says the dean's right. It was a fake."

"How about—" But at that instant Rick pushed his way through the main doors of the administration building. To their inquiring gaze he responded by running a comb through his grown-out butch. "Changed my mind. But not about that. I just didn't want to—"

"Get kicked out," supplied Linda.

Rick ignored her. "Nobody's buying us," he said to Rennie.

"Lots of people in the Bible heard voices," said Rennie stoutly.

"So did Joan of Arc," added Linda.

Rick turned his head. "And look what happened to her!"

The door to the board room opened, and they were ushered into the handsomely paneled room. Portraits of founders and patriarchs looked down sternly from the walls. Thick Persian rugs of considerable antiquity covered the floor. In high-backed chairs around an oval-shaped table sat the Bible faculty, six strong, with Dean Mallory at the head.

Chairs for the three students awaited them at the foot. It was an atmosphere of solemnity and dignity such as a Bible college can sometimes uniquely convey, and for which many Gothic cathedrals could be said to struggle in vain with their arches and flying buttresses.

Shades were drawn in such a way that the sunlight struck the students in the eyes, making it difficult for them to see the faculty and increasing their feelings of alienation. Then the Bible scholars rose to their feet and introduced themselves informally. Some light, friendly expressions made the students feel that the pressure was lifting. All were seated, and the meeting began with the dean leading in prayer.

"Now," said Professor Oberholzer, the head of the Bible faculty, who was seated on the dean's right, "we want to emphasize to our young friends that this is in no way an inquisition. We came together to consider other matters this afternoon, and we shall just treat this as a friendly preliminary exchange."

The trio began to feel uneasy again.

"Let me present our students properly," said Dean Mallory. "These remarkable young people flew back yesterday from Virginia after a very-well received performance on CBN Network. Renaldo Lopez and Linda McDowell are music majors, and Rick Ramsey is a student in telecommunications. They have just presented our school with their first album," and he held it up.

"And I understand they believe the world is coming to an end tomorrow afternoon?" asked Profesor Nilsson.

"Well, not—" began the dean.

"I wonder why this couldn't have waited over till Monday,"

continued Nilsson. "That would have taken care of the matter nicely."

"Without complicating the weekend," added Professor Langham.

Rick and Rennie exchanged dubious glances, but Linda spoke up: "We may be out of town Monday."

Everyone laughed.

"Well," said Professor Oberholzer, "I suggest we hear from the students whatever they wish to share with us about this episode on the plane or wherever it was."

The students were silent.

"Tell them what you heard, Linda," urged Dean Mallory.

Linda suddenly looked very Indian. "We were on our way from New York," she said, "when we were hit by lightning. Then we began to drop real fast and we heard this talk. That's all I know."

"Talk about what?" inquired Professor Oberholzer.

"It sounded something like an invitation."

"An invitation to what?"

"Well—to God!"

"It said that after two days, judgment was going to be executed on the earth," said Rick.

"And everybody was to come into the ark," added Rennie.

" 'After two days.' After what two days?" persisted Oberholzer. When no reply came forth, he continued, "What did you make of 'coming into the ark?' "

"We thought it just meant, 'Come to Christ,' " said Linda.

"She could be right there, technically," put in Professor Langham. "Ever since Tertullian and Jerome, typology has used Noah's ark as a classic symbol of the church."

"A refuge from judgment," agreed Professor Nilsson.

"A metaphor of salvation," agreed Professor Chernowith.

"We all know that," said Professor Oberholzer impatiently. Turning to the students, he said, "You are Christians and you read your Bibles or you wouldn't be here. Now tell me, why would God go against His own Word, which states that when Christ appears for His church He will come suddenly, unexpectedly, without warning? The Gospels state plainly that He will not announce His arrival in advance, and that He warned His disciples against any date-setting."

"Not only that," added Mr. Arleigh, "but Christ told us that He does not even know the time of His return. Only the Father knows it."

"You see," said Oberholzer, nodding his head like a rooster closing in for the kill, "Christians have been deceived by this kind of millenarian foolishness for centuries. Here's what the record says: When the elect are removed at the Rapture, the Restrainer is also removed. Then comes the great apostasy of the church. The world will be gripped by a tremendous buildup of evil power, and the man of sin will be revealed. This is the Antichrist, the world dictator. Then we shall see—"

"The ten nations coming together," said Mr. Arleigh.

"And the Great Tribulation," said Professor Nilsson.

"And the Battle of Armageddon," said Professor Langham.

"And the return of Christ the Judge," said Professor Chernowith.

"And the setting up of the Millenial Kingdom," said Mr. Baum.

"And the lake of fire, and the new heaven and the new earth," said Professor Nilsson.

"Now you can see," said Professor Oberholzer, "if all these things have to take place according to the written Word of God, what you heard yesterday had to be spurious."

"Bogus," said Mr. Arleigh.

"Counterfeit," said Professor Nilsson.

"Specious," said Professor Langham.

"Phony," said Professor Chernowith.

"Simulated," said Mr. Baum.

"Only yesterday," Professor Oberholzer continued, "the *Times* carried an item about a supposed lost fragment that turned up from the heretical Gospel of the Hebrews, saying that Jesus told His disciples He would give advance notice of His return. . . ."

"Impossible," said Mr. Arleigh.

"Pure legend," said Professor Nilsson.

"Pseudepigrapha," said Professor Langham.

"And even if it were true," added Professor Oberholzer, "it wouldn't affect the timetable of prophecy in the slightest."

"You're telling us, then," said Rick, "that we've been duped. That's what the dean said. And that's what I think."

"The voice may have been demonic," nodded Professor Oberholzer.

"More likely just an electronic trick," said Mr. Arleigh.

Rennie spoke up hesitantly. "I'm not so sure, sirs. I think we ought to be out warning people. He's got to come sometime."

Dean Mallory cleared his throat. "I think it's time we drew this matter to a close. Let me read to you a passage from Second Peter that applies here: 'Seeing then that all these things shall be dissolved, what manner of persons ought you to be in all holy conversation and godliness, looking for and hasting unto the day of God.' We all know the signs given in prophecy, and we all know that while Jesus could come at any time, He warned us against speculation and false voices. But notice what Peter says. He asks, if the Lord is coming back, what kind of persons should we be? And his answer is that we should be holy. We should be peaceful and loving. We're to be filled with the Spirit."

"I challenge that," said Professor Langham. "Nowhere does the Apostle Peter say we're to be filled with the Spirit. That's Paul's word."

Professor Chernowith added, "And you forget that by this time the Holy Spirit has already been removed."

"Now I challenge that," objected Professor Nilsson. "Never is the 'Restrainer' of Scripture referred to as the Holy Spirit."

"Oh, I'm sorry, you're wrong there. But then, you've always been wrong there," countered Professor Chernowith.

"Gentlemen, gentlemen," soothed Professor Oberholzer, "let's not—"

"You just went to the wrong school," snapped Professor Nilsson.

"Why would you pop off with a statement like that when it's clearly not Scriptural?" demanded Professor Langham of Dean Mallory.

The discussion continued with mounting rancor until Professor Oberholzer stood and, raising his voice above the battle, said, "My recommendation is that these young people enroll next semester in Mr. Arleigh's course in dispensational studies, where all these subjects are taken up in detail."

"Amen!" said the dean.

But the young people had slipped out of the room.

"Well, now we got it straight," declared Rick Ramsey as he and his companions stood on the front steps of the Administration Building. "They think we're nuts, and I say they're right."

"If you ask me, they're nuts," said Rennie.

"I feel like yesterday's omelet," said Linda.

"Listen!" Rick was combing his hair fiercely. "This whole thing has probably put us on the faculty hit list. I'm going to bug out right now."

"You can't do that," protested Rennie. "We're on TV tomorrow."

"Not me."

"Why not?" asked Linda, alarmed.

"Because I can't handle it, don't want it, and won't do it."

"But all we're gonna do is sing."

"Oh, no!" Rick jabbed his finger at Rennie. "He's got some big deal going on about giving out a warning to the television audience. I heard about it. And I don't want any part of it!" Putting his comb in his pocket, Rick walked off.

Rennie laughed ruefully as he watched him depart. "Now what do we do?"

Linda looked at her watch. "They say why pray when you can worry? How about if we meet in front of the library at four o'clock and go from there?"

12

"I'll get back to you, Miss Embree, or one of our people will," said the voice on the golden telephone. "What's your room number?"

"The Huntington suite. Gréen Tower."

"We'll do what we can."

"Thank you. Remember me to Mrs. Fairbank."

Charlotte Embree hung up and turned, momentarily pleased with herself, to face the panorama from her window. She had stormed the citadel of power; the president of Intercontinental Airlines had interrupted his golf game to address her complaint.

The telephone rang; it was Ralph at last. "I'm downstairs, about to take the afternoon off."

"You—" sputtered Charlotte.

"You wanted me to look in on your franchise in Malibu," Ralph continued easily, "then I thought I'd go out to an amusement park near Ojai. See if it's any better than Coney—"

Charlotte recovered herself. "What do you mean, you're about to take off?" she thundered. "Where are those proxies?"

"The cousins weren't home."

"That's ridiculous. You told Alison—"

"I mean the other cousins, Harry and JoAnn. They hold most of the cousins' stock, and they're in Oregon. Won't be back for a week."

So it was going to be one of those days, after all. Or was it life closing in? "Come up here," Charlotte ordered. "I want to see you." She hung up.

In a few minutes Ralph presented himself at the door of the suite. "I warned you to call from New York before you tried to set this up," he said with an urbane smile.

"That's hardly the point," sniffed Charlotte. "You've got to arrange to go after them."

"Why? They don't have the proxies with them."

"Who did you talk to? Lou?"

"I think that's her name. Louise Embree."

Charlotte assumed the role of a field general regrouping after a disastrous skirmish. "Does Lou know where to reach them?"

"She didn't have an address, just Enterprise, Oregon. Staying in a motel, she thought, while they look at some property."

"Call Triple A. Get a list of the motels. If you can reach Harry, he can call Lou and tell her where the proxies are, and then you can fly to Oregon and get their signatures."

"Why the rush?" Epstein appeared amused. "You'd think the world was coming to an—"

"This is terrible," burst out Charlotte. "I've already fired Irwin."

"You WHAT?" Ralph suddenly lost his smile. "How could you do that when I didn't have the—"

"Don't just sit there," interrupted Charlotte. "Get on the phone to Lou. You could have done this last night. Where were you? Why didn't you call us back? You could have saved me all this."

"I—" Epstein paused. "Firing Irwin was not my idea, Charlotte."

"Never mind. Where were you?"

"To tell you the truth, I went to the synagogue."

Charlotte was flabbergasted. "The synagogue? I thought you told me—"

"—that I hadn't been since my bar mitzvah. So what? He was a good speaker. I enjoyed it." Charlotte turned her back and looked out the window while he continued, "He talked about the twelfth principle of faith and get this: it's the belief in the coming of Messiah, the Son of David. Talk about coincidence!"

"I don't want to hear about it. Aren't you going to get on that phone?"

"Sure. Where's Alison?"

"Who knows? She's disappeared."

"Do you want me to page her?"

"I've already done it."

"I'll phone from my room." Ralph was reminded of his firm's six-figure retainer. "I guess I'll have to put off my little jaunt into the country until tomorrow."

"Tomorrow you should be on your way to Oregon." Ralph started toward the door when a knock was heard.

Standing in the doorway, to her amazement, was Irwin, smiling and cool. "Yes, Irwin?" Charlotte's apprehension made her voice sharp. Then recalling her manners, she said, "Oh—this is my attorney, Mr. Epstein. My brother." The men shook hands, after which Ralph arched his eyebrows at Charlotte and left.

Irwin looked around the suite admiringly. "Well, Sis, you picked yourself a gorgeous spot."

Charlotte left the window and walked back to her desk. "How is the convention?" she asked pointedly.

"Just getting started." Irwin lit a cigarette. Something in his manner betrayed an Embree-like confidence he had not shown at lunch. To Charlotte it was a taunt, a bugle in the camp.

"Since you're here, let's take a look at your letter." She put on her gold glasses. "You say you've worked out a plan."

"It'll be ready Monday."

She looked up. "A plan isn't going to make up for all that's happened, Irwin. I'm going back. I mean, *way* back."

Irwin found a chair. "We had a pretty good home life, didn't we? You were my kid sister—I teased you a lot. If you mean the time you got whipped because I—"

"I'm talking about the whole growing-up process," said Charlotte quickly. "You were a boy. You were fourteen months older than I. You were taller, stronger, could run faster, swim farther, and do everything better than I. And you could make me do anything you wanted. Don't you remember? When we played handball, if by some fluke I beat you, you made me play over again until you could beat me."

Irwin sat with his hands clasped over his stomach and wished for a drink.

"Dagger's Dungeon," she continued, warming to the challenge, "does that ring a bell? It was a manhole leading down to the sewer main and had side vents. You told me there was treasure down at the bottom, and you got me to crawl down into that hole. Then you ditched me. Don't you remember that?"

"Vaguely. Why bring it up now? Every family has memories they try to forget."

"I didn't forget. And I didn't really grow up. I sucked my thumb till I was eleven years old. You kept telling me I was second-rate, and I've still got the scars."

"I saved your life once."

"I knew you'd bring that up. It doesn't change a thing."

"What if I said I'm sorry?"

"For what? For all the times you twisted the skin on my wrists until I screamed? It was that kind of treatment that made me into the person I am. I remember going to bed thinking how I would twist your arm some day, and become so powerful that nobody would ever hurt me again."

Irwin looked at her with amusement, and blew some ashes off the end of his dangling cigarette as she continued.

"After Dad died, I got to thinking, someday I'm going to get hold of that company and Irwin will be *out*. So now you come lolling around, saying you're sorry and you have a plan. Well, you can take that plan and—" She ended abruptly as an inner voice reminded her that the proxies were still outstanding. Where was Alison? "I have to call the desk."

"Wait," said Irwin, "we're not through." Charlotte paused, her hand on the telephone. "You're probably right, being my kid sister wasn't that easy. But I didn't make Dad change his will, if that's what you mean by my 'pulling something.'"

Charlotte took her hand off the phone. "Who did then?"

"He did it himself. It was his idea."

"That's a lie!" said Charlotte quickly. "You never mentioned it."

"You were informed. I've got all the records."

"This better be good," said Charlotte, settling back.

Irwin lit another cigarette. "It was about a month before Dad died. He knew I was in trouble with cash flow and the banks were putting pressure on me. He told me then that if the business went, everything went."

"I want to see those records," interrupted Charlotte.

Irwin nodded. "You know in his original will he left you and me each 25 percent of the stock he owned in the company. The cousins got the rest from Uncle Ben."

"Go on."

"Well, at the time the stock wasn't doing too well—still isn't. But Dad had some negotiable securities of his own and some cash in the bank."

"Of which I saw nothing."

"Neither did I. With Mother gone, Dad planned to divide the estate between us, fifty-fifty, but under the circumstances he felt he had to protect the stock. So he liquidated just about everything and put the cash that was supposed to come to us back into the corporation."

"But surely that was just a loan."

"You're right. It was originally; but just before he died he forgave the loan."

"He did *what?*" Charlotte shouted.

"He said we didn't need the money as much as the company did. You remember you were going through a divorce back east and he didn't want the family inheritance to become involved. He never did like Casper. He said I'd have a job with the firm, and he knew you had a good head on your shoulders and would come out on top."

"I don't believe it. He knew I needed that money."

"He said he couldn't sleep thinking about it, and it was undermining his health. But he promised he'd explain it all to you."

"He never did. Neither did you."

"Oh yes I did."

"This whole thing sounds like a cock-and-bull story," Charlotte snorted.

Irwin smiled. "It's the truth. Dad took the easy way out. There wasn't a thing I could do about it."

"What do you mean? You could have let me know. I was here for the funeral."

"Yes, and you flew to San Francisco right after the service. But I did write you at the time and filled you in. I remember because I put it in a Christmas letter and sent it to your home."

"I get thousands of Christmas cards," said Charlotte. "I seldom read them."

"Apparently."

"I do have a telephone."

"Sister, trying to ring you is like trying to ring the Oval Office."

Charlotte deliberately turned her back and stared out the window. "So now you're a martyr. Wasn't it John the Baptist who had his head cut off?"

"But my head isn't off yet." Irwin rose and buttoned his jacket.

Charlotte spun around. "What does that mean?"

"It means, sister, you may have spoken a bit too soon at lunch today. Or so I've learned."

The red light on the telephone began to flash. "Don't bet on it," Charlotte muttered as she picked up the receiver. Irwin stepped to the door.

"I'll be back tomorrow to hear your speech."

But his sister did not hear him. "Hello, Alison?" she was saying.

"It's your cousin Harry, calling from Oregon. How are you?"

"Harry? I'm glad you called. My lawyer's trying to get hold of you."

"I know. I talked to Lou this morning. She said a Mr. Epstein was out to see her. What's going on?"

"I'll let him tell you about it. Where can he reach you?"

"I've already got the word. Lou says you want to buy out the cousins and Epstein's advising us not to sell."

"He's *what?*"

"That's what Lou said. He talked to her this morning and said he'd changed his mind overnight. He's sending her back the papers."

"He didn't tell me that when I saw him. There's something wrong. He must be—"

"I agree Charlotte, something is wrong. That's why I called. Lou says the man told her you have some kind of vendetta against your brother."

"Harry, listen. She's got it all mixed up. Irwin was just here."

"I hope you're right. Irwin's a fine fellow, Charlotte. He drinks too much, but he's helped out our family many times. Right now he's having a little cash flow problem, but we're going to stand by him, and I think you ought to, too. Instead of taking his company away from him, you ought to be helping him."

"Did she tell you that?"

"It doesn't matter. I just thought I'd let you know, Charlotte, that we're not selling. JoAnn sends her love to you."

Charlotte put down the receiver and stared out the window at the angry redness in the western sky.

13

*F*ollowing Alison's instructions, the taxi driver pulled his cab to the curb in front of the Rose of Sharon Church. "You shouldn't wait here alone," he said.

"I'll be all right," she assured him. But the wait turned out to be a long one, giving time for reflections that were not always comfortable. The image Alison sought to present to the world was of a calm, prudent, sober, intelligent lady, but she had never succeeded in convincing herself. As she strolled up and down the sidewalk, wondering what she would do if the unthinkable happened and she really did have to face the Lord, certain actions loomed up in her mind and made her meditation so unbearable that she was glad to see a car approaching.

The Reverend Jordan Foster parked his Cadillac and stood looking curiously at Alison as she walked up to him. "Reverend Foster?"

"Yes indeed." He extended his hand with a smile. "You are—?"

"Alison Pitt-Barr. I was with you on that wild flight yesterday."

"I remember now. You wore a cap."

"A Scottish tam."

"Well, my goodness! And you've come down here. . . . I hope you haven't been waiting long."

"I know how busy ministers are. Can we talk?"

"We can sit in my car."

"I'd really like to see your church."

Jordan Foster looked embarrassed. "The truth is, ma'am, I've been trying to find a key to get in myself." They walked to the front door, where he fumbled with the lock and shook his head. "I guess I'll have to go around the side, if you'll excuse me."

Alison trailed after the minister and watched curiously as he jimmied a ground-level window, crawled in, and emerged slightly rumpled through the door to the furnace room. "We can get up to the sanctuary this way," he said, brushing himself. "You'll have to accept my apology, Sister—is it Barr-Pitt?"

"Call me Alison."

"Well, Sister Alison, somebody or something has been after me ever since I got off that plane." He led the way upstairs into the simply furnished auditorium. "I came home and learned that the deacons had called for my resignation. Now I find they've changed all the church locks—" He tried a door. "—even on my study. Let's just sit in one of these pews."

"Why would they do that?" asked Alison.

"Oh—" Foster sighed. "My wife and I are estranged; that's part of it. The gossipers have been at work."

"A rum thing." Alison scanned the room, taking in the Bible texts painted on the walls.

"Let's talk about what brought you down here," said Foster.

"I watched you on TV. You were smashing! Then last night I read that piece about some lost Gospel they found."

Foster nodded. "They showed it to me at the studio."

"When I was a little girl in Scotland," Alison said, "I was told if I had a spiritual problem, I should have a wee chat with the minister."

"All right. Where do we start?"

"I want to know if that voice we heard was for real."

"I'd like to know that myself. Very much."

"Let's say it was real. Then I want to know why."

"Why?"

"Yes. Why us? Why would God pick the likes of us to tell the world what He was going to do? I didn't notice any saints on that flight."

Jordan laughed. "I doubt if we were a sanctified crowd."

"Would you say we'd been had?"

"You know," Foster mused, "when God spoke in the Bible, He didn't single out the high and the mighty. He picked on small-fry like us."

"It may have been Oral Roberts."

"Or the Devil."

Alison's face darkened. "Not auld Hornie," she said in a thick accent. "I don't gie him an inch."

Foster mounted the steps to his pulpit. Placing both hands on the rails, he looked down at Alison. "Let's suppose we'll be with Jesus tomorrow afternoon. How do you stand?"

"Not ready. Up to my neck in thistles!"

"*You're* not ready! How would you like to have to present Him with this church? And be the shepherd who had to crawl into his own sheepfold through a window?" He held out his hands dramatically. "Here you are, Master. Here's your black-and-blue bride. Sorry about that." He stepped down from the pulpit. "Let's just hope there's no Testament of Daniel, and that somebody piped in that business about the ark."

Alison dabbed at her nose with a bit of tissue. "And where does that leave us?"

Foster smiled. "Frankly, I don't want Him to come. Not now. As soon as we get this mess straightened out, I've got some big plans."

"Can you tell me?"

"We're going to build two new halfway houses for young people coming out of prison. The first check will be here next week."

Alison warmed to his enthusiasm. "Isn't that exciting!"

"I'll have a chance to do something for my people."

Alison's expression changed. "Maybe it won't happen. What about your family?"

"I've got three boys."

"Do they know God?"

"One does."

Alison said, "I have a daughter, but I don't know where she is. I gave her up for adoption when she was born."

"Let's pray," said Foster, just as a rattling was heard at the front door. "That'll be the choir. We're getting ready for a musical tomorrow at Griffith Park." He started for the door, but stumbled on some hymnbooks piled in the aisle. As he stooped to pick them up he said, "I'd like you to meet my mother."

"I'd love to," said Alison.

"She says she's got her heavenly bags all packed and is ready to go."

Alison gave a silvery laugh as Jordan reached for the handle of the church's front door. At that moment it opened and a large black man burst in, followed by two uniformed policemen.

14

The large man confronted Jordan menacingly. "How did you get in?"

"This is my church, Deacon Warburton," said Foster quietly. "I'm your pastor."

"You mean it *was* your church and you *were* my pastor," announced Warburton loudly. Turning to one of the policemen, he said, "He's yours. Take him away."

Before the officer could move, Alison stepped in front of Warburton. "I beg your pardon," she demanded, "who do you think you are?"

The deacon looked down, surprised. "What's all this?"

Alison stretched to her full height and put an edge in her voice. "I am a visitor in God's house, and it occurs to me that this intrusion is out of order. Constable," she addressed one of the policemen, "do you have a warrant to do this?"

"Ma'am, we just got a call to see what the trouble was," responded the officer.

"Who informed you that there was trouble?"

"Dispatcher reported a break-in."

"That's right. This man broke into the church," said Warburton. "I can show you where—I was watching."

"You're the minister?" the officer asked Foster.

"I am."

"You don't have a key?"

"Well, it's—"

"What difference does it make?" interposed Alison. "I telephoned the pastor for some counseling, and we met here by appointment. Did you expect us to talk in the street?"

"Take him away," urged Warburton, "let him cool off."

"This is just an investigation," the officer reminded him.

Hearing a noise, Warburton stepped back and looked out the door. As he did so, the entrance was filled by a group of young and middle-aged people who came trooping in, laughing and joking. The mood of the new arrivals changed abruptly when they caught sight of their minister standing between two policemen. The word was passed outside, and a gray-haired man who appeared to be the choir director quickly entered.

"What's going on?" he demanded as he sized up the group. His question was echoed by several dozen singers who pushed in and crowded around the officers.

"What are you doing to our pastor?"

"They going to arrest him?"

"You can't do that. This is God's house."

"What right you got busting in here?"

"This is a free country, man."

"You're off your turf."

"Move, baby, move. Out the door."

"Call the D.A."

"He didn't do nothing."

"Get out. Get out. Get out!"

The chorus began to swell. Two women started shouting hysterically. Another screamed. Some young men moved toward the center and threatened to become physical. The two officers put their hands on their revolvers.

At this point Jordan Foster, sensing the need to defuse the situation, spoke to the choir director. He in turn spoke to Deacon Warburton. The deacon nodded, nudged the two officers, and made a path to the door for them. As they stepped outside, a choir member slammed the door.

"Just a minute," said Jordan Foster. "Leave the door open. You folks go on inside. There's no cause for alarm." As the noise level diminished, Foster spoke to Alison, then went out to the curb where the officers were sitting in their patrol car, talking with Warburton. "Please accept our apologies," Foster said, but got no response. To Deacon Warburton he added, "Leroy, would you like to come in and enjoy the music?" Warburton chose not to reply.

Inside, Jordan found Alison listening to the choir, and he tapped her on the shoulder. "The church office is open," he whispered. Once seated in the office, he told her, "You can wait until practice is over, or I can take you back to your hotel now."

"We're not through," Alison objected.

"Oh?" Jordan caught himself. "That's right, we were going to pray."

"Pastor," said Alison, her voice trembling, "I've never told this to a living soul, but I am a cheat." Foster listened quietly as she went on, "I owe a lot of money to the federal government— tax dollars. My employer used me as a dodge, and I went along with it. It's been three years now."

"But if it wasn't your money—" Foster began.

"Oh yes it was," said Alison fiercely. "I was paid and never reported it. Like everybody else, I was trying to survive."

"And you want to—"

"There's more." Alison was sobbing now. "My life is cursed, and I'm out of the kingdom. Will you pray for me?"

"I will if you'll pray for me. Whatever you've done, I've done forwards and backwards and bottom side up." As he began to pray, strains of music floated in from the choir:

> *"Oh, precious is that flow*
> *that makes me white as snow;*
> *no other fount I know,*
> *nothing but the blood of Jesus."*

When they returned to the auditorium, the choir director tapped his music stand and turned to the pastor, who assisted Alison up the pulpit steps and faced the choir members with her. "When the enemy comes in like a flood," he said, "then the choir comes in like a tidal wave!" Amid the laughter he continued, "Let me present Miss Alison Pitt-Barr, a fellow-passenger with me on the flight from New York yesterday. She has come for prayer."

The choir did not welcome her with applause. Instead it picked up,

*"Just a closer walk with Thee
Grant it, Jesus, is my plea. . . ."*

In the moments that followed, the choir kept a soft accompaniment as Jordan Foster led in prayer. He prayed for the services on the Lord's day, for Alison, for his mother, his wife and sons. Then he prayed for the choir, for Deacon Warburton, and for the whole congregation. The choir resumed its practicing, and Foster stepped into his study to pick up some books. As he did so, his telephone rang.

"Pastor Foster?" asked a male voice.

"Yes."

"This is Arvie Erickson. I spoke to you as we were getting off the plane yesterday."

"Oh yes, I remember. I'm sorry, Mr. Erickson, but—"

"Reverend, you gave me something to read and I was wondering if I could come and talk to you about it. Tomorrow."

"I'm afraid not. Tomorrow is a busy day. Is it something urgent?"

"It's for a term paper I'm working on."

"Then perhaps it can wait."

"I'm sorry to have troubled you, Reverend."

"Wait a minute. Didn't you inform me that you were not a believer?"

"That's correct. Not your kind, anyway."

"Then there's no point in talking to me, is there? You need to talk to God."

"I beg your pardon?"

"You need to have a talk with God. I suggest you go out in

the hills somewhere. Talk to Him, and then you can drop over to my place and we'll talk. Now, if you'll excuse me, I'm just on my way out. . . ."

Putting down the receiver, Jordan Foster rejoined Alison and escorted her out of the church. They found that the deacon's station wagon and the patrol car had left. Getting into the front seat of the Cadillac, they were startled to hear a voice from the rear seat. "Don't move, don't say nothin'." Alison sat frozen. Jordan glanced in the mirror and saw a tense young face that was saying, "Now just start up and go where I tell you. Drive to the next corner and take a right." The minister recognized the voice of a small-time junkie and neighborhood pusher who had a lengthy record in juvenile crime. Something cold was pushed against the back of Jordan's neck. "Feel that? One slip and I'll blow your head off."

At the same time a hand seized the top of Jordan's head. "You hear me?"

Until that instant Foster was prepared to obey his assailant to the letter, though he realized his chances of survival were dicey. The hand on his head changed everything. He couldn't believe it. Only a few hours earlier his mother had made a solemn prophecy that such a sign would occur. And here it was fulfilled—by a thug! Jordan's response was to jam his foot on the throttle and swerve the heavy car into the street at such speed that his would-be kidnaper was flung back, firing his pistol into the car roof. Only her seat belt kept Alison from being hurled against the window.

"Slow down or I'll kill you!" yelled the youth.

"Listen, home boy," Jordan called out, using a tone he normally saved for the pulpit, "I don't know what it is you want, but tomorrow afternoon this whole world is coming to judgment, and for you and me it might just as well happen right now. So how would you like to go off the end of Pier J with me? Huh, boy?" He spun around a corner and headed south toward Long Beach with all tires squealing.

As the car accelerated, the face in the rearview mirror became contorted. Suddenly a gun butt struck Foster on the head and a hand reached past him for the ignition keys. Foster's response was to fishtail the Cadillac back and forth across the empty street, bumping up on sidewalks, while the youth in the rear seat fell back screaming and cursing.

"Throw your gun into the front seat," shouted Jordan.

"Pray to Jesus!" added Alison in a choked voice.

Instead the youth began to pistol-whip the minister from the rear. Alison watched in horror, not daring to interfere. A red traffic light loomed ahead; Foster sped through it and made a sharp right turn, throwing his passenger against the left rear door. The youth grasped the door handle as he attempted to regain his balance, but another twist of the wheel loosened his grip and he was thrown to the opposite side.

A police siren was heard in the distance. Jordan swerved and made another sharp right turn in the direction of the oncoming patrol vehicle. This time the youth's body struck the left door and it opened, spewing him into the street. Foster immediately applied his brakes and stopped. Leaping from the car, and telling Alison to remain where she was, he hurried to where the young man lay crumpled against the curb. As the officers approached, Jordan looked up and pointed to the gun lying on the sidewalk.

15

Maybelle Lewis was in good spirits. At the civic reception for President-elect Raymond Phillips in the Bonaventure's Sequoia Room, thanks to Mrs. Phillips, she and Reginald had met virtually the entire administrative faculty of Pacific Institute. She was aware that Reginald had slipped away after going through the line, but he had a key to their room and she was not about to pursue him. In fact, she was feeling the stress of surrogate parenthood sufficiently to require a quiet cup of tea. She made her way to the Sidewalk Cafe, where she sat happily anticipating the telephone call she would be making that evening to her daughter and son-in-law in Schenectady.

Meanwhile her grandson, free to pursue the goals of unfettered genius, had made an electrifying discovery. As he entered the atrium lobby, he saw standing by the "lake" and talking to two men none other than Vasily Mechikoff himself, the king of all the spies. With flight bag firmly in one hand, Reginald now undertook the Great Stalk. It involved studying the underwater lights, watching the yoyo-ing glass elevators, wandering past the exhibits, but always keeping his eye on his man. In another part of the atrium lobby he espied his grandmother at a table with a teacup in her hand, but he kept out of her sight.

And now came a break: one of the men talking with Mechikoff went to a telephone. Mechikoff broke away from the other and walked toward the lounge area. Was he heading for the men's room? He was! Reginald could not believe his good fortune. Making sure he was not under surveillance himself, he tracked his man into the elegant, gleaming lavatory and looked around. It was empty except for an elderly gentleman using a paper towel at the end of a row of sinks. Apparently the spy king had entered one of the stalls. Reginald placed his flight bag on a shelf and pretended to wash his hands.

When the older man left, Reginald lifted a tape recorder out of his bag and carried it to the built-in paper towel rack. Switching it on and turning up the volume, he lowered it by a cord into the used towel slot. Hearing the sound of running water from one of the stalls, he hastily made his exit.

Vasily Mechikoff was washing his hands at a bowl when his ears were assaulted by a stentorian voice: "LET THE PEOPLE KNOW AFTER TWO DAYS I SHALL EXECUTE JUDGMENT AND JUSTICE ON THE EARTH. BUT LET THOSE I HAVE FORMED FOR MYSELF COME INTO THE ARK."

For Vasily, the shock of the repeated message left him frozen. Then he looked around wildly for some source, but could find none. The tape recorder had shut itself off after the announcement, leaving him no clue. Vasily wiped his hands, placed the towel in the receptacle, and stared at himself in the mirror. He was profoundly shaken. Hearing the words again confirmed certain sentiments that had been at the back of his mind—if not, indeed, in his viscera—ever since he heard the words on the airplane.

As a good cadre, he had reluctantly accepted Moscow's assessment: this was code language. It could very well be part of a sinister propaganda move against the forces of world revolution and particularly against the U.S.S.R. Malof had guessed that right-wing extremists were behind it, and he was probably right. Yes, no doubt. *But in the washroom Vasily was alone,* with no Malof, no KGB, no trade mission, no foreign office to direct or interpret; and he became convinced what he had heard— twice—was none other than the voice of God.

In his youth, before he traded faith for expediency and adopted the colors of antireligious ideology, Vasily had heard the story of his father's conversion. Plowing behind a horse in a Soviet Georgia wheat field as a young man, Vasily's father (so the family tradition went) literally saw the heavens open as God spoke to him. After his father was taken away, Vasily's mother often reminded her children of the incident until it took on a mystical quality.

During his brief journey to America, Vasily had hardly given a thought to the possibility of defection. He loved Mother Russia. His wife and daughter lived in a comfortable apartment near the Hermitage in Leningrad. Following his assignment on the West Coast he was expected in Washington to inventory the software in the Soviet embassy, after which he was to return home.

All that was now suddenly, irretrievably changed. Life would never be the same. Nothing mattered—nothing—except getting out. Opening the restroom door a crack, he spotted an exit sign and disappeared into an alley. Behind him, he left his uneasy comrades in the atrium lobby, his family, the Amtorg Trading Company, and the Union of Soviet Socialist Republics.

Once out on Figueroa Street, Vasily hurried into a taxi and requested to be taken to an Eastern Orthodox church by an indirect—and speedy—route. The driver obliged, and after a hair-raising ride the taxi arrived in front of St. Basil's Greek Orthodox Church. Dismissing the driver, Vasily entered the sanctuary, lighted a candle, and carried it to the altar. He had not become a believer. He had a hundred reasons to deny the existence of God; his indoctrination had been massive and thorough. But somehow, in a very personal way, eternity had now broken into time, and he was more than confused, he was alarmed. He sat in a pew and remained there for some time, staring at his candle.

After watching his spy king disappear, Reginald reentered the washroom and, much to the astonishment of some Japanese tourists, retrieved his tape recorder from the towel disposal. He then returned to his grandmother's table where he listened with proper respect to her verbalized indignation. But as he followed her back to their tower elevator, Reginald was internally jumping up and down with satisfaction. Score two for the monkey demon! Los Angeles was turning out to be a blast.

At the elevator Reginald's euphoria suffered a setback when a tall, heavily bearded man with a bald spot followed them into the cage and stared at him with piercing eyes. Embarrassed, Reginald occupied himself with the flashing numbers and tried to think where he had seen that face before. But when they got off at their floor, the man stayed on, and the cloud passed.

16

Midafternoon found Frank Medeiros back in the Operations wing of Intercontinental Airlines, visiting the Weather section. Thompson, the meteorologist in charge, was off-duty, but his jocular young assistant, Doug Prucha, a transplant from southern Missouri, informed the captain he was "happy to be of service—what service?"

Medeiros went to the point. "What I want to know, Prucha, is what you can tell me about that weather system around Pike's Peak yesterday afternoon. I'm looking for any unusual atmospheric or seismic disturbances, and anything else you can find."

Prucha went to his computer, which put him immediately in touch with the National Weather Service. After trying several combinations he reported, "You sure took on some heavy weather. Snow, hail, four inches of rain on the lower slopes. Nothing else I can see."

"Any earthquakes?"

"No earthquakes, no volcanic eruptions, no falling meteors. Sorry, Captain."

"How about a voice?" (Medeiros thought to himself, What a ridiculous kind of probing for a future airline executive!)

"A what?" Prucha suppressed a laugh.

"A voice," repeated the pilot feebly.

"Weather around here doesn't talk that much. Did you hear something?"

"We picked up a signal, some guy talking about the end of the world and stuff. We're trying to locate it."

This time Prucha laughed. "Have mercy! What frequency?"

"Not sure."

"Can't your people run it down?"

"We're checking."

Prucha lit his pipe. "I was going to suggest NORAD, but that don't sound like NORAD to me. More like the Hollywood Revival Center!"

Medeiros' eyebrows went up. "NORAD. What about it?"

"Well, you know, North American Air Defense Command is doing odd things in the middle of Cheyenne Mountain, and the Air Force itself is conducting experiments around here all the time. But it looks to me like you picked up some joker—not that NORAD doesn't have a few around."

"The FAA has asked for an irregularity report," said Medeiros. "Tell me more about these odd things."

"Well, for one, they're superimposing communications signals over laser beams. When that happens, you never know what kind of result to expect."

"Could they possibly create a—"

"An audio disturbance? They might. You just don't know, and they won't talk—to me anyway."

"You don't have any contacts in Colorado?"

"Just weather people. And all they talk about is weather— wait a minute. Let me check something." Moving to his computer, he spent a few minutes punching keys, then called the captain over. "This might work for you. Sunspots."

"Sunspots?"

"Yep. They've been active for the past month. You know what they can do to our electromagnetic signals."

"Bulge the atmosphere? Harmonics?"

"Correct. Just the other day we got an anomaly report you wouldn't believe. A pilot was trying to put down in Algiers, and he was getting landing instructions from Miami International. Outstanding!" Prucha laughed again.

"Sunspots. Why didn't I think of that? It happened to me in Vietnam."

"All it takes is an inversion layer," said Prucha.

"I'll just keep sifting around. Appreciate your time."

"That's what I'm here for. When's your report due?"

Medeiros paused at the door. "Tomorrow morning."

Prucha took the pipe from his mouth. "Have you really analyzed what you heard, Captain?" he asked seriously. "Wouldn't that yield a clue?"

Medeiros shook his head. "You wouldn't believe it, Prucha. It was just a lot of garbage."

It being Saturday, Maintenance could not come up with any leads. Captain Medeiros found himself driving home, wondering whether "garbage" was after all a fair description of what they heard on the plane. It occurred to him that if the voice did have a divine origin, that would explain why the tape failed to record it. But such speculation was pointless, and besides, it made his skin crawl. What he really needed was something to palliate Roark Maddox. Sunspots were a more useful, and certainly a more sensible, hypothesis. What sunspot activity does to audio reception was known to every ham operator.

An electrical storm in outer space, however, could hardly

account for the kind of jerk who would get on the airwaves and transmit doomsday warnings. And there was always the connection with the lightning strike. He needed time, lots of time, to check it out; and that, Captain Medeiros realized grimly, was what he did not have.

17

*L*inda was stretched lazily on the library steps, a closed Bible in her lap, and was listening to a mockingbird concert when Rennie joined her. "I tried to pray," she said. "Too many hassles."

"Me too."

"My roommate said she heard we'd been suspended."

Rennie tapped her Bible. "Find anything?"

"I was looking up this verse: 'Always be prepared to give an answer to everyone who asks you the reason for the hope that you have.' But it doesn't tell you what to say if nobody asks."

"Or what to say if they do ask. I can't find Rick."

"Don't worry about Rick," said Linda.

"Why not?"

"Worry about us. Rick doesn't believe it. So O.K., he's honest. We say we do, but we're not doing anything about it."

"Well. . . ?"

"O.K., let's try it. Let's warn some people and see how it goes."

"What'll we warn 'em about?"

"About getting straightened out before the Lord comes."

"This is a Bible school. They're already supposed to be straightened out."

"Nah. If they're like the ones in my dorm, they're not ready for God, not by a whole lot. All we're ready for is cheerleader tryouts and boyfriends and homecoming and a new diet."

Rennie yawned, put his elbows back, and basked in the

sun's warmth. "You're right. This school's not ready." Linda
looked at him and smiled. The mockingbird finished his song
and departed for the Science Building. Rennie spoke again.
"O.K., let's try it. See what happens."

"I don't think I can," confessed Linda. "I never liked to
corner people."

"Me neither."

"Well, you're the man. Why don't you start?" She opened
her Bible. "I'll give you a verse."

"We don't need any more verses. We need a kick in the
pants."

"Ready?"

"Ready. Lord, help us!"

Rennie waved and whistled at a male student bicycling
slowly past the front of the library. Tall and bespectacled, he
stopped rather awkwardly when he saw them and began munch-
ing an apple.

"We got a word from the Lord," Rennie said, "and we
wanted to share it with you."

"Yeah? Whuzzat?"

"See, we were on this plane yesterday and we heard a voice
saying He's coming back to earth soon, maybe even tomorrow."

The cyclist looked over Linda and Rennie and took a large
bite. "Sure," he said, "I know." He continued on his way.

Two male students emerged from the Music Building. One
espied Linda and came over to speak to her. He found himself
listening with amazement to the story of Flight 803. "Interesting," he said when Linda finished.

"What's interesting?" demanded Rennie.

"That God would select people like you to spread the
news." He walked off.

A diminutive student in cut-off jeans sauntered past carrying
a jumbo-sized sack of popcorn into which he dipped periodical-
ly. Rennie had played chess with him, and so he tried again. He
told the story of the plane incident and then asked, "Mickey, if
Jesus came, would you be ready?"

Mickey offered some popcorn to Linda. "When?"

"Like maybe tomorrow?"

"What kinda odds you puttin' up? I mean, what are the chances like on a scale of one to ten?"

"Turkey, either you're going with Jesus or you're not!"

"I'd put it about one point five," said Mickey, dipping into his sack as he wandered away.

"This isn't going to work," decided Linda. "We've got to—there goes Debbie!" She took off after a plump girl just emerging from the library and brought her to where Rennie sat. "You know each other."

"Oh, sure."

"Did you hear about us being on CBN?"

"Oh, we watched it," gushed Debbie. "It was fantastic."

"Well, you know, we were flying back when we were hit by lightning and we heard this voice saying Jesus was coming back."

"No kidding! When?"

"Maybe tomorrow."

"That's weird," said Debbie. "Tomorrow I'm playing for a wedding—my roommate's sister. Is it ever going to be something!"

"Don't forget to put oil in your lamp," said Rennie.

Debbie stared at him. "What does he mean?"

"He doesn't mean anything," said Linda hastily.

"I've got to go." Debbie looked at Rennie. "I don't think that was very nice." She raised her voice. "Who do you think you are?" A number of students emerging from the library at closing time began to cluster around the group. Rennie and Linda got to their feet and repeated their story of the airplane flight. One of the students broke in and began arguing.

"Jesus Christ can't come tomorrow," he said. "If He were, Zeke would have told us."

"Who's Zeke?" asked Rennie.

"He's our teacher down at the Soul Center."

"That's a cult."

"It's not either a cult. We're Christians."

"I know about you," said another student. "You use surveillance and thought control. You turn kids into programmed robots."

"You need to get straight on Scripture," said the first student.

"If Jesus does come, He won't come here," spoke up another.

"Where will He come?" demanded Rennie.

"At the Mount of Olives. It's all in the Book."

"Our preacher at home is always talking like that," said a girl student.

"My folks are pre-Trib, but I don't go for any of that stuff," said the girl next to her.

"So what if Jesus comes back?" said a student wearing a Calvary T-shirt. "It wouldn't bother me. I'd face it."

"I hope He comes before midterms," said another.

"We're not a cult," repeated the first student. "Take that back."

"Why should I?" asked Rennie.

"You're an enemy of the truth."

"You're full of the stuff they put on lawns."

The head librarian emerged from the building just as Rennie and his adversary were squaring off. "I say, what's it about?" he asked mildly. "Seems a bit serious."

"It's nothing," said Linda.

"You've turned your back on God," said the first student.

"You're off the wall," said a student standing beside him. "You'll end up in the pit of hell."

"I say," the librarian spoke up, "it's all right to talk about spiritual things, but let's not let them get out of hand!"

But the brawl had already started, and while a growing number of students crowded around the flailing arms and legs, two students strolled away, one of them remarking to the other, "If He does come, I'm wondering if they'll carry it on all four networks."

"Probably Canadian too," nodded his companion.

18

Rick Ramsey sat in a booth of the Student Union Annex staring at a Pepsi and drenching himself in glum thoughts. As usual he was by himself. Unexpectedly he was joined by Jennifer Cochran, a new student from Bisbee, Arizona, who had spoken to him in chapel a couple of times.

Jennifer had a Spanish mother from whom she inherited her pointed chin and olive-black eyes and the dark hair she wore in long pigtails. On campus she was described in one all-encompassing word: "cute." Her girlfriends had warned her about Rick, whose negative disposition was already a topic of conversation. Their comments had only roused Jennifer's curiosity.

Rick looked up and smiled. The chemistry of youth was soon at work, and Rick began painting for her his canvas of woe: his parents didn't approve of Calvary and wanted him to transfer; the song he was working on didn't jell; and his biggest gripe—the classes he was taking.

"When I got saved," he said, "it was a whole new scene. God, music, the Holy Spirit, Jesus—everything fell into place. I found out what life was all about, and it was beautiful. I wanted to go out and save the world, get groups together, start them praising the Lord. I got with Rennie and Linda down at the Chapel, and we really had something going. I mean, we were out on the boulevard, and kids came around by the thousands. It was so different from the church I grew up in. Man, we had the beat.

"So then I end up in this place, and you know what it is? It's a training course for club directors. They don't care anything about Arcadia, or Los Angeles, or California, or the rest of the world. They want us to go out and start little clubs of middle-class Christians and be the directors. Build up a Sunday evening program. Set up a budget. Organize a drama group for quote young people unquote. Teach the Bible. You know, if Jesus

Christ were to come back on this campus, He'd be bored to tears."

Jennifer, who had ordered a root beer float, fiddled with the straw in her cup. "I hear you think He's coming back pretty quick."

Rick snorted. "That was a scam someone tried to pull on the airplane yesterday."

"You didn't believe it?"

"Naw. We were set up."

Jennifer laughed a high, tinkling laugh. "It's gotta end some time, Rick. Or don't you believe that either?"

"Sure I do. I just got back an A paper in eschatology."

She was laughing again. "I wonder if Francis of Assisi got an A in eschatology."

Rick was irked. "Francis was a Catholic."

"So what?" Rick remained silent, and Jennifer decided she had passed the point of sympathy. "Why don't you bust loose?" she asked.

Rick opened his eyes wide. "What?"

"I said, bust loose. This is the world, man. You're in it up to here. I mean, what's the point of being a Christian if you—?"

Rick blinked. "And how do I bust loose?"

"I mean, you're in a trap. You're right, this school is a trap. But the whole world is a trap." Not for nothing had they elected her president of Bisbee Youth for Christ.

"So? I'm in a trap."

"You don't have to be. There are ways—"

"I've prayed about it. Don't think I haven't."

Jennifer rolled her eyes. "Hah! I read somewhere most prayers can be answered either by a bunch of money or a kind friend."

Rick stared at her, eyebrows raised. "Don't you believe in prayer?"

"I'm talking about a trap, man. You're tied up."

Rick slumped. "I know it."

"Only one Person ever sprang that trap."

"And He's in the glory."

Jennifer's eyes blazed. "Like so much! He's here."

"O.K., He's here. So what do you mean, 'bust loose'?"

"Did you know Linda and Rennie are all over the campus telling about the plane and all?"

"Dumb." Rick sipped his drink.

"Sure, they're wrong, maybe. And your folks are wrong, and the school's wrong, and everybody's wrong, and here you sit, plastered all over with Bible verses and tied up in tape. And I say, bust loose!"

"Bust loose from the Bible? Is that—?"

"Good grief, no. Bust loose from what people are doing with it. Just go out and be a human being, Rick. There's a beautiful green earth out there, full of people and animals and trees and lakes and flowers and beaches. Why don't you just love people? Try another song. Kiss the sky. Just *be!*"

Rick looked at her narrowly. "Be filled with the Spirit?"

Jennifer's eyes were Christmas lights. "That's it! That's the way to face the end of the world!"

Rick looked at her for a long minute. "You know, when we first heard that voice, it sounded real."

"Maybe it was."

"But you don't think what Linda and Rennie are doing—"

"Why scream? Why not dance?"

Rick dropped his head. "Can't do it."

"Why not?"

He sighed and slipped back into his phlegmatic mood. "I dunno."

Jennifer hesitated a minute, then threw back her head and wailed, "Owoooo! Owooooooo!"

"What are you doing?" whispered Rick, looking around.

"I'm a coyote feeling sorry for myself. Mourning my creaturehood. Owoooooooo!"

People in adjoining booths looked over amusedly. Soon other caterwauling sounds began to echo through the annex. Rick became embarrassed. "All right, drown it. What are you trying to say?"

Jennifer stopped. "I want you to go back to them."

"You're out of your gourd. I told you what it was!"

"I want you to go anyway."

"Do you know what they're up to? We're supposed to sing on local television tomorrow morning, live, and they've got some idea of taking over the station and warning the world. And they want me on the console."

Jennifer's eyes were again sparkling. "Do it!"

"I'm not going to mess with it, Jennifer."

As he spoke her name, she suddenly became quiet. Neither spoke until she said, "I've been watching you, Rick. I think—" But she never told him what she thought. Instead she leaned forward and, cupping his face in her hands, kissed him slowly and fully on the lips.

Whistles and whoops began to emanate from the nearby booths. Rick, stunned, laughed in spite of himself. "Wow! What does that mean?"

Jennifer smiled demurely. "Guess."

"Guess what? You mean go back?"

"That's right."

"Why?"

"Because you're in a trap. You're like Lazarus, all done up in bandages, and I want you to turn loose. And I'll be there to watch you!"

19

Jordan Foster parked his Cadillac in front of the Inglewood condominium complex and rang the door chime. He was admitted by Paula Marie Ives, who was expecting him.

"What held you up?" She offered her lips for a kiss.

"What didn't! How are things with you?"

From the touch of his lips and tone of his voice, Paula Marie sensed immediately that things with him were in disarray. She retreated to the kitchen and began preparing coffee. He followed her. "Just a glass of water, please. We've got to talk. Time's limited."

"What's your problem, sonny?"

Jordan looked around at the tidy kitchen and the tasteful line drawings and furnishings in the living room beyond. "Paula Marie, I've got to say it and I don't know how to say it. I feel I'm in the middle of a soap opera."

She turned off the burner and walked past him to sit in her favorite chair. Reaching for a cigarette, she inquired, "Which is bugging you, Jordan? Your wife or your church?"

"Neither." He followed her into the living room and sat on the circular sofa. "I guess you could say it's my mother."

Paula Marie blew a cloud of smoke. "Your mother? What in blazes has she got to do with us?"

Jordan looked at his watch. "She's—well, I can't say, I tell you. But we both know this is wrong. It's hard to come up with it, but we're finished."

Paula Marie's black eyes snapped. "Finished? We haven't even started! Why? Just tell me why?"

"Because all we're going to do is hurt people, and we're not really helping each other. It's just wrong, Paula Marie. It's sin."

She crushed her cigarette angrily. "Sin!" Then just as quickly she switched her mood and came and sat by him. Putting her hand on his knee, she asked, "Jordan, sugar, how could anything as beautiful as what we were planning be sin?"

But Foster did not respond to her. "Somehow I've got to find a way back to what I want. Try to see what I mean. Right now I can't call myself a pastor. . . ."

Paula Marie's look was scornful. "I never intended you to be my pastor, Jordan. You're my lover."

He looked up quickly, noticing her perfect teeth as she smiled. "You're marvelous. The sweetest thing that ever came my way. It has nothing to do with you, Paula Marie."

"Oh, no. Nothing to do with me!" She stood up and reached for his glass of water. "I'm just the sweetest thing that ever—how would you like it if I showed up in your church tomorrow and shared a thing or two?" She drank half the glass of water and threw the rest in his face.

Jordan did not move, but let the water drip from his chin. "I won't stop you. But I know now I can never be part of it. I've got to be true to myself."

"What do you mean 'true'?" she demanded. "What's 'true'? I said I'd be true to you. Isn't that enough?"

Jordan shook his head sadly. "Nothing we have is true."

Paula Marie returned to her chair and studied her long purple fingernails carefully. When she looked up, her voice had hardened. "I don't happen to share your point of guilt, and I could care less for your Rose of Sharon Church or your mother either." She stood up. "You came here looking for love, Jordan Foster, and you found it. And there's more where that came from—a whole lot more. I don't know what it is you want to get back to, but I won't stand in your way. Only do me one favor, will you? Don't throw dirt."

Jordan stood facing her, afraid to touch her. "Good-bye, Paula Marie," he said weakly. "Like Mom says, I just ran off on a siding."

She walked to the door and opened it. "Some siding! I know you, Jordan. You'll be back. You'll get over this business, whatever it is. Take a good look!" She clasped her hands behind her head. "You're not looking at air bubbles. What I've got, you won't find in your old Bible."

Jordan started to speak. "I—"

Paula Marie interrupted. "Good-bye. And don't forget, when you walk out that door, I'll never call you or come after you."

He stood on the tiny cement porch and turned. "What I've been trying to tell you is that—"

But she had closed the door.

20

When Alison entered the suite's parlor-sitting room she found Charlotte at the antique desk in what appeared to be a frozen rage.

"Where have you been? I've tipped the hotel upside down looking for you."

"I'm sorry. I should have left a note."

Charlotte's voice could acquire a timbre that quailed many a tearoom manager. "Alison, I brought you on this trip because I needed you. You're acting very strangely." She held up the rough draft. "This speech has been ready for hours."

"I'll take care of it," said Alison without moving.

Charlotte worked her mouth. "Do you have our plane tickets?"

"I have." Alison opened her purse.

As she took the envelope, Charlotte said, "Ralph couldn't find the cousins."

"I thought—"

"Lou was the only one home."

"Great. That means your brother is still—"

"Ralph says he went to the synagogue."

"Who? Your brother?"

"Ralph, you clod. Now he wants to chase off to an amusement park and leave me stuck. Synagogue. I'll synagogue him. I'm sorry I ever came on this trip."

"Why?" Alison looked up. "What have you done?"

"Get on that speech." Charlotte stood up and began pacing. "I want to practice telling those good old boys, 'Think big. Think big.' "

Alison seized the moment. "What you're doing to your brother is not so big. I think it's rather small."

An icy silence ensued. "I'm not aware that I asked your opinion."

"Did you fire him?"

Charlotte switched the subject. "How many more of these executive lectures are set up?"

"Two. Tulsa and Buffalo."

"Well, cancel them. I don't have to do this. They need me more than I need them."

"Did you fire him?" Alison repeated.

"I gave him a month's notice."

"But without the proxies—" Alison leaned back and gave a shriek of laughter.

"Very funny," said Charlotte acidly. As Alison began warbling a snatch of Scottish song, she added, "Shut up, you idiot. I'll pick up those proxies. I can buy and sell that whole tribe of cousins. They talk big, but they'll come around."

Alison walked over and perched herself on the edge of Charlotte's desk, a playful gleam in her eye. "So you think I'm an idiot."

"I think your religion has your brain in a time-warp," retorted Charlotte.

Alison explored the inside of her cheek with her tongue. "What would you think if I told you I've written to the I.R.S.?"

"What about?"

"About my not reporting three years of consulting fees."

Charlotte's face turned white. "Did you send it?"

Alison looked out the curved window. "Just setting my house in order, Charlotte."

"Did you send it? You know I wrote you checks for one hundred and fifty thousand dollars."

"All I got was fifteen thousand. You saw to that."

"They'll want to see the checks. Why in heaven's name—"

"To be honest."

"Honest! You cleared your conscience by smearing mine, woman. Don't you realize that?" Charlotte went to the tiny refrigerator and poured herself a glass of vodka. "When they move in, they'll turn up our Grand Cayman trust and probably the Swiss bank account." She pointed her glass at Alison. "You Judas! Get out, I don't want to talk to you." As Alison moved toward the door of her bedroom, Charlotte looked at the envelope in her hand. "Wait!" she said, setting down her drink, "there's only one ticket here."

"That's right," said Alison.

Charlotte's expression changed. "That means you're going to heaven, I suppose. And are you planning to leave your daughter behind?"

Alison stopped at the door and leaned against it. "Just what do you mean by that?"

Charlotte seated herself. "I know where Pamela is and have for years."

"You? How?"

"I'm on the board at Booth Memorial. Who do you think took care of your hospital bill?"

Alison's shoulders slumped. "And all this time when I've been trying to find out—"

"You weren't supposed to find out. You gave her up. But I can tell you she's well taken care of."

"Where is she?"

"You give me that letter, if you haven't sent it."

"*Where is she, you hellcat?*" Alison was crying now. "The one thing I've wanted in this life, and now I find you've kept it to yourself all these years. Why? So you could blackmail me?"

Charlotte's composure returned as Alison lost hers. "Don't be silly. You do as I say and stop all this nonsense, and you'll see your daughter, I promise you."

Alison tried to pull herself together. "It doesn't matter now," she said at last. "It's too late." She turned into her room and closed the door with a click.

21

Sipping a gin-and-tonic and watching inane football in their two-room suite at the Bonaventure, President-elect Raymond Phillips reflected that of all the issues facing his new administration at Pacific Tech, only one was making him uncomfortable. That was the domestic predicament in which he was trapped. If the college presidency was a majestic oceangoing vessel, Colleen was a leaky scow. Her behavior at the "think tank" he found most unsettling. Instead of effacing herself, a mate about to be discarded, she had captured the imagination of everyone. At one stroke she had made herself into a campus personality, so that while he would be endeavoring to build his West Coast image with prize-winning scientists, she would be written up in the student paper as more important than he was.

It was obvious that before he could dump Colleen, he would have to cut her down. But how could he do it? Getting out of his chair, he went over to the well-stocked little refrigerator in the corner and took out an orange drink and two glasses. He placed them on the tray with his bottle of gin, poured the orange drink into a glass, and added some ice. At that point Colleen emerged from the bathroom and paused to say goodnight. Raymond turned off the television and invited her to sit down. "I've poured you some orange juice," he said, pointing. "Tell me something. Why did you say what you did this morning?"

Colleen settled on the divan and pulled her robe around her. "You keep asking. It seemed the natural thing. I was brought up with a sense of fair play."

"I can't believe there wasn't more to it."

"Believe what you wish."

Raymond reached for his drink. "I think you did it so I couldn't ship you east after the inauguration."

Colleen threw back her head and laughed. "You're not shipping me anywhere, Mr. President."

Raymond studied her closely. "You realize of course it wasn't your place to say anything."

"My remarks were not unappreciated."

"But you paid no attention to what you were doing to me—how you made me feel."

"You were in trouble, and I bailed you out."

"I could have handled it."

"I see what's bothering you, Raymond. You wanted to unload me, and now you feel you can't." While Phillips sat drinking glumly, she continued, "Take heart, lover. I may be out of your way tomorrow. Well out."

"You're bonkers," said Phillips.

Colleen stretched herself on the divan. She was still an engaging person. "*You* tell *me* something, Raymond. Do you ever think back to when you were studying for the ministry?"

"Not oftener than I can help."

"I do. I remember the hours you used to spend on your books, the talks you gave in little churches. That's why I married you, really. I loved to project myself as a minister's wife."

"I'm perfectly aware of why you married me," muttered Raymond. "You were in an intolerable family bind, and I was your escape hatch."

Colleen ignored him. "You had that one unfortunate clash with Professor Dilby, and it threw you. Such a silly thing. You were late turning in a paper, I think."

"An arrogant birdbrain," Raymond almost shouted.

"After that your interest in theology, in God and everything, kind of eroded. Very strange."

"You missed the point—you usually do," retorted Raymond. "My interest didn't erode, it evaporated. I just bought into the field of higher criticism. Jonah, I found, was a mythical folk hero—and I was *persona non grata*." He drained his glass. "That school was a waste."

"Oh, but you used to inspire so many people when you'd go out to speak on Sunday. Everyone said you had a real gift."

"Will you get off it?" demanded Raymond in exasperation. "It was all role-modeling. Just a flash in the pan. I could see I'd been carried away. Science was always my field."

"You disappointed a lot of people."

"They got over it."

"I didn't."

Raymond filled his glass. "I went into seminary because I wanted to change people, redirect their behavior, but I was paddling up a blind slough. Science will decide the way the world goes."

"What about your motives?"

"I've quit talking about motivation. What we need now is something we can take hold of and say, 'This fits. This works.'" He picked up the institute prospectus for the coming year.

"Don't let me keep you up, Colly. I just thought you'd like some orange juice."

Colleen ignored the drink and stood up. "Raymond," she said, "did you ever dream about evil?" He seemed not to be listening. "I had a horrible dream last night. There was this evil thing—kind of like a demon—and it was crawling up your back. I can't stand to think of it!"

"Charming, I'm sure," commented Raymond.

"Something's happening, Raymond. I'm frightened, because we all love you so. You're such a brilliant, gifted person, but for years you've carried this thing—I don't know—some kind of grudge against the Almighty. . . ."

Raymond got out of his chair. Holding his drink he stood with face flushed, balancing on his toes. "Sit down," he ordered. "I've had about enough of you and your Almighty. I should have checked out of this ten years ago. An albatross around my neck—that's what you are! I've watched you go downhill ever since, wandering from one crowd to another, one slogan to another, and now one church to another, for God's sake, parroting whatever the 'in' language happens to be. Sure, I went to seminary. I sat in those classes and listened to the cant about miracles. Axe heads floated, sundials went backward, water turned into wine, people jumped in and out of their graves. It wasn't so easy to retrain my mind after all that, and get back my scientific outlook." He looked at her. "And you—you were a weight, holding me back. I'd see you coming home from Bible study, starry-eyed, telling me Jesus is the answer. Well let me tell you, lover, Jesus didn't even know the questions!"

Raymond resumed his pacing as his wife sat with tears streaming down her face. "I resented what you did this morning. I resent what you stand for, the way you have dropped out of our culture. I particularly resent the way you have influenced our children to become pious nonentities." Colleen interrupted in protest, but he overrode her. "Don't contradict me—I know how they feel down inside. They've admitted it. They're more honest than you are." He walked to the window. "This thing that happened to you on the plane was so typical. Every time I turn on television somebody is giving out a wacko prophecy about the end of the world. King Hussein laces his shoes cross-ways, and there it is in the Bible. The Common Market admits Ruritania, and now we're six verses from the end times." The gin bottle being empty, he brought a fresh one from the refrigerator. "I am so turned off by all these voices and threats, but the first time you hear something, you fall for it." He paused and glared at her. "I've known for a long time that I didn't love you. Now it has come to where I don't even want to be around you. So now you can go to bed and have a good time sobbing and then pray yourself to sleep. And tomorrow you can climb a tree and wait for Jesus to come and pick you up." He carried all the glasses but one to the sink by the refrigerator. "The sooner you're out of my life, the better. I'm going to restore the years the locusts have eaten. Don't wait up for me; I'll sleep out here." He went into the bathroom and slammed the door.

Colleen sat for several minutes, fixing her eyes on nothing in particular. Never since she had been married had she felt so alone. Their son Stephen was now married six months and already launched on a banking career in Boston. Their daughter Janet was a senior at Bryn Mawr and engaged to a dentistry student. Her mother was in a Catholic rest home, and her father was no longer living. That left Raymond, concerning whom Colleen was ready to admit defeat. After twenty-four years the parting appeared imminent and inevitable.

While growing up in a Roman Catholic family, Colleen had clung for years to the dream of becoming a nun and going to India to teach. By the time Raymond entered her world, boys had become her chief interest and churchgoing had become desultory. The way Raymond talked about God, his vision and enthusiasm rekindled the dead fires of her devotion, and she followed him with delight. After marriage, when he withdrew from seminary, she continued to believe in him, confident that he would make a sensational contribution to his generation. Only after the children came did she realize how completely her husband had discarded Christianity, so that she was left with the total responsibility for their spiritual upbringing. The cleavage in their marriage widened, and Colleen began sipping wine to fortify herself. Her faithful efforts with the children proved successful; they became firmly established in their beliefs, while she turned into a melancholy casualty.

Something was intruding upon her reflections. It was the freshly opened gin bottle Raymond had left on the tray directly in front of her. Over three years had passed since she had taken a drink, and she knew well enough that those years represented no victory. She was an alcoholic for life, and the battle would go on, day after day, until she winked out.

She suspected that the bottle had been left intentionally, but she was in no mood to fight. She reached out her hand, drew it back, then reached again. She filled the empty glass, stood up, and in three gups drained it.

22

By the time Raymond Phillips emerged from his bathroom shower, Colleen had dressed and left the suite. Distraught and battered in spirit, she took the elevator to the lobby court and wandered about staring at the painting exhibits. In the piano bar she could see and hear people laughing and occasionally singing.

She approached the desk. "Is there a chapel in the hotel?"

"A chapel?" repeated the night clerk. "No, ma'am, I'm afraid not. All we have open are the bars and the cabaret. I can give you a card showing where the different services will be held tomorrow. . . ."

"No, thanks. Is there a church nearby?"

"Of course. There's one right up the street."

It was a warm evening, Figueroa Street was well lighted, and within ten minutes Colleen found the church, an imposing stucco structure dating from the 1930s. The massive doors were (as she expected) locked. Slowly she retraced her steps to the hotel, and this time, when she entered the atrium lobby, the chummy atmosphere of the piano bar was too strong for her to resist. She sauntered in, perched on a stool, and ordered a double Scotch and soda.

As the contents of the glass went down her throat, Colleen reflected sardonically that the stream of high purposes and strenuous labors of her past two decades had trickled down into sand. The equation of life had worked itself out to zero.

Another glass, and her perspective underwent a radical change. The struggle was over. She felt a new kind of peace in which the anxieties and tribulations of the past two days faded out of sight. She was able, she felt, to concentrate more clearly on what was important—the tremendous message she had heard on the plane. How lucid it seemed now, how palpably true! If it were true, then, that the last weekend was upon them, why should she be so mortally upset over a broken marriage relationship? Was she not safe in the hollow of God's hand? Safe . . . safe . . . she felt almost jaunty!

A bearded, scruffy-looking character, some years younger than herself, came and sat down beside her. "Remember me?" he asked pleasantly.

Colleen peered at him in the subdued light. "Not really. Wait . . . yes . . . this morning. . . ."

He nodded. "I'm Zoltan. I was your tour guide through the 'think tank.' "

"Of course. What are you doing here?"

Zoltan smiled. "I might ask you the same thing." When Colleen chose not to respond, he continued, "I guess I'm like a lot of other people. I'm here because I can't think of anything better to do. This Pentagon takeover is creating a lot of turmoil in the research division."

"I didn't think it was that definite."

"It's definite. They just won't release it. They're afraid of the students."

"What kind of turmoil is it creating?"

"Well, divorce, for one thing. Our rate is up three times over the other departments. That's a fair reading."

Divorce! Colleen cringed inwardly. "What's the reason for it?"

Zoltan wrinkled his generous nose. "We look down the road and we think, what's the use? Who cares about the rules?

We've lost hope. At least—I've lost hope." He studied his glass. "That Star Wars protest you saw today was just the tip of the iceberg. What people don't wake up to is that the whole social structure is being dismantled. The West is finished. Look at art, literature, music. And the idiot box. You can make out the death wish everywhere. If I were a believer, which I'm not, I'd say it's the end of the world."

That again! Colleen took a whimsical approach. "What would it take to make you a believer?"

Zoltan shrugged. "Hard to say."

"The end of the world?"

"I don't want to talk about it. Life is mysterious—let's leave it there. I happen to like my lifestyle. It suits me."

"Are you happy?"

Zoltan stared at her and shook his head slowly. "Happy? When the courts took my children? I see it as part of the dismantling. So here I am, left with—*la vie!*"

"*La vie?*"

He smiled and held up his glass. "I'm thinking about what the old Malay doctor said in Somerset Maugham's 'Narrow Corner': 'Life is short, nature is hostile, and man—'" Here Zoltan drained his glass. "'—is ridiculous.'"

"You're not married now?" asked Colleen.

He barely shook his head, then looked at her. "You made quite an impression on campus today."

"Thank you."

"Bailed out your husband neatly, I thought."

"I wouldn't say that."

"I would." After another silence, Zoltan said, "I was watching when you were studying the paintings. I'm an artist myself. Got a few nice things—at least I like them."

"Is zat so?"

"You might want to look at them. My place is just down the way."

I'm dizzy, thought Colleen, but not that dizzy! She couldn't believe her ears. A school employee propositioning her—and tomorrow her husband was being installed as the new president! Something in her felt wicked and daring enough to respond to the offer, but there were prior claims upon her wobbly con-

science. What should she tell this character? Should she clue him
in about the events on Flight 803? She had told Raymond that
she believed it. This second drink convinced her that she did in
fact believe it. But would this Zoltan believe it? She rejected the
idea out of hand.

Zoltan watched with amusement as she hesitated. She
glanced at him and turned away in astonishment and dismay.
What had she got herself into? God, help me! she thought.
Make this jaybird flap his wings and take off. How could I ever
have imagined—? What would the children think of me—?

The thought of her children brought Colleen up short.
Stephen and Janet—they needed to be told. And there it was, a
way out. Thank you, God! "Where's a tel'phone?" she asked the
bartender, who had also been watching her.

"Right over there."

Colleen finished her drink. " 'Scuse me," she said and left.
As she walked to the corner of the lounge, she found her steps
weaving a bit. The struggle to find her son's telephone number in
her purse—and then her card—was almost too much. With a
reeling head, after innumerable delays and massive confusion,
she heard Stephen's voice answering sleepily.

"Hello."

"Steve?"

"Yes.

"This your mother, darling."

"Hi, Mom. What's up?"

"How're you all?"

"Oh, fine. What—"

"Dear, I'm terribly sorry to get you out of bed, and I
wouldn't have done it if it wasn't terribly important. You see,
your father and I were on this plane yesterday, and we were
struck by lightning over the mountains, and then this message
came on an' it told us the Lord's comin' back tomorrow afternoon. . . ." She hiccuped.

"Oh, Mom!" The voice of her son rang with despair. "Why
did you do it?"

"Do wha'?"

"You've been drinking. . . ."

Colleen wept into the telephone.

23

Alone in her room in the Huntington suite, Alison telephoned room service, then seated herself at her desk. Pushing her typewriter aside, she wrote out a series of tiny messages on plain paper in her neat Scottish hand. Once finished, and with a potful of hot tea inside her, she took them to the lobby court.

At the main desk Alison arranged to use a copying machine provided for weekend guests when the gallery offices were closed. She then borrowed some transparent tape and a pair of shears from Arturo, the bellman. Back in her room Alison sat on the edge of her bed and cut the duplicated sheets into small squares, each of which contained her message in writing. She then gathered up the squares, tucked them into her purse with the tape and shears, and again tiptoed out of her room. She noticed a light under the door to the sitting room, but ignored it.

Spotting Arturo in the lobby court, she gave him the shears with several of the small paper squares. "Tell your friend not to put them in every box," she cautioned, "just here and there, and when no one is around. We certainly don't want to make any trouble, do we?"

Alison then left Arturo to his well-palmed intrigues, and for the next hour she quietly decorated the Bonaventure Hotel with the squares of paper. In the hours to come, the staff and guests would be finding them taped to elevators, escalators, mirrors, menus, counters, even luggage. They appeared under coffee cups, affixed to bar stools and shop windows, afloat in the fountain pool, even tucked inside tourist brochures. Each message was in her handwriting and each read:

"Jesus Christ may be appearing this weekend
for those who love Him. Are you prepared
for this event? He loves you. John 1:12."

Because it was late in the evening, no one paid much notice
to the preoccupied little lady guest in the plaid suit who, when
she spoke, had such a delightful accent. She just seemed to be
everybody's aunt.

At midnight the sparrow stopped fluttering and returned to
her penthouse nest, her rented Selectric III, and Charlotte's
speech. Three hours later she said her prayers and was into what
she expected might be her last short sleep on earth.

24

As soon as Arvie exited out the door of the Alpha Chi house
that evening, Mary Zlibin made a furious attempt at escap-
ing. Two of the sisters caught her, and a wrestling match ensued
on the floor of the fraternity's living room which was quickly
broken up by the house's male complement. Finally subdued
after inflicting her quota of bites and scratches, Mary was again
trundled upstairs, this time by the men. She was deposited in
Arvie's room, where the sisters ordered her to undress and don a
pair of Arvie's pajamas. She was then escorted to the bathroom
for a much-needed shower and put to bed. Five minutes after
her door was closed, a sister stationed outside opened it to find
Mary halfway out the window to the fire escape. A leg-pulling
match followed, which Mary lost. The window was wired shut,
and she was again ordered to bed.

At ten minutes to midnight, dressed in his skivvies, Arvie
opened the door to his room. "Are you awake?" he whispered.

Mary raised herself on an elbow. "I figured you'd be in."

Arvie snorted. "Don't get ideas." He snapped on a light. "I have a skin condition and forgot my medicine."

"Syphilis?"

"Pruritus."

Mary stared at him curiously. She looked almost demure in his outsize pajamas. "Why are you doing this?"

"I happen to want to."

"Do you really think I'm worth it?"

"Matter of opinion."

"I know—you're taking pity on a victim of society because you think you're better than the rest of us poor slobs."

"To tell the truth, I am." He seated himself backwards on a straight chair. "You just served an ace."

"Oh, yeah? I met a phony like you once. Rich guy with a long nose, said he was from Connecticut. He didn't want to do anything, just wanted to be in the same room with me. Said he went to church, but sin fascinated him. He liked to hang around it. Wanted to feel unclean. Spent his money, got nothin' for it. Looked me up two or three times and talked about himself. Said he liked to weekend in strange towns and cruise chicks like me. What a wacko!"

"Was his name Ulysses?"

"I forget. But you're just like him."

The timbre of Arvie's voice changed slightly. "Why do you say that?"

"Look at you. You're not a man—you're just a snooty, stuck-up thing. You want it and you don't want it, and you sit there like a bug-eyed frog. I'd respect you more if you were a preacher—no, I wouldn't. I don't trust them either. But you don't seem to have any guts. I mean, I'm nothing, I'm a whore, but you—"

If he was offended, Arvie didn't show it. Instead his manner became almost friendly; he seemed eager to talk. "You're right about one thing: I don't know what I want." He stared at the trophies on his dresser. "I mean, things come pretty easy to me. Student body president in high school, freshman athlete of the year, tennis captain, pro offers—too easy. It was my mother that got me the athletic scholarship. And now she's dead, and I've got this blah feeling." He shook his head. "I don't know, I'm just looking for answers. That's not why I picked you up today. But yesterday, when I saw you on the plane and knew you were in a mess, something clicked."

"Yeah. I remember when I was eleven I told my Sunday school teacher I wanted to be a missionary and go to Africa."

Arvie was silent a moment. "I'm not sure what I can do, or if I want to."

"You can be a doctor and help sick people."

He looked at her penetratingly. "If I were a doctor, I'd say you're sick."

Mary bristled. "I'm not sick, you dummy. It's the whole system that's sick. Everybody's cheating. It's all rotten. These cops. You know my first trick was a lousy cop? You can't trust anybody. I can't."

"I thought you wanted out."

Mary laughed harshly. "There's no way out."

Arvie snorted. "You're a fool. You don't have to go back."

"No, I don't. But I'm going, and when they come after you, they're going to cut you open like a muskrat."

He studied the label on the bottle in his hand. "I caught a muskrat once."

"Yeah?"

"When I was a kid I ran a trap line—skunks and rabbits and stuff. But I quit it."

"Why?"

"Guess I felt sorry for them. Some of them would die just from fright."

"And now you're feeling sorry for me," said Mary. "You want to spring my trap. But if you'll hand me my duds, I'll spring my own trap."

Arvie's mood seemed to change again. "Oh, no," he said, getting to his feet, "it's all over, remember?"

Mary sat up and planted her feet on the floor. "Let me tell you this. I was six years old when I got real sick, and they flew me in to a hospital in St. Paul. And I remember a lady came to see me and told me Jesus was going to send an angel to my bedside. She said that angel would stay by me day and night and protect me, and maybe take me to heaven to be with Jesus." Mary wiped her nose on a blanket. "He never showed up."

"So?"

Mary gestured downward with her thumb. "That old bag was a liar."

"How do you know?"

"When you're in hell, you know."

Suddenly Arvie was lighthearted. Ah, ha!" he cried, grabbing a towel off a rack. "I just figured out my destiny. You thought I was going to be one of your tricks. Well, you're wrong. Know what I am?" He draped the towel over his head. "I'm your angel!"

Mary snickered. "And you're gonna shoo everybody else away from me with your old tennis racket so we can make out on a cloud-bank, huh?"

The supercilious smile had returned. "We'll just have to wait on that, won't we?" He wrapped the towel around him.

"Aren't you going to reform me?" asked Mary mockingly.

"I don't think so. I did think for a while, maybe I can give this gal a lift. I should have known that you didn't want a lift. Guess I was out of character."

"Then we can call this thing off, and I can go?"

Arvie stifled a yawn. "Unfortunately, no. I've told these people I'm taking you to Ojai and, baby, to Ojai we will go."

"So you think I'm worth salvaging."

"I wouldn't say so. You're what Lucretius calls floating atoms. Junk in space."

"Kidnaper! Toadeater! Eggsucker!"

"Good night." Arvie flipped off the light and closed the door behind him, not noticing as he did so that Mary was making a face at him and sticking out her tongue.

25

Just before midnight Saturday the black Cadillac entered the parking lot of Rose of Sharon Church and the Reverend Jordan Foster, after a cautious surveillance, stepped out. He opened the church's front door with a borrowed key and flicked on a set of lights. Then, walking down the center aisle, he dropped to his knees at the Communion rail.

Through Jordan's mind raced one image after another: the voice on the P.A. system . . . the grilling at the airport . . . the television interview . . . the visit with his mother and her strange blessing . . . Alison saying, "You're skirting the issue, Reverend" . . . the uproar at the church . . . the young man with the gun, and the hand laid on Jordan's head . . . the garbage on his porch . . . Paula Marie standing in the doorway . . . and then back again to the commotion on the plane, and the voice. . . .

After a few minutes Jordan stood up and faced the back-lighted stained glass window over the altar, with its stylized representation of the Good Shepherd and the sheep.

"God! Spirit of God!" He spoke the words softly.

He began walking slowly around the sanctuary, his eyes on the carpet. After a while he stopped in front of the altar window and held up his hands. "You're telling me something, Lord, and I can't hear it. I can't hear. All I hear is people!" He dropped his hands. "How many times have I had a chance to preach Your power and didn't, because it wasn't there?"

He knelt on one of the carpeted steps. "Jesus," he said finally, "You made a mistake. I don't belong. You made a mistake. Do you hear? A mistake!"

For ten minutes he remained in a kneeling posture, until it seemed that one by one the images in his mind melted away. He looked up and whispered, "I want to get off this siding. I want to be *clean!*"

Another pause, for how long he could not have said. Then one word was breathed: "*Abba!*"

And with that, Jordan Foster prostrated his body on the carpet of his church.

THREE

SUNDAY

1

At 6:15 A.M. Mary Zlibin worked past the air mattress parked outside her door and tiptoed downstairs to the pay telephone booth in the Alpha Chi house. After talking briefly, she made her way back to the room. Half an hour later she emerged and found Arvie waiting outside.

"Breakfast?"

"I never eat breakfast."

"Then you can watch me eat."

Mary gave him a withering look, walked down to the lounge, and seated herself with a copy of *Esquire*. Arvie rejoined her shortly.

"How'd you sleep?"

"What do you think?"

"Why did you use the telephone this morning?"

"Oh, I called home. Collect."

"Who'd you talk to?"

"Mom. Who do you think?"

"How are things?"

"They're still yelling at me."

Arvie examined her battered complexion with distaste. He had slept little outside her door, and was becoming increasingly aware of his folly, not to say risk, in becoming involved in Mary's messy affairs. He was ready to opt out of the whole episode. He could, of course, simply open the front door and let her go. But now the word had spread, and he had the house to consider; his credibility as a campus leader was at stake. The sooner they left for Ojai, the better.

"Ready to go?"

Mary pushed back a lock of her hair and glared at him.

179

"Why don't you lay off, honcho? Go play angel somewhere else."

In spite of himself, Arvie found her fascinating. Somewhere there had to be a chink in her armor, and he persisted in looking for it. He tried persuasion. "Come on, Mary, for pete's sake, shape up."

"Why? I don't need you to clean up my act."

"Is your aunt's address in your purse?"

"No, but I have a pack of Lifesavers." Hearing a car engine racing, she glanced out the French windows at the street, then jumped up and made for the door. Arvie followed her gaze and saw a black Lincoln Continental moving slowly past. He reached the door ahead of her and grabbed her arm as she fought to free herself.

"Lemme go, my ride's here."

Arvie stood with his back against the door. "You lied. You never called your mother."

"Sure I lied."

"Why?"

"Because you wouldn't give me any bread."

"Look, I'm your friend."

"I have no friends!" Mary suddenly reached out and ripped her fingernails into his cheek. Arvie picked her up, threw her over his shoulder, and headed upstairs. He carried her kicking to his room where he tossed her on one of the freshly made twin beds. While Mary laughed scornfully at him, he dabbed as his bloody face with some tissue, then shouted through the open door and accosted an underclassman on his way downstairs. "Do something to move that black Lincoln hanging around in front. Now!"

Mary leaned back against the wall. "I warned you!"

Through the open doors came the sound of fists being pounded on fenders and water squirting from a hose. A car engine roared, and there was silence.

"Now let's go," said Arvie to Mary, applying a Bandaid and looking grim.

"No!"

"I'm not going to mess with you any longer, you little witch. You got me into this thing."

"Oh no, I didn't. Don't you lay that on me."

"All right, I'm not going to argue the point." Arvie reached into his closet and took out a baseball bat. "You told me they're on my case now as well as yours, didn't you!"

"Probably."

"And it won't make any difference whether I turn you loose or not, they're still out to clean my clock."

Mary shrugged.

"Suppose we keep you here. What'll they do?"

"You can't tell. If they thought you were holding me as a hostage, they might throw a bomb. Might even torch the place."

Arvie picked up his notebook and stared at it. "I wonder," he said, "what all this has to do with apocalyptic literature."

"Gimme a cigarette," said Mary. He tossed her a pack from the dresser top.

"I think," he said, "I'd rather be shot at for what I did do than for what I didn't do. I guess that's not a very good motive. You're not a very good motive."

"You really are a pompous ass."

"It's hard not to be a pompous ass around you. I've given up trying to help you. I'm thinking about my own skin now."

"Nothing new about that."

"For somebody who's stupid, you seem to know a lot."

"Nobody helps me."

"Why should they, with those claws? Get your purse. My wheels are out back."

2

At 6:18 A.M. Sunday, Captain Medeiros was on the telephone, calling his flight engineer, Barney Bricklebine, in Westwood. "Barney?"

Bricklebine sat on the edge of his king-sized bed yawning as Mrs. Bricklebine pulled a blanket over her face. "What's up, Captain?"

"Did you pick up any sunspot activity while you were on that flight?"

Barney was suddenly wide awake. "Are you kidding?"

"I am not."

"Sunspots? You mean about that hit we took?"

"I mean any time. Did you run into a lot of static?"

"Boy, I don't remember any. Sunspots have more to do with radar than with radio, don't they?"

"Our radar was out." Medeiros' voice had an edge.

"I know. . . ."

"I'm just asking if you had any distortion or blackout."

"Well, just for a few seconds after the antenna—why don't you talk to the aerospace people? They know about sunspots."

"Barney, our weather crew tells me there was unusual sunspot activity yesterday that could have created overlap and caused the wrong frequency to feed into our VHF."

"Maybe under abnormal conditions . . ."

"Precisely. I know sunspots can cause mixed signals to reach halfway around the world. It happened to me once in Nam. That voice that was supposed to be from God could have been piped in by the Vatican."

"It could have come from Mary Poppins, but it didn't."

"I've worked up my report. Will you listen to it?"

Barney slid off the bed onto the floor. "Fire away."

"The unusual audio reception reported by passengers and crew on Flight 803 at approximately 1500 hours Friday, September 13, was caused by atmospheric radio distortion, due to an abnormal ionized ceiling, the effect of sunspot activity in the electromagnetic field. A lightning strike had destroyed the radio antenna and caused the number three engine to flame out. A key toggle switch in the cockpit shorted out, allowing the P.A. to transmit reception into the cabin. Flight Communications Center has been requested to launch inquiry with the Federal Communications Commission and the U.S. Air Force to determine the source of the transmission. A copy of this request is being forwarded to the office of Over the Horizon Radar."

"Sounds pretty impressive," said Bricklebine, "but what's this about a toggle switch?"

"I'm still checking it," said Medeiros evasively.

"Find a glitch?"

"I'll let you know Monday. You think this will take care of it?"

"Boy, Frank, I don't know. Did you check the station telephones? Maybe somebody . . ."

"They haven't been tampered with."

"What about the voice recorder? That ought to tell us something."

"Blank."

"What?"

"I don't mean the whole tape, just a segment that included the voice. Whatever it was, it didn't record."

"I don't believe it." Bricklebine sounded awed.

"Look," said Medeiros, "I don't care if what we heard came from Saint Peter or Brigham Young or Tom Brokaw. All I want is something I can put together that will shut up Maddox."

3

Charlotte Embree spent most of the night twisting and squirming on her ornate bed, reconstructing her last conversation of the evening. Did Alison actually mail the letter? Would it be in character for her to do it? Would she dare, knowing the inevitable consequences? Or did she do it on the impulse of some latter-day revolt?

For fifteen years Charlotte's attitude toward her private secretary had been set in concrete. She had nothing but approval for Alison's taciturnity which kept big secrets inviolate; for her handling of detail and her personal loyalty. Charlotte could trust Alison as no other. Alison protected her from intruders, warned her of impending difficulties, maintained her schedule, and many times resolved staff problems in her absence. Alison could be tough, and Charlotte liked that.

But Charlotte's benign feelings never let her forget that Alison was an employee, and such admiration as she felt was always seasoned with contempt. The social gulf between them, she felt, was as real as it would have been in Scotland. Alison was her aide, her servant whose station in life depended on her benefactor. As a recent immigrant from Scotland, Alison had gone to work for Charlotte at a ridiculously low salary; but by working long hours and attending evening classes she had made her way to a post of considerable influence in the company. Charlotte knew all that; but she also knew she had rescued her from an impossible situation.

So it was always there—the gap between them. By a condescending nod, by a turning of the head, by an inflection in the voice, and above all, by supremely ignoring her, Charlotte kept whispering daily to Alison, "You are my lackey. I salvaged you. Don't presume upon my magnanimity."

Such ingrained behavior masked whatever affection Charlotte felt, and smothered any temptation to show it. Most of the time Charlotte treated Alison as she would an old shoe. She took her for granted, stepped on her, wore her out, and missed her terribly when she could not be found.

According to Charlotte's clock radio, in six hours she was due in the California Room to deliver her speech. Suppose Alison did mail it, what could be done? The I.R.S. would start a massive probe; teams would start gathering information, examining franchise arrangements, bank loans, cash transfers, overseas contacts. Leads would be followed, and the roof would fall in. But suppose she didn't? If she didn't (and it was possible), then Alison would have to be contained . . .

When she finally drifted into a nightmarish sleep at 5 o'clock, Charlotte had almost convinced herself that she was safe for the moment; the letter had not been sent. Two hours later she awoke a desperate woman, sensing that her life, her business, everything was in jeopardy. She rose up and jerked the window curtains furiously. Her speech that morning was forgotten. Nothing mattered but the letter.

At 7:58 A.M. Charlotte had bathed and was clad in a silk

robe when her telephone rang. "A Captain Medeiros is in the atrium lobby to see you," said the switchboard operator.

"Ask him what he wants."

"He says he is here at the request of the president of Intercontinental Airlines, responding to an inquiry you made."

Charlotte looked at her watch. "Tell him I'll join him in ten minutes."

Descending in the glass elevator, Charlotte struggled to compose herself. It was a situation that ordinarily she loved: dealing with an adversary when she held the advantage; and Frank Medeiros was a foe worthy of her steel. Once they were seated in the lobby court, he took a formal tack.

"I understand, Miss Embree, that you registered a complaint regarding your flight last Friday."

"Yes," countered Charlotte, "and I will make another about being disturbed before 8 o'clock on Sunday morning."

"We certainly regret any inconvenience caused you by the turbulence. . . ."

"You know perfectly well what I'm talking about," interrupted Charlotte. "You had that wild voice coming over the loudspeaker with all kinds of threats about hell and judgment. It has had personal repercussions involving members of my staff."

"There was a technical problem in our radio reception," said Medeiros easily. "Those things happen." He took a typewritten sheet from his pocket. "This report might be of interest to you."

Charlotte studied the draft of the irregularity report, then returned it to him. "You've covered yourself well."

"They're talking about a citation for our emergency landing."

"Congratulations. Of course your report doesn't say anything."

"I beg your pardon?"

"I mean, where did the voice come from, Captain? Where did it originate?"

The pilot's composure was a bit strained. "It may have been a transmission from some religious radio program in the South or Southwest. We're looking at Alabama."

"Does that make sense?"

"Oh, yes. We even think it might have been a church play of some kind."

"That's not in your report."

"It's only a supposition. We haven't located it. All we're saying is that we received an unusual transmission due to conditions in the atmosphere."

"You had something about a switch not working. Was that a supposition too?"

Medeiros ran his hand over his mouth. "Some wires may have been fused. We're bringing in a crew in the morning to go over all the equipment."

"I see." As she prepared to leave, Charlotte adopted a milder tone. "I'm relieved about one thing. You seem convinced that the voice business has a technical explanation."

"Absolutely convinced."

"And we're not talking about mysterious voices from outer space."

"We live in a scientific age, after all," said Medeiros, rising.

"I couldn't agree more." Charlotte sounded almost mellow. "It was very kind of you to come and bring me this explanation." She held out a jeweled hand. "I shall write to Mr. Fairbank and express my appreciation."

"Happy to be of service," said Medeiros.

"Good day." Charlotte swept out of the lobby court and returned to the Green Tower elevator.

4

At 8 o'clock Sunday morning a three-year-old Volkswagen entered the parking lot of the Beth Eden Rest Home in south central Los Angeles. Lucy Townville, a deaconess from Rose of Sharon Church, emerged and hurried up the ramp to assist Arlowene Foster, who was having trouble with the heavy glass front door. Arlowene was attired for church in a violet dress, rose-colored hat, and cloak to match. Besides her cane, she carried a large paper parcel containing presents for her grandchildren.

It was Arlowene's first attempt in months to go anywhere except to church. The Volkswagen conveyed her to nearby Watts, where it stopped in front of an apartment that was home to Vivian, her son's estranged wife, and their three boys.

Vivian came to answer the bell, wearing a terrycloth robe and sloppy scuffs, with a towel around her head and a pancake turner in her hand. She opened the door and her mouth simultaneously. "Mother Foster!"

Sister Lucy saw her charge inside the door, excused herself, and drove off to the church. Arlowene seated herself in the most comfortable chair in the apartment and came to the point: "Vivian, I want you to take these boys and go home to your husband."

Vivian, shocked, fired back, "Mother, if that's all you came to say, you're wasting your breath."

"I ain't wastin' nothin,' " retorted Arlowene, resting her hands on her cane. "I'm here because God wants me here, and because you and Jordan are out of His will."

"These boys don't want any part of their daddy," asserted Vivian.

"Where are they?"

"Two of 'em are back there watching TV. Danny's asleep."

"Has Jordan talked to you?"

"He called up."

"Well?"

"Oh, he was real laid back. You know Jordan. Said he was sending over a check. I asked, 'When?' "

"Vivian," said Arlowene, "you love Jordan. I know you do."

"I did once."

"He came to see me yesterday. Are you listenin'? He believes the Lord's comin' back and he wants to set things right."

Vivian's eyes opened wide. "That don't sound like Jordan. Long as I've known him, the Lord's comin' was the last thing on his mind."

"I tell you he's shapin' up," said Arlowene stoutly, "and he needs you in church this mornin'."

"Oh, I'm sorry, Mother Foster." Vivian flourished the pancake turner. "I've been through enough. I don't want any more sweet goop. If Jordan sent you over here, tell him forget it. Tell him go mess with his woman and leave me alone."

"You look here!" Arlowene's eyes were blazing. "Nobody said nothin' about seein' you. And nobody sends me anyplace. I came here because this thing has gone on long enough, and because when the Holy Spirit works a man's heart, I know it, and you better know it. Seein' you was God's idea, right in the middle of the night. I got up at 6 o'clock and called Sister Lucy."

Vivian finally sat down. "You think I want to be shamed any more in God's house, listening to that hypocrite?"

"Vivian," said Arlowene pleadingly, "I know you don't believe me, but I'm asking you to believe God. He told me to get myself over here because He's goin' to put this family back together. He's got His man where He wants him."

"Jordan? I thought this was the day they were going to kick him out of the church." Vivian's tone was sardonic.

"No, the Lord won't stand for it." Arlowene reached out and took Vivian's hand in both of hers. "I want you to bring the boys and come this mornin'."

"You mean so he won't lose his job?"

"I'm not workin' on Jordan's job. I'm workin' on his soul."

Danny, the youngest, wandered into the room in pajama bottoms. "Well hi, Grandma," he said sleepily, kissing her. What's goin' on?"

Arlowene patted his cheek. "I was just tellin' your mother I want you all to come to church this mornin', son."

"Are they going to let *him* preach?" demanded Vivian.

"He's the preacher."

"We ain't been in a long time, Ma," said Danny.

Vivian studied him. "Who's going to run you over?"

"Nobody 'cept you," said Arlowene.

Vivian said, "Dear God. . . ," then choked, and the tears came.

Arlowene got herself to her feet with difficulty and embraced her daughter-in-law. Danny took the hand with the pancake turner and kissed it. Closing her eyes, Arlowene said, "Bless your heart. . . . Father, You promised to take the sting out of this child's heart. I'm askin' You now to keep that promise, and to do somethin' about her man. Lord Jesus, prop him up!"

5

The sleep she had sought after a long day did not come easily to Alison. As she lay tossing in her elegant queen bedroom, an endless variety of phantasms floated through her mind. A sweet, solemn teenage girl came walking out of a building, holding out her arms toward her . . . A black choir sang spirituals while she argued with a tall policeman . . . Charlotte's stern countenance glared at her from behind an enormous desk . . . She, Alison, was sneaking from table to table in the Sidewalk Cafe, slipping apocalyptic notes under coffee cups, acting innocent but feeling terribly guilty. . . .

As the sky at last began to brighten, the thought of seeing her daughter became so exciting to Alison that she tried resolutely not to dwell on it. To imagine that a new love might come into her life at this late date, the love of a young human being who would be her darling, who would be the flesh of her flesh, and would cherish her and stand with her against the world—it was almost unbearable. It didn't seem to matter that Charlotte had cruelly kept the secret from her all these years; what did matter was that life was about to start over in a beautiful way.

And yet—it would never happen if she mailed that letter to the I.R.S. That's what Charlotte had said: "I promise you will never see that girl if I can help it!" Writing the letter had been a purgative experience for Alison. She was sure God was in it, that it had to be done. But that was before her daughter had suddenly materialized out of the unforgotten, before she learned that the letter she had written would probably flag an audit and destroy the Embree empire.

And what about the Lord? Was He coming back, or was it all a put-on, in which case . . . She gave up trying to sort things out and went into an old breathing-prayer exercise she had learned from her grandmother in Scotland. And as it had so many times in past bouts, sleep came at last to Alison.

After a quick breakfast downstairs, Charlotte returned to the Huntington suite, determined to handle the Alison affair coolly and astutely, no matter what the outcome. She entered the parlor-sitting room and found Alison dressed and seated at the antique desk, collating sheets of paper.

"Have you had breakfast?" Charlotte asked in a casual tone.

"Yes, thank you." Alison continued her shuffling.

"Then you're all set."

"Set?" echoed Alison.

"I believe this is the day the world is supposed to whatever."

Alison ignored her. "Here's your speech. Two copies."

Exasperated by her secretary's indifference, Charlotte dropped her mask and abandoned her good intentions. "Did you mail that letter, Alison? If not, where is it? I want it."

Alison rose and walked toward her bedroom. "If there's anything else, I'll be back after church."

Charlotte turned livid. "You little snipe! Are you trying to eight-ball me? Is this the way you show gratitude?" The door to the bedroom closed, leaving Charlotte stalking restlessly about the room. A plan! She had to have a plan. Like a djinn from a bottle, a trick Irwin had once pulled on her leaped into her mind, and she stepped into her bathroom to examine the fixtures. Now that her thoughts were moving, she went into action. A Mexican maid in housekeeping was soon on the dead run for the suite with a ball of heavy twine. Concealing the ball in a towel, Charlotte entered Alison's bedroom without knocking and found Alison slipping on her coat.

Charlotte steadied herself against a chair and put a hand to her brow. "I've been trying to go over these pages," she said. "Do you have some aspirin?"

Without replying, Alison went immediately into her bathroom and dipped into a small bag of medicines. While she was thus occupied, Charlotte quietly opened the door leading from Alison's bedroom to the circular corridor, and just as quietly drew the bathroom door shut. Before Alison realized what was happening, Charlotte had lashed the two doorknobs together. When Alison tried to open her bathroom door, she found it jammed; she had been made a prisoner in her penthouse privy.

As always when she became the victor in a situation, Charlotte now dropped her voice to a purr. "You sit there, dearie, and think about what you're planning to do. Unless, of course, you want to give me that letter."

There was no response. Alison gave one more tug at the doors while Charlotte tightened the lashing.

"Don't try to scream, there's nobody up here. You brought all this on yourself, you know, with your pathological obsession about Jesus coming back. I told you there was nothing to it. The pilot of our plane talked to me just now and told me they've traced the voice to some radio station in Alabama."

Still no response.

"Now, when I get back," Charlotte continued, "we'll go out for steak and lobster. Then after I get the letter we'll go look up your daughter. How does that sound?"

Charlotte's explanation was interrupted by the sound of the buzzer at the main entrance to the suite. As she hurried to the hall corridor to see who it was, she was accosted by a florid, agitated middle-aged gentleman. "Miss Embree! You're on in fifteen minutes!"

"Shhh," whispered Charlotte, "there are people sleeping. Hold the elevator for me."

If Alison heard the visitor, she made no sound. Charlotte dashed back to her desk, picked up her speech, took a final look in the ornate mirror, and left. Alison continued to perch quietly on the edge of the bathtub, and eventually began humming. Soon she was singing softly an old Scottish tune:

> *"Ca' the yowes to the knowes*
> *Ca' them where the heather grows,*
> *Ca' them where the burnie rows,*
> *my bonnie dearie."*

Within her Alison felt a strange exhilaration, not unlike that of a long-pent prisoner released from her cell. She apprehended that somehow her years of indenture were over and finished. Emancipation was hers, forever.

6

Maybelle Lewis and her precocious grandson were enjoying Sunday brunch in the lobby's so-called Sidewalk Cafe when Reginald found one of Alison's messages under a coffee cup. Reaching to another table, he uncovered a similar message under the cream pitcher.

Maybelle was annoyed. "Now what are you up to, you scamp?"

"Lookit, Grandma! End of the world! Here's another!" He spotted a slip of paper on the floor.

Maybelle raised the ornate glasses that dangled from her neck chain. "My soul and body! Somebody agrees with me!" She looked up. "I wish I knew who was writing these messages. I think it's cute. I'd send her a doll." She studied one of the slips. "It's a woman's handwriting all right."

"And you know what, Grandma?" Reginald's sleuthing instinct was alive. "I'll bet whoever wrote this stuff was on that plane with us Friday. Don't you think?" He rubbed the writing with his finger. "They ran it off on a copying machine."

Maybelle lowered her glasses. "It's very strange, all these things, Reginald. I don't know what they mean. Can't put my finger on it."

Reginald, on his part, was wondering just how much cre-
dence his grandmother now placed in the message on the plane.
His electronic high-jinks could backfire and make family trouble. "Are you going to see your doll collectors?" The question
was intentionally provocative.

"If you want to go, go. You're excused."

Reginald wasted no time launching his fact-finding probe.
He started at the mail desk, making a display of the slips on the
counter. Did the clerk know about these? He did, and was
properly apologetic. Did he know who wrote them? He did not.
Did he know who might have used the hotel copying machine
the night before? The clerk was showing signs of annoyance.
"Sorry, we don't give out that information."

Reginald then approached Arturo, the bellman, and asked
what he knew about the lady who put notes around the atrium
lobby. Arturo stiffened and fixed a hostile eye on his young
inquirer, then walked away. He had already been grilled by an
assistant manager and was knee-deep in lies. Reginald pursued
his investigation while studying the people wandering about the
vast lobby, thinking that whoever was doing it, might still be
doing it. No likely suspects emerged. The shopping galleries
were empty, it being Sunday; but what about the upper floors?
He decided to "feel the place."

Reginald's plan was to start at the top of the towers (which
were interconnected) and work down floor by floor; perhaps he
would catch the lady in the act. He took the glass elevator to
the top of the Green Tower and found himself facing the Huntington suite east. As he wandered around the circular corridor,
he observed that a door to the suite was wide open and seemed
to be tied. He examined it more closely, and was startled to hear
someone singing behind the door.

"Hello," he said, not knowing what else to say.

The singing stopped. "Can you help me? I'm caught in
here."

The flight bag was resorted to, and a Boy Scout knife was
produced that quickly separated the doors. Alison emerged and
stared at her rescuer. "You were—"

Reginald was equally astounded. "I saw you—"

Alison began a laugh that reached the edges of hysteria. Reginald's laugh was more tentative; he was looking around the room for slips of paper. This must be the person, he decided.

"Weren't you with a white-haired woman?" Alison asked at last.

Reginald nodded. "My grandmother."

"And what did she think about the voice on the plane? Sit down!" Alison pointed to one of the luxurious chairs in her room.

Reginald sat down gingerly, holding his flight bag. He felt his joke had gone far enough; more deception simply meant more hassling and trouble. But when it came to confessing the prank, fear held him back. "Who tried to tie you up?"

"Let's not talk about that. Let's talk about you. What's in your flight bag?" Alison had noticed how he clung to it.

Reginald brightened. "If I played something for you, would you promise not to tell?"

"Oh, I promise."

Reginald reached into the bag, pushed a switch, and the words came out: "LET THE PEOPLE KNOW THAT AFTER TWO DAYS I SHALL EXECUTE JUDGMENT AND JUSTICE ON THE EARTH. BUT LET THOSE I HAVE FORMED FOR MYSELF COME INTO THE ARK."

Alison, shocked beyond belief, sat down on the edge of her bed. "What is this?" she asked feebly.

"It's a stunt, kind of." Reginald shut off the machine.

"You mean, you did it? You?" He nodded. "Why? I can't believe it—how could you—in all that confusion?"

"I know," said Reginald meekly. "I wasn't expecting the storm. It just happened. I—"

Alison finally adjusted herself to reality. "Why would you do a thing like that? I mean, what was the point?"

"You promised not to tell on me."

"That's right, I did. What's your name?"

"Reginald."

"Reginald what?"

"Reginald Tibbets."

Alison moved to a comfortable chair. "All right, Reginald

Tibbets, let's have the whole story. I'm not interested in how you did it. I want to know why."

"I—uh." Reginald swallowed. "You see, ma'am, they make me go to church every Sunday, and I hear everybody talkin' about the end of the world and Jesus comin' back—you know, real flaky—" Here he tried to make his voice deep and hollow, but only succeeded in cracking it. " '—He's coming soon, He's coming soon—' but nobody seems to act like it's gonna happen. It's a cover-up. Our church doesn't want the Lord to come, we got a long-range planning committee. You'd think He wasn't coming for a zillion years."

"So you decided to speed it up!"

"Naw, I just thought if somebody gave out the word it was really gonna happen, well, I'd like to see what everybody would do. That's when I got the idea. Make it scientific-like."

"An airplane."

"Why not?"

"Where did you get all that business about justice and judgment?"

"Out of the Bible." Reginald explored a nostril with his finger.

"Whose voice was it?"

"Mine. I used a distortion filter."

"Well!" Alison stood up. "You certainly will have some explaining to do."

"You won't tell on me?"

Alison studied the anxious face. "I don't quite believe you, Reginald. I'd say you're holding something back. You didn't cook this up by yourself."

Reginald swallowed. "I don't know what you mean."

"Let's go meet your grandmother."

"You won't spill it? Promise?" He clutched her arm.

"No, that's your job, sonny. Wait a minute." She struggled with the twine on the doorknob and tossed it on the bed, after which they walked out the door. As they passed the mail chute, Alison dropped in a letter.

7

"And I take great pleasure," said the chairman, "in presenting to you one of the fabulous success figures of our decade, Miss Charlotte Embree. Miss Embree is a pioneer innovator who has put together a sense of history, a demand for diet foods, and the buying power of women to create a whole new concept in the restaurant field. She has many imitators, but she remains number one. Let's welcome the founder and president of Victorian Tearooms as she comes to address us on the subject, 'The Executive Use of Power.'"

Her jeweled earrings swaying, Charlotte was in form with her opening lines: "I have been advised that the world is going to self-destruct sometime today (laughter). Dr. Samuel Johnson once said, and I quote, 'Depend upon it, sir, when a man knows he is to be hanged in a fortnight, it concentrates his mind wonderfully'" (more laughter). The rest was a collage of bluff quotes from *Fortune* magazine: "Keep up an unrelenting demand for constantly improving performance . . . liquidate anyone who is not in complete control of the facts . . . force out managers who can't handle the pace . . . leadership is demonstrated when the ability to inflict pain is confirmed." The executives decided she was a tiger, and gave her a rousing ovation.

After leaving the California room, Charlotte took the escalator to the lobby and was shocked to find Alison seated in the lobby court, visiting with Maybelle and Reginald. Since there was no point in going to the suite, and she had no desire to become involved with strangers, Charlotte was forced to take a seat in the lobby court and wait—something that grated noticeably upon her disposition. As for Alison, she was blissfully unaware that Charlotte was nearby.

"We're renting a car and driving out to this amusement park," Maybelle was saying. "Would you like to join us?"

"What park is that?"

"I believe it's called The Ark."

"*The Ark?*" Alison felt a tremor through her body.

"Yes. Curious. Reginald seems possessed to go. I told him if he didn't try to rewire the hotel I'd take him." Reginald waved his flight bag at Alison puckishly.

"I'd love to go," said Alison. "Your grandson did me a real kindness, and I hope to be able to return the favor. But today I'm afraid I have other plans."

"Are you O.K. now?" asked Reginald in a tone that was, for him, exceedingly solicitous.

"Thank you, yes."

"What did he do?" asked Maybelle wonderingly.

Alison sighed and stood up. "I'll let him tell you about it." She spotted Charlotte waiting severals chairs away, looking like an Amazon queen about to pronounce judgment. Alison excused herself and left Reginald to inform his already-mystified grandmother that this was indeed the lady who had placed notes under the coffee cups, that she had then been locked in her bathroom, and that he had arrived to rescue her. . . .

"Well!" pronounced Charlotte as Alison seated herself.

"I mailed it."

"I see." Charlotte's mouth was a jagged line. "In the mail chute? Today?" Alison nodded. "So you have blown me away."

"Just a minute, Charlotte," protested Alison. "Aren't you being a little dramatic?"

"You know nothing, of course, about a betting operation that we've been conducting at our Chicago restaurant for the past two years."

"What are you talking about?"

"We've been catering to very exclusive clientele, but I didn't report the income. Now you've got the feds alerted, and I can end up either leaving the country or going to jail."

Alison was stunned. "Why wasn't I informed?"

"Why should I tell you? What business is it of yours?"

"I had no idea—I only wrote about my holding back—"

"You had no idea? I had no idea that my private secretary would do a thing like this to me."

Alison was quiet for a moment. Then she asked, "What about my daughter?"

"Yes, what about her?" Charlotte got up and walked to the registration desk, where she summoned a clerk. "I would like to retrieve a letter that was dropped in the mail chute today by mistake."

"Your letter, madam?" inquired the clerk.

"I believe my secretary's name is on it."

"I'm afraid we have no way of helping you."

"Hasn't this ever happened before?"

"Yes, it has happened before, but the man to see is the one who collects the mail. He'll be here at ten o'clock tonight."

"At ten o'clock I will be on an airplane for New York."

"I see. But you say it's not your letter."

"That's right."

"Then it wouldn't do any good for you to stay over anyway. Your secretary, or whoever mailed it, is the one who will have to ask for it. Sorry."

8

For Rex Apgar, owner of KBEX-TV, Channel 33, it was a day of celebration in his campaign to "Reach the Coast with the Most for Jesus." His station was being linked for the first time to a Midwest Christian network, and already his staff was working on a replacement motto. The superspectacular Sunday package he had put together would be carried live by satellite to viewers all the way from California to Texas to Minnesota.

Ever since the station opened the doors of its impressive new Santa Monica studio that morning, people had been flocking in. Most of them were there to see, in person, Eli Pixley, the southern rock singer who had just brought out his Christian testimony in song. It was the hottest religious platter of the month, and Eli would be singing some of the more popular numbers from it.

The program included videotaped greetings from many of the leading Christian celebrities of North America. Pixley's final number would introduce a taped ten-minute evangelistic message by an exciting young preacher from Sydney, Australia. To please the Southern California viewing audience, Apgar had invited The Lofters as home fare. The host who would emcee this dazzling talent was the well-known Robbie Cronk, a TV personality who had settled at Channel 33 after a peripatetic career in the networks.

Half an hour before air time, the bank of thirty telephones was fully staffed by volunteer counselors and the audience section was overflowing. In a ready room down the hall, Eli Pixley was seated while a makeup girl did what she could with his rather gaunt profile. "You cover 'em zits, sister, or I'll shore be unhappy," he told her. Pixley was attired in a gold lamé suit with pearl-studded shirt and Frye boots, and carried an expensive guitar.

Across the hall in a side room The Lofters were getting their act together at last. Rick had rejoined the group at dinner the night before, and was showing the kind of enthusiasm he had displayed at Restoration Chapel, before they had enrolled at Calvary College. Now he was saying, "Let's put the Spirit into this. Let's bust loose!"

Linda looked at him sharply. "Why did you really come back?"

"To sing. That's all. That's our thing, let's do it."

"What about the other?"

"Let's go for it!"

"You know," said Rennie, "the more I hear people telling me I'm crazy, the more I believe it."

"Rennie's got one strong point," said Linda. "Nobody believes it; therefore it's going to happen.

"Who hath believed our report?" said Rick softly.

At 10 o'clock the cameras were loaded and rolled into position, and the floor manager and studio director were at their posts. Robbie made his appearance on the television screen to canned applause, and then brought on his special guest, Eli Pixley, who was greeted with whistles and stamping feet. After puffing Eli for two minutes, Robbie introduced The Lofters and he and Eli retired to studio chairs off-camera.

As the lights went up and the tape in the number one camera began to roll, Rick, Linda, and Rennie led off with one of their old favorites, "I Wish We'd All Been Ready." They were grouped around the foot of Channel 33's famous "Golden Ladder," a colorful bower intertwined with artificial pansies and begonias. With the help of guitar and traps, the song moved nicely down to the final bars of the chorus, when the tension among the singers increased. Linda watched Rennie for a signal. Was this the time? In a few seconds the red eye would wink out and they would be off the air.

Just before the song ended, Rennie nodded his head. Linda quickly climbed up two rungs of the "Golden Ladder," holding her microphone. The surprised number one cameraman followed her movement as Linda announced in a shaky voice, "Friends, I have a special message for you. Jesus Christ is coming back, possibly today!"

Robbie Cronk, seated at the other set, swung his head around and stared at Linda, who was continuing to extemporize on the end of the age and the imminent return of Christ. Robbie then turned to the floor manager, who was signaling the program director in the console room and running his finger across his throat. Instead, the program director put the camera on Robbie.

Caught off-guard, the emcee rallied lamely with a studio smile. "Amen, glory!" he said, raising his voice to drown out Linda, "there's a message in that song for all of us like, 'I wish we'd all been ready.' Every Christian in this day and age ought to be ready for the Lord's coming back, don't you think, Eli? We don't know when it will be, but we sure need to be ready."

Linda, unaware that her microphone was dead, was now paraphrasing verses from the third chapter of Second Peter.

"Yes, sir," said Eli Pixley, "I reckon I'm about as ready as I'll ever be. Me and my little ole git-tar got our white cloud picked out up there in the wild blue yonder."

By this time the floor manager and his assistant were struggling with Rennie and Rick in a strenuous effort to get Linda off the Golden Ladder. Her response was to climb several rungs higher and elevate her voice to a higher pitch. Since the ladder was never intended for human use and was now swaying dangerously, the attempt to remove her had to be given up.

The program director, however, had had enough. Finding that Linda's noisemaking was interfering with the reception of Robbie's patter, he had the console switch abruptly to its backup film. Thus the television screens in nearly a million homes were now introduced to the antics of Ranger, the Gospel Horse, who was presented as a sure-enough born-again bronco.

All of the confusion began to amuse the studio audience, but it greatly dismayed Eli Pixley, who rose up in righteous indignation and demanded, "What's goin' on? I'm supposed to be next. What are y'all doin' to me? I came here to sing my song for Jesus. You tryin' to cut me out? I don't guess you will!" When no one seemed to pay attention to him (the chief interest being the Golden Ladder), Eli seized his guitar and strode across the studio floor to where the assistant floor manager was arguing with the assistant studio director. On his way, his boot caught in a cable and sent Eli sprawling. As he did so, the basted left sleeve of his lamé jacket came loose. Picking himself up, the rock singer retreated to his ready-room and locked the door.

By now several volunteers had abandoned their telephones (which were ringing furiously) and crowded around the Golden Ladder to hear more from Linda. Rick, thoroughly enjoying himself, tossed her a Bible while Rennie held the swaying ladder. Linda waved the Bible and shouted, "Listen to what the Book says: 'For as the lightning comes forth from the east and appears

202 / The Doomsday Connection

as far as the west, so also shall be the coming of the Son of Man.' Would you believe, we were on a plane last Friday flying from east to west when we were struck by lightning and heard this voice telling us that . . ."

A fresh assault was now launched on the Golden Ladder. Rick and Rennie were shouldered out of the way by studio personnel, and Robbie Cronk began to clamber up the rungs after Linda. Realizing that her time was up, Linda shouted, "Listen, it's true! Remember Mary in the garden—they didn't believe her either!"

So agile was Robbie's pursuit that Linda inadvertently stepped on his head, disturbing his toupee. Robbie then descended in disarray, knocking over a large bowl of artificial hydrangeas at the base of the ladder. The studio audience, well into the spirit of pandemonium, applauded.

Gradually the dust settled and the stage was cleared. Linda descended the ladder and joined Rick and Rennie as they waited stoically for the forces of retributive justice to catch up to them. As the switchboard was continuing to light up, the counselors reluctantly returned to their telephones. Eli Pixley was coaxed back on the studio floor. The studio director and floor manager began putting together the pieces of their superspectacular. At the console the program director was taking orders from Rex Apgar, who kept well out of sight.

The remainder of the spectacle's airtime was devoted to the remarkable cavortings of Ranger, the Gospel Horse, who pawed the earth three times for the Trinity, four times for the Gospels, and five times for the number of stones David used in his shootout with Goliath.

Meanwhile some of the viewers in Lompoc, California, and Sulphur Springs, Arkansas, and Terre Haute, Indiana, and Spooner, Wisconsin, had heard enough of Linda's shrill proclamation to begin asking questions. What was going on? Was it true? Was the Lord Jesus coming back?

Today?

9

Never since he quit working for the white man had the Reverend Jordan Foster been so humiliated. At a closed meeting of his congregation he listened to the charges brought against him by a special investigating committee of deacons.

The chairman, Leroy Warburton, declared that Jordan had failed to account for church funds amounting to $3,800; that he had been derelict in his hospital visits; that he had engaged in political activities without the consent of the church, thereby neglecting the souls entrusted to his care, including the youth and elderly; that he had absented himself from stated meetings and generally been discourteous toward members of the congregation. As to his personal life, it was well-known that his home was in disrepair and had become a poor example to the church.

"Brothers and sisters," said Deacon Warburton after detailing the charges, "we in this church have honored Reverend Foster as a preacher of the Word and as a man. We have respected him for his good qualities and loved him as a Christian brother. I regret that it is my sad duty to present these facts for your consideration and action."

As Warburton was speaking, Jordan Foster sat with bowed head and watched his life pass before his eyes. He saw the little town in west Texas where he had grown up; felt the first stings of discrimination from the owner of a candy shop; listened to his father's footsteps as he packed a suitcase and walked out for good one night humming, "Bye, bye, blackbird."

A face came before him. It was the summer youth worker from San Angelo, a white man who befriended him and won him back to God. He studied his hands—powerful hands that had won a batting championship and led his high school team to the county title; hands that had worked in Texas fields, and then brought him a scholarship to Baylor University. As the reading of the indictments continued, he felt the perspiration at the back of his neck.

He was being called upon to respond to the charges. What could he say? A lot of them were true; some were not. If the conviction of the Spirit to his heart was true, and God was going to wrap things up, what difference did any of it make?

He rose from his chair and faced the congregation. "Brothers and sisters in the Lord, I came here six years ago as a son of peace and your servant for Jesus' sake. During these years I have sought to present Christ to you by precept and example. I realize now that I have failed. My conscience has convinced me that I am unworthy of the honor bestowed upon me as undershepherd of our Savior's bride. I will not answer the allegations, but I ask your forgiveness as I submit to you my resignation and beg leave to depart as I came, as a son of peace."

A slight commotion occurred at the rear of the church. Mrs. Arlowene Foster, wearing her rose hat and cloak, white gloves, and violet dress with white ruffle, made her way down the center aisle with a flourish of her cane, followed by her daughter-in-law and three grandsons. They walked clear to the front row, where other worshipers made room for them. Arlowene acknowledged the gesture with a queenly nod.

Now everyone was seated, and Jordan Foster was exchanging glances with his wife. Deacon Glasscock, who was not a member of the special committee, rose to speak. "Mr. Chairman, to get this matter properly before the church, I would like to move that the pastor's resignation be accepted, and then speak to that motion."

The motion being duly seconded, he proceeded, "I am not prepared to vote on this matter, Mr. Chairman, until some of the charges you detailed have been responded to. With your permission I would like to address the pastor." Permission being granted, and Jordan having stood to his feet, Glasscock asked him, "Is it true, Reverend, that certain church funds in the amount of $3,800 are unaccounted for?"

"It is not true, Brother Glasscock," replied Foster. "I have called for an audit of the church books by an independent firm that will show every penny of the Lord's money properly designated and none misspent."

"And is it true, Reverend, that you have been engaging in politics while minister of this church?"

"It is not true. My trip to Washington last week was not political. I was invited by the President of the United States to a special conference on prison work. Last month some gentlemen from Sacramento came and waited on me, but I did not consent to engage in politics or run for any office, nor would I without the approval of the whole church."

Deacon Glasscock sat down and Deacon Haines arose. "Would the pastor please respond to the other charges?" he asked. At that point a young woman member of the congregation stood in the rear of the church and shouted, "Ask him about Paula Marie! Ask him! Don't let him off! I say the man is a scoundrel!"

Arlowene, seated in the front row, bristled, turned her head, and thumped her cane. Jordan, who had been standing by his chair, now entered the pulpit and grasped its sides with his powerful hands. "I want to commend Sister Saunders for her courage in speaking up. She said I was a scoundrel. No, I am not a scoundrel or an adulterer, but I am a sinner. I have broken my vows and violated God's law. I am sorry. You gave me many opportunities, and I failed you. Those chances won't come again." He paused and looked down at Vivian in the front row. "But my greatest sin is not with people; it is that I forsook the Fountain of Living Water. My pride and ambition made me too busy to pray except in public, and caused me to neglect my personal study of God's Word."

Jordan stopped, took out a handkerchief, and wiped his eyes. "Brothers and sisters, you see what I am. God has been dealing with me for two days. I ask forgiveness from you and my family, and please allow me to resign."

He sat down. No one moved. Other handkerchiefs began to appear in the pews. Finally Deacon Warburton rose and asked, "Are you prepared to vote?"

The choir director raised his hand and asked to speak. "Mr. Chairman, the Bible tells us that God does not despise a broken and contrite heart. It tells us that if a brother commits a trespass and sincerely repents, then our orders are to admonish him and if he changes his ways, to restore him to fellowship. I believe what our pastor says. I believe the Spirit is working in his heart.

"I therefore propose a substitute motion. Pending the time of the audit of our church funds, I move that action on Reverend Foster's resignation be postponed for thirty days, and that meanwhile this congregation go to prayer and build up some support for this man of God."

Several voices were heard seconding the motion. "Is there discussion from the floor on the motion to accept the resignation?" A retired minister, who was too deaf to hear any of the arguments, rose to give a peroration on the symbolism of Noah's ark which the congregation endured with loving patience, as it had endured his remarks in the past. There being no other comments, Deacon Warburton called for discussion on the substitute motion. "Are you willing to accept the substitute motion in place of the motion to resign?" A show of hands indicated a majority was willing. "Are you ready to vote on the substitute motion?"

On this crucial vote, Vivian was not among the overwhelming number of those present who lifted their hands in support. Arlowene noticed it and gave her daughter-in-law a dig with a good-sized elbow. Vivian's hand shot up, followed by the hands of her three boys. A scattered number responded to the chairman's call for those contrary-minded.

"The motion is carried," announced Deacon Warburton. "The motion to accept the offer to resign is dropped." This caused some parliamentary confusion, during which Jordan Foster stepped down and held a tender reunion with his wife and boys. Bowing to the inevitable with good grace, Deacon Warburton pounded his gavel at last and declared, "There being no further business, these proceedings are closed and the meeting is adjourned."

10

Alison inserted her key in the door of the suite and opened it with the scary feeling that she was doing it for the last time. The days of luxury accommodations were over; in the future she would have no money, no job, no place to go—and no daughter. She thought of Abraham in the Bible, who "went out, not knowing whither he went." And yet she was not depressed; far from it. The letter was in the mail, and she was free.

The red message light was flashing on the telephone by the antique desk. Alison picked up the receiver. "Hello."

"I have a call for Miss Embree."

"Her secretary speaking."

"This is the switchboard. Will you accept the call?"

"Who is it?"

"It's a Miss Pamela Osborne."

Alison's heart played hopscotch inside her ribs. Pamela was the name she had given her daughter before putting her out for adoption. "Miss Embree is not available, but I will be happy to take the call."

"Hello," said a young voice, "Miss Embree?"

"I'm her secretary," said Alison tremulously. "May I take a message?"

"I've been trying to locate somebody, and I thought Miss Embree could help me."

Alison's thoughts were racing wildly. "Miss Embree is not here at the moment. Can you tell me about it? Perhaps I can help."

"I don't know—I have to talk to Miss Embree."

"Yes. Well, my name is Alison Pitt-Barr. I'm her personal secretary. If you will give me the message, I will ask her to call you."

"It's just that I read in the paper that Miss Embree was speaking at the hotel, and I remembered seeing her name on some paper at the home where I stay. I just thought—"

"Yes?"

"Maybe she would call—"

Alison panicked. "Yes. Wait—don't hang up, Pamela. Is there something Miss Embree can do for you? What can I tell her?"

There was a pause. "It's about my mother. My natural mother. I thought she could help me find her."

Alison closed her eyes. A touch of vertigo made her sway. "Where are you staying?" she managed to ask.

"At the Loma Vista Home for Girls in Redlands."

"Is that near Los Angeles?"

"It's east—I think about a hundred miles."

At that point an operator broke in to ask Pamela for additional coins. Alison quickly wrote down the telephone number and told Pamela, "I'll call you back." She then raced to her bedroom, leaped across the bed to the telephone, and returned the call. By the time Pamela answered, Alison had devised a plan of action.

"I know Miss Embree will want to talk with you," Alison began. "Only last night she was telling me about you."

"About me?" Pamela sounded puzzled.

"Oh, yes. Now, you're living at the Loma Vista Home—is that right?"

"Yes."

"And did you ever live in a home near Rockford, Illinois?"

"Oh, yes."

"And before that?"

"Before that I lived with the Osbornes."

Alison was madly checking her purse to see how much money she had. It was all she could do to keep her voice from screeching, "I'm your mother, Pamela! I'm Alison! I've wanted you for so long, been looking for you, tried to find you, prayed for you, ached for you! Praise God, darling, I love you, love you, love you. You're my daughter! My child! I've found you at last!"

Instead Alison spoke softly and distinctly, keeping herself well in check. "Now listen carefully, Pamela. We're so glad you telephoned. One of us will be coming out to see you this afternoon. Will you be there?"

"Yes."

"Let me have your address. I don't know whether to drive or take a plane—"

"They have helicopters that fly out here, I think," said Pamela.

"It may be by helicopter, and it may be by hot air balloon. Just promise not to leave until I—until one of us gets there."

"And you think you know where my mother is?"

Alison's hand went to her throat. "I think so."

"I promise. I'll be glad to see you." Pamela's voice wavered as she hung up.

Tossing her suitcase on the queen-size bed, Alison began gathering up papers and emptying drawers, so elated she could hardly think. "It's God, it's God," she whispered to herself.

"I didn't have to look, He sent her looking for me. It's from His side!" She flung herself across the bed and for two and a half minutes let the tears flow. Then she rose up, repaired the damage to her face, and was soon on her way down the glass elevator and out onto Figueroa Street.

11

Gus Krieger sat with Frances in the back row of the Congress Hall auditorium. A fresh bandage decorated his cheek, and the cross of nails Commissioner Hilliard had given him was resting on a clean shirt. A fanfare of trumpets, led by Major McCorkle, opened the morning worship at the Salvation Army's Los Angeles citadel.

As far as Gus was concerned, whatever went on up front was O.K. with him. Nothing was bothering him today. For the first time in a long stretch, his prospects looked good. He was among friends, including a special friend. The past was strangely distant. He felt protected from danger. The salvation songs, the testimonies by the soldiers and visitors, the time of prayer, and the solo by Mrs. McCorkle were all pleasantly absorbed; they fit his mood. That God could do anything with his life seemed unlikely, but it wasn't the first time he'd been surprised. Meanwhile, if the end was coming . . .

Major McCorkle now stepped to the platform where Commissioner Hilliard was sitting with the divisional commander and his wife. McCorkle called Gus Krieger's name and asked him to step forward. Gus was reluctant to move, but after the second appeal he walked slowly to the front. "Here's a person I want you to meet," Major McCorkle was saying. "You know, the way God works is amazing. Just last night we met this brother at the Bonaventure Hotel—but I want him to tell you about it. Gus, tell us what happened."

"You ought to know," said Gus, "you were there."

"Would you just share with the folks about it?"

"Why should I?"

"Well, to glorify the Lord," said Major McCorkle rather doubtfully.

"I don't know what to say."

"You were in your room—" prompted the major.

"Shall I tell 'em who I was expectin'?"

Major McCorkle glanced at his wife. "We came in by surprise," he told the congregation briskly, "and we had a great prayer time, and Gus asked the Lord to come into his heart." He turned to Krieger. "Thanks so much for coming up." A handshake followed, and the trophy of grace was escorted off the platform. He returned with considerable relief to his seat beside Frances.

A bit later Major McCorkle presented the divisional commander, who in turn introduced Commissioner Hilliard. The commissioner delivered some jovial amenities and greetings from India, after which he preached a homily on the text, "Endure hardship with us like a good soldier of Christ Jesus." As the talk wound to its close, Major McCorkle rose to announce the closing hymn. Before he could speak, however, Gus Krieger stood up in the back row and called, "Can I ask the colonel—the commissioner I mean—a question?"

"Of course, Gus," said Major McCorkle hastily, "right after—"

"Why didn't you say anything about the voice we heard on the plane?"

Commissioner Hilliard rose to his feet. "Thank you, Augustin. It was good of you to remind me. To be candid, I have been so busy with meetings and receptions since I got here that there just has not been a moment to discuss the matter with my colleagues as I planned to do. But I have placed it at the top of the agenda for tomorrow morning when I will be meeting with the divisional commander and his staff. I can assure you of that."

"But what if it's too late, Colonel?" insisted Gus, continuing to stand.

"Perhaps we can arrange a meeting with you and Commissioner Hilliard later today," said Major McCorkle. "Thank you for that. And now, let us all stand for the benediction. . . ."

Frances and Gus were among the first to emerge from Congress Hall after the service. Frances was joined by two of the women soldiers, to whom she introduced Gus. As they stood chatting in the sunshine about the street meeting planned for that afternoon in Pershing Square, a black Oldsmobile drove past on Ninth Street. To everyone's horror, gunfire erupted from the vehicle.

Gus, who had apparently been watching the car, leaped in front of Frances, then spun around crazily and fell in a crumpled heap on the sidewalk. Blood spurted from his neck, then ran down his shirt and over the cross of nails he was wearing. Frances, screaming, sank to the ground beside him and attempted to stanch the wound with a handkerchief.

Major McCorkle, hurrying out of the hall, immediately ordered an ambulance. "Did anyone get the license number?" he asked the stunned bystanders. Someone did. The major then knelt by Gus and turned him on his back to administer mouth-to-mouth resuscitation. "Start praying," he ordered those around him.

It was too late. Even though the skies had not split open, Jesus had come for Gus Krieger.

12

"They're back there." Mary's voice was taut as they headed toward Thousand Oaks on the Ventura Freeway.

"They can't be!" The Camaro leaped forward under Arvie's foot. Then, "How far back?"

"Four cars, maybe."

"What lane?"

"Same as ours."

"Two guys?"

"I think so. Been tailing us for miles."

Arvie pulled into the fast lane. "I'm going to blind-side 'em." He darted in front of a Fruehauf semi-trailer in lane two and cut to the outside lane. By staying ahead of the semi he became invisible to cars on the inside lanes. Before the Lincoln could get its target back in line of vision, Arvie had peeled off at the first off-ramp and was on his way north. Cutting back at Janss Road, he got on state highway 23 heading for Moorpark. The Lincoln, unable to maneuver to the outside lane, was forced to continue on toward Camarillo. It was easy—too easy.

"They'll never catch us now," said Arvie with a satisfied air as the highway led them past the settled area into open country. "What are these guys like?"

Mary looked at him, green eyes glittering. "Mean!"

"Yeah? Who are they?"

"They picked me up at the airport. I think the driver you saw was in prison with Lennie."

"Who's Lennie?"

"He's a guy in New York."

"Oh?" Arvie tried to remember what he had read about

Minnesota girls being transported to New York to become prostitutes. "Was he your pimp?"

"I lived with him for a while."

"Is he the one that beat you up?" Out of the blue, things began to fall into place. "I get it now. He beat you so bad you decided to run away, so what did you do? You rolled some poor guy and took his money and caught a cab for Kennedy Airport."

"He nearly killed me."

"Why?"

"He'd been shooting up."

"How'd he track you down?"

"He knew about my aunt. I found out later he was on his way to the airport when I got on the plane. He checked my flight and called his buddy in L.A."

Arvie looked at his gas gauge. "We snookered 'em. We ought to be at your aunt's in an hour."

"It won't do any good."

"Why not? You'll be safe enough there."

"You don't understand. When you're in, you're in. They've got you. This is all a waste."

"We'll see about that. Talk some more."

But Mary slumped into a sullen silence.

Tooling through Moorpark on Highway 118, Arvie headed his Camaro north on Balcom Canyon Road, winding over a 1,000-foot ridge. Patches of chaparral dotted the brown hills that rose steeply on either side of the narrow road. As they crested the summit, they were suddenly alone. They were only four miles from the heavily traveled arterials, but the route was totally deserted.

Pulling off the road onto a wagon track just below the top of the ridge, Arvie parked where his car was virtually concealed from view. Ever since he had left Thousand Oaks, and the magnificent Topatopa Mountains had appeared in the north, he had been thinking about Jordan Foster's remark on the telephone—"I suggest you go out in the hills somewhere. You need to have a talk with God." The idea seemed inconceivable at the time, but here he was, and here were the hills.

"Let's take a walk," he said to Mary. "You've been strung out long enough."

Mary looked at him. "You nerd!"

Arvie walked around the car and opened the door. "Come on!"

"You're not gettin' any sex out of me."

Ignoring her remark, Arvie said, "We're going to lie low and let them run their tails off. Do they have your aunt's address?"

"Just Ojai."

"Then we'll take a back way. I know this country. And I figure, instead of sitting in the car, let's go for a walk!"

"No!"

Arvie held up her purse, dangling it on a finger. "Better come!"

Slowly and reluctantly Mary stepped out and took back her purse. Arvie locked the car and, keeping her ahead of him, pointed the way up a steep, barren hillside. They struggled to the top of the canyon to find themselves in a different world. After navigating a broken fence, they wandered silently through a pleasant sloping meadow, following a narrow trail that led toward a high rock outcropping in the distance.

Mary, finding her boots unsuitable for this kind of hiking, carried them in her hand. The trail was not too rough, the afternoon was sunny, the air clean, the breeze light and warm, and the scenery spectacular. Her body responded; her bare toes curled in the soft earth, and she began to feel better in spite of herself. At the moment she was resigned to following Arvie's lead, but had given up trying to fathom his motives. Sexually he was either gay, which she doubted, or else a harmless weirdo or a romantic idiot. He seemed determined to unload her at her aunt's, although she had told him repeatedly she had not the slightest intention of staying there. The need for cash and the desire to get high had killed the impulse that sent her west in the first place.

"Watch it. Back off!"

Arvie picked up a stick and pointed at a young diamondback rattlesnake, coiled on the trail and displaying its forked tongue while moving its head from side to side. Three rattles quivered on its tail. Mary stared at the reptile without the slightest trace of fear.

"Let's just walk around," said Arvie. "I used to kill them back in Orange County, but now I leave them alone. They belong here more than we do." Mary stepped off the trail and they continued their walk, with Arvie turning and looking at her curiously. "You didn't seem bothered."

"Why should I? It's the two-legged snakes that bother me."

Arvie continued, "They told us in psychology that people who scream at snakes are usually afraid of their own sexuality."

"Sex doesn't scare me." A cottontail leaped out ahead of Mary and disappeared into the brush. "You know what scares me?"

"What?"

"Dying."

Arvie was intrigued, and dropped back alongside her. "Why do you say that? It's part of nature, just like that rattler."

"No, it's not. Not when the Devil's got your soul."

They passed an abandoned satellite tracking station and ascended a series of gentle hills that brought them to the base of the bold peak.

"I've got to stop," puffed Mary for the first time.

"Put your stuff here," said Arvie, indicating a small, low cave. "We're going to climb." And climb they did, both of them, scrambling and leaping from one smooth igneous rock to another, Arvie reaching a hand to Mary as they went up the side of the steeper boulders. At last they found themselves on a flat crag not far from the summit, and stopped to look. This was the California most visitors never see except from an airplane. Tiny mountain daisies, sprouting between the stone cracks, trembled in the afternoon breeze. A lizard eyed them, performed a couple of push-ups, and twitched out of sight. A tiny thrush chirped its objection to their intrusion.

"Sit down," said Arvie, leaning against a towering boulder. "This is great."

"I'm pooped," was Mary's rejoinder.

But Arvie was waxing loquacious. "Looks a little like Montana. My folks came from there." He persisted despite Mary's

216 / The Doomsday Connection

obvious disinterest. "Mother took us back there once and showed us where she and Dad started ranching after he came back from Korea. Fabulous country."

"Where is your dad?" asked Mary, for something to say.

"Dead. Killed."

"Really? How?"

Arvie ignored her and stepped to the edge of the crag, where he surveyed the pastoral scene below them. His thoughts moved from his father's death fifteen years earlier to his mother's funeral the past week. A chilling sense of loss gripped him as it had at the graveside in Hartford. After a moment the shudder passed; the warm, hazy sunshine again caressed him and brought him back to the present. He realized with relief that the immediate threat of pursuit was gone, and that Mary had asked him a question. He came and sat beside her.

"They moved to California before I was born. Got a place in Pauma Valley and started growing oranges. Did real good. We were small—my sister Virginia was seven and I was five—when Dad got up one night and surprised a burglar." He paused. "About a year after that Mother sold the ranch and we moved to San Fernando."

"You mean he was shot?"

Arvie nodded. "Four times. They got the guy and gave him life, but he's out now."

"Do you remember your Dad?"

"Yup."

She was silent. Arvie cupped his eyes and peered down the trail toward the canyon. "I was out this way once before," he said. "I was a freshman. Some guys at the house brought me out here blindfolded and I had to find my way back without any money." He smiled reflectively as he went to the edge and studied a sparrow hawk circling above them, buoyed by the warm air currents. "Looks better in daylight." A sharp noise shattered the peace; a formation of Blue Angels was passing over. As he studied them Arvie remarked, "I guess we're all heading toward the end."

"How do you know?" Mary was immediately interested.

"Oh, everybody's getting the bomb. It's bound to happen."

"All I know," said Mary, "is that my feet hurt."

Arvie knelt and began massaging the balls of her feet. He noticed how dainty and beautiful her toes were, now dusty from the trail. "Let's have some fun, Mary," he said, and Mary decided that the expected moment had arrived. But he went on, "Let's say today really is Doomsday. We've only got a few hours to go. I mean, that's it. What's the first thing we do?"

"Find a fast-food place."

"Oh, come on. Food won't make that much difference. What else?"

"I don't know what you're looking for, but I'd snort some coke. Some good coke."

Arvie looked her over carefully. "You know what I'd do?"

"What?" Mary returned his gaze.

"Well, first of all, I'd just start to relax."

"That's neat. I like it. You start to relax with two hoods after you."

"Hoods?" Arvie was indignant. "We're playing a game. What about all the other things? Inflation, pollution, abortion, evolution, the Russians, the bomb—even the Superbowl. All down the tube. Fantastic!"

Mary stood up. "I think you're missing some dots off your dice. We'd better get back before it's dark."

But Arvie was again leaning over the edge. "You can start back if you like. I came up here to do something." Jumping up, he attacked the nearest boulder and was soon scrambling upward. In a few minutes he was straddling a sharp rock at the top of the outcropping that seemed to rise above the others. He faced the wind coming from the ocean and let his eyes sweep the view to the west and north. For a quarter of an hour he stood motionless, then turned his head and watched Mary slowly working her way down the rocks and starting along the trail back to the Camaro. Now Arvie did something most uncharacteristic of him. Raising both arms, he shouted into the wind, "God! Why did You destroy my dad? Why did You do it? And now Mom. All I ever did was hate You, but all she ever did was love You. And what I want to know is, why?"

He stood with the warm westerly breeze whipping the tears from his face. His hand reached to the shoulder he had hurt during his climb. Syphilitic, Mary had called him, a pompous ass. What would his mother have said if he had walked in the door with Mary? Stupid question. His mother believed in God, and that too was stupid. Only up here, looking out over the rolling vista of hills dropping to the ocean, it didn't seem so stupid. Creep, she said. What a mess she was. Said the Devil had her soul. Typical cop-out. Only a month back Arvie had informed his mother that he couldn't accept the kind of God she believed in; that Lucretius had made him an agnostic.

That left the basic question: What was life for? Tennis matches? Nobody seemed to know—or care. But why had his parents bothered to bring him into the world? He assumed they had something in mind. He wished now he had asked his mother. What would she have said? That all his parents had done with their hard-working lives, they had done for him and his sister Virginia? Probably. That those early struggles planting the orange orchards were not for themselves, but for *him*. He still had his hands in the air, but he was moaning softly. "I don't know . . . I don't know!" It didn't make sense. There was nobody left he could turn to—nobody! He was captain of the team, life was supposed to be so great—and it was merely disgusting.

He dropped his arms; there was no help there. Something Brenda had said came floating back: *true joy is being used for a mighty purpose.* Arvie grunted. Purpose for what? In the distance below he made out the sparrow hawk soaring above the low hills, hunting for field creatures with unconscious grace. A thermal draft bore it upward and it lay on the warm air with wings fully spread, motionless except for a trembling at the tips. Then it turned and headed toward his crag, and Arvie caught a flash of red. It passed over him, wheeled suddenly, and dove directly down upon him, uttering shrill cries and swooping past his head so that he was forced to duck.

Protection! he thought as the fowl disappeared behind a boulder. It has a nest here. An idea gripped him: maybe that was it. Maybe that was it! Maybe his purpose in life—he sucked in his breath as self-discovery caught him in its rapture—was to take what his folks had given him and use it to help somebody else. Maybe that was what was missing in life, and this screeching bird had shown it to him. His job was to take what equipment he had been given, not to fill the universe with tennis balls, but to protect someone who needed it. Not to achieve greatness, but to share goodness. He didn't remember that in Lucretius.

It was as if a surgeon had lanced an angry boil on his neck or someplace, draining the poison that festered in his soul. To his amazement, he felt no more hostility toward God. Self-importance (the real root of his arrogance) was brought down to earth. He and the sparrow hawk were one. But a question came to him: if he was to do for someone else what his forebears had done for him, where did he start? He didn't bother to look for an answer. Instead he climbed off the crag and began sliding down one boulder after another. "Mary!" he shouted, his whole body electric with vitality. "Mary! Wait up!"

He needn't have yelled. Mary had witnessed the whole scene from below. To her, Arvie had dissolved into a knight in her child's storybook. Was he really praying up there? She knew it was all so much crap; prayer had never helped her when they were beating her up; he was only brainwashing himself. And yet there he was, bounding toward her, the one guy in her life who didn't fit into her grim codification. Stupid as he was, there was something about him that was from beyond, something that set him apart from what she knew of the world and its ills and pills and snakepits.

She watched as he approached, fascinated, unable to take her eyes off him.

13

A distinguished audience was listening to the new president of the Pacific Institute of Technology and Science in the Greek theater on Sunday afternoon. Raymond L. Phillips, Sc.D., LL.D., wearing his robe, hood, and full academic regalia, was delivering his inaugural address. Behind him on the platform were the representatives of some twenty institutions of higher learning, including several college presidents and chancellors.

A taxicab turned into the parking lot adjoining the Greek theater and drove slowly up to the steel gate. A loudspeaker was relaying the new president's address, and Colleen Phillips, in the backseat of the taxi, asked the driver to pause. She was wearing dark glasses, not to protect her eyes so much as to act out the remorse and guilt she was feeling over her fall from grace.

Now Colleen rolled down a window in order to hear what her husband was saying, or (to be precise) what he was reading from his manuscript.

"We know from archaeological evidence that primitive man, prehistoric man, instinctively attributed the events surrounding his daily life to the manipulation of supernatural powers. Every tree had its god, every stream its spirit, whether benign or malignant; every hilltop had its magic ring where numinous objects were propitiated and worshiped.

"In our day such simple credulities have been dissolved in the glare of open knowledge. The so-called demons that once infested the environment have been exorcised, if I may so speak, by the steady advances of science. The Holy Spirit of the Bible turns out to be merely the collective unconscious, bubbling up out of the folk memory of the race. . . ."

As Colleen listened, she realized that the end of a long and sometimes beautiful marriage had come, and this was her good-bye to her husband. The words he was speaking were erudite and impressive, but to her they were concrete blocks, walling her off forever from her life partner and the father of her children. They sounded so cold, so massive, as if they had been deliberately chosen to crush the tiny tendrils of her faith. But whatever Raymond's faults of conduct, and the depth of his apostasy, and the harshness of his cruelty toward her, it was not Raymond who sent the tears rolling down her cheeks from behind the dark glasses. It was her own collapse, her weakness, the destruction she had brought on herself, that overwhelmed her as she sat in the taxicab this Sunday afternoon.

Near the chain fence some twenty yards away stood a group of demonstrators who were being quietly but carefully watched by security police. These were the no-nukes, placard-carrying students who were protesting the policies of the new administration. Two of the students approached the taxi.

"Mrs. Phillips?" asked the large, red-bearded student whom she had seen at the think-tank the day before. Colleen's lips trembled, but she did not reply.

"How are you?" asked the girl alongside him with a disarming smile. She was still wearing the designer Levis and the T-shirt emblazoned with "P.I.T.S." "We liked what you said yesterday." Her placard read, "DON'T TRASH THE EARTH."

"Won't you come over and say a word to us?" asked the man pleasantly. "We weren't planning anything, just registering a presence."

Colleen rolled down the window another three inches. "I'm afraid I can't now. Thank you, though. Something happened last evening that changed the picture for me a little."

"I wish something would change the Pentagon," said the girl.

"Are you O.K., ma'am?" asked the man.

"I'm O.K. It's just that it seems nothing has any meaning for me any more—except God, maybe. I read that once somewhere. 'Our life has no meaning in itself; it has meaning only in relation to God.' "

"Well, we're in a battle to save God's creation," said the man. "We could use some help from people like you."

"I was in it," said Colleen, removing her glasses and revealing her dark circles. "That was what I was living for. I marched, and paraded, and carried my sticks. But now it all seems a little naive. What's the point? I mean, it's out of our hands. I can't even save myself."

"The earth is all we have," said the girl. "What else is there? We've got to stand up for it."

Colleen shook her head wearily. "I don't know. For me, it's come down to a question of justice and mercy. The one isn't working. I don't know about the other."

"Meantime we blow up," said the man.

"No!" For the first time Colleen raised her voice. "God's not going to let it happen."

"You mean—?"

"I mean He's going to take it back!"

Colleen spoke to the driver, replaced her glasses, and rolled up the window. In the background her husband's voice could still be heard: "Once it seemed that science was turning loose on our planet immense new powers beyond the ability of mere human beings to control. Here at this institute we have proved that such is not the case. Through the peaceful use of nuclear energy, nature is being harnessed and redirected to protect and preserve all that is best in the environment. . . ."

The taxi moved out of the parking lot as the students went back to their silent protesting.

14

Taking the South Mountain Road at the bottom of Balcom Canyon, Arvie drove across the Santa Clara River and into the town of Santa Paula, where he and Mary began looking for a gas pump. What they found, at the first service station they came to, was a black Lincoln Continental.

"Look!"

As Arvie glanced where she was pointing, his spinal cord went glacial. Whipping the Camaro into an alley he blurted, "Did they see us?"

"They got eyes and they ain't stupid." Mary's ugly mood had returned.

He swung south onto Harvard Boulevard. "Were they gassing up?"

"Probably. Couldn't prove it by me."

"We'll have to get on 150 and go for it."

"Come on, sailor!" Mary pointed to the gas gauge. "That thing's bobbing around empty."

"Can't help it. We're not staying here with those birds in town." As they paused at a traffic light he added, "They may think we took the freeway to Ventura." He turned right and headed north. Two more lights and they were on the shortcut for Ojai, sixteen miles away. "Got your aunt's address?"

"Nope."

"Don't try to fake me out. I know it's in your purse."

Reluctantly Mary took out her aunt's letter. "You're an ass. Why should they go to Ventura? They can read the map. They'll just tail us into the sticks and run us down. Why don't you drop me off now? I've had enough."

"And leave me to explain where I dropped you? If I thought—"

"Hey!" Mary swung her head around as a sign flashed by. "That sign at the airport. Remember?"

"What sign?"

"The Ark. You know."

"What about it?"

"Six miles straight ahead."

Arvie pressed on the throttle and bent over the wheel. "Yeah. 'Come to the Ark.' Why not?"

"Instead of Ojai?"

Arvie looked at the gauge. "Never make it. Guess I faked myself out."

"I guess you did. Big John Wayne."

"You don't think much of me, do you?"

"I like you sometimes. Sometimes you're like the south end of a horse going north."

"See 'em?" he asked as she glanced back.

"No, but they're there."

Arvie checked his rearview mirror for the twentieth time. "I could have taken you to the police station."

"And turn me in?"

"Oh, let's drop it, shall we?"

"O.K., stud. You let me out of this clonker and we'll drop it."

Arvie was silent as he watched the signs indicating the approach of the amusement park. Taking an off-ramp, he followed the entry lanes to The Ark's parking lot. He grabbed a ticket and drove to the main park entrance, where the Camaro's engine began to cough and sputter.

"Let's go," he ordered as they coasted into a space for handicapped parking.

"For gas?"

"Not now. No time. Come on!"

They ran toward the ticket kiosk and slipped into line just before two dozen passengers were discharged from a chartered bus. Mary turned toward the lot entrance and clutched Arvie's arm. He looked back and saw the black Continental idling slowly past the entrance.

"I knew it!" Mary's voice was dead.

Four persons were in line ahead of them, and the nearest gentleman now spoke to Arvie. He had dark wavy hair and wore a Brooks Brothers suit. "Well, well, how interesting!"

"I remember you." The woman standing next to him was laughing as she spoke to Arvie. "I was your flight attendant." To Mary she added, "I changed your seat, didn't I?"

Mary was speechless and Arvie nearly so. "You were on that—" He paused. "I can't believe this!"

"Nor can we," said Ralph Epstein, smiling. "We just met in line a few minutes ago."

"Why did you come way out here?" demanded Arvie.

"I don't know, really," said Ralph.

"I don't either," added Sally Carstairs.

Mary was pulling at Arvie's sleeve and pointing to the end of the line. Ralph noticed she was trembling and asked, "Is anything wrong?"

Arvie spoke in a low voice. "There's a guy just joined the line back there. See him? Heavyset."

"I see him."

"He's a hood. We think he's tailing us."

"What does he want?"

"He wants her." Arvie nodded toward Mary. "He may have a gun."

By now Epstein had reached the ticket window, and he

quickly placed three twenty-dollar bills on the counter. "Four adult." Turning to Arvie, he said, "You take my friend Miss Carstairs and meet me—" He turned to the clerk. "—what's the name of your restaurant?"

"Ham's Burgers. Just inside."

"Wait for me at Ham's Burgers." To the clerk he said, "Will you call security? It's an emergency!"

Arvie, Mary, and Sally entered the park and followed the "Ararat Trail" into an open area. In the center was a small-scale, bright-hued replica of what the artist Gustave Doré conceived as Noah's original ark. Beyond were fairy-tale rides, shooting galleries, roller coasters, overhead skyrides, and the usual features of a pretentious southern California amusement park. The ark itself was seated in a circular moat about six feet wide and two feet deep. A sign at the entrance announced it was designed for children of less than two cubits in height, a cubit (it said) being a foot and a half. A cable track led across the moat, by means of which plastic animals conveyed the diminutive riders into the ship. These colorful lions, rhinos, leopards, giraffes, and zebras were mounted at the gate by the children with the assistance of uniformed attendants. Once strapped in, each with an accompanying adult, they rode across the moat two-by-two and disappeared into the mysteries of the ark. A few minutes later they reappeared, still mounted, through the mouth of a bilious-looking floating monster advertised as "an exact replica of Jonah's whale."

A huge sign on a low building to the left announced the home of "Ham's Burgers." While the other three stood and waited in front of the restaurant, Ralph Epstein talked with two security guards, who promptly telephoned the sheriff's office in Ojai. When the heavyset man reached the window, he was issued a ticket and allowed to enter the park. He quickly spotted Mary, and sauntered toward the carousel nearby. Within a few minutes a sheriff's vehicle arrived, and two deputies entered the park and walked over to where the man was under surveillance. A deputy spoke to him.

"We'd like you to come with us." He pointed to a nearby screening area.

"Kiss off," replied the man.

The deputy's response was to grab him and shove him against a fence, while his partner frisked the suspect and quickly located a snub-nosed .38 automatic revolver in a shoulder holster. As the three men walked through the return gate to the patrol van, the detainee colored the air with a few choice execrations. This tableau was watched from behind the wheel of the Lincoln Continental by the man Mary knew only as "Lennie's friend." When he saw the deputies close in on his partner, the man quietly backed out of his parking space and drove to the west end of the lot, where he reparked and got in line at the west end ticket office.

"I don't think you'll be bothered any more," said Ralph Epstein as he joined the waiting group. "How about sampling the delights of Ham's Burgers?"

"Don't you wish it," said Mary. "There's another one."

"He was waiting outside in a Lincoln Continental," explained Arvie apologetically.

"A partner?" asked Ralph Epstein.

"Partner my eyeball," blurted Mary. "He's the man! The other guy's nothin'."

"He's probably taken off by now," said Sally.

"Maybe," said Ralph. "Too much heat."

"Should we tell the sheriff?" asked Arvie, seeing the patrol van about to leave.

"There's nothing the sheriff can do until the guy makes his move," said Ralph.

"Meanwhile, do we have to stand here?" demanded Mary. "Can't we take off?"

"We've got to decide," said Ralph. "Let's just go in here where we can sit down and get this thing together."

A string of small, latticed arbors, each open at the top, provided outside bench seating for the patrons of "Ham's Burgers." Ralph led the way into the arbor nearest the ark, which happened to be empty. When they were seated he said, "First of all, do I understand you're out of gas?"

"That's right," said Arvie.

"Mary can go with me. Where were you taking her?"

"To Ojai. Her aunt's place."

"I don't want to go to my aunt's place," said Mary.

"She's scared," said Arvie. "She doesn't know what she wants."

"Let's get out!" said Mary, standing up. "That guy's in here, I know he is."

"Sit down, Mary," said Sally.

"That's right," said Ralph. "Your ambivalence isn't helping. We've got to work something out. I can run Mary into Ojai, and Sally can stay and help Arvie—that your name?—get gas. Then I can come back—"

"Arvie doesn't need me," said Sally. "I'm going with you."

"I was thinking I might be tailed if that whoever-it-is is waiting outside. Didn't you say they followed you all the way out here?"

Arvie nodded. "All day long. I shook them once, but they caught up with us in Santa Paula."

"And apparently they have some kind of hold on Mary." Ralph glanced at Mary, who lit a cigarette.

"Hold on her?" echoed Arvie. "Look at her! They beat her up, but she won't talk about it."

Mary blew smoke at him.

"Well, we've got to get her to her aunt's, that's certain," said Ralph. "Why don't we all go? There's room."

"What about a sheriff escort?" asked Arvie.

"I wonder if it's necessary. If Mary's right, they've probably picked this man up by this time."

"Hah!" said Mary.

"So," Ralph continued, "let's just slip quietly out of here and—"

It was precisely at the moment in the discussion that the man known as "Lennie's friend" walked into the arbor and stood before them.

228 / The Doomsday Connection

15

Captain Frank Medeiros rolled his white Corvette alongside his wife's Mercedes in the driveway of their La Habra executive mansion, leaped out, and hurried to the front door. Working the door's lock combination, he opened it and gave a shrill whistle that was echoed by a mynah bird in the kitchen. Going directly to his den, he seated himself at his desk, drew a fresh yellow pad from a drawer, and began scribbling.

Tracy, his young blonde wife, appeared in the doorway in shorts and halter and "go-aheads," holding a drink in one hand and a teddy bear in the other. "You called?" she inquired archly.

"I need to make a will."

Tracy stared at him. "Are you all right?"

"Of course."

But he was not all right. His sallow countenance was even paler than usual. The tight mouth under the clipped mustache was working nervously. The piercing black eyes that usually took in everything were now filmed over—a fact concealed by the sunglasses he was wearing.

"You act drunk," said Tracy. "Want some coffee?"

"No. Where's my old will?"

"I saw it yesterday in the safe."

"Get it."

"What for?"

"What for?" Frank mimicked her tone. "You'd better make one too."

"Why should I?"

"I'm telling you, it's going to happen. We're wiped out."

Tracy's instinct was alerted. "What's going to happen? Who's wiped out?"

Frank leaned back in his chair and twiddled his pencil. "You know that thing on the plane?"

"Yeah. The world coming to an end and everything. Some kid—"

"That's what I thought. Or some preacher. But I couldn't prove it. Anyway, I've been to the library, and on the way home I got this premonition."

"Premonition? About what?"

"I saw something."

"What was it?"

"A sunspot."

"Sunspot? What does that mean?"

"I dunno. But I saw it, and from what I found out this morning, I knew it was a premonition."

"Maybe it was dirt on the windshield. The car wash is open till 6."

Frank began writing on his pad. "Who do you want your teddy bear left to?"

Tracy tossed her teddy bear onto a blue velvet sofa and set down her drink. "Over my dead body," she announced, fist on hip. "Don't you try giving away my teddy bears. Are you sure you went to the library?"

Medeiros looked at his wristwatch. "We've got just a few hours, that's all."

"Look, if you haven't had a drink, I'm going to fix you one."

"Don't."

"Then get hold of yourself."

He continued writing. "Shall we leave half the property to my nephew and half to your sister?"

"I'm going to call the doctor."

"No time. We've got to think this thing through. There's all that booze in the bar, and the safe deposit, and all that stuff in the garage . . . and that property in Gustine."

"Are you serious?"

"Course I'm serious."

"But if the world's coming to an end, that takes care of everybody, doesn't it?"

"You tell me. You went to Sunday school once."

"Then what's the point? There's not going to be anyone around to leave anything to!"

Frank reached into a desk drawer and took out a cloth-covered black box. Opening it, he lifted out an old-fashioned pocket watch with a gold case. "See that?" he asked, opening the case and winding the stem. "My grandfather's. I'm not giving that to anybody."

Tracy put an arm about his shoulders and seated herself in his lap. "It's going to be O.K., Frank. You had a bad flight, and you're tired and upset over this new job deal and everything." She stroked his hair. "I've been worried about you, you know."

Frank relaxed for a moment, then gently dislodged her and stood to his feet. "You can forget my new job," he said. "I've got to think fast. I spent my whole life acquiring all this, and I can't give it up. I've worked too hard for it."

Tracy plopped on the sofa and lit a cigarette. "So you want to give it all away, and you don't want to, and there's nobody to give it to anyway. What makes you think my sister will be alive after you're dead?"

Medeiros put both hands to his cheeks in a distracted manner. "It isn't that. You know me—I'm a man for method. I've just got to be ready. Check out the alternatives. Formulate a plan with an out, and put it into action."

"Well," said Tracy, cigarette in mouth, as she stepped over to the bar, "if you're not going to have a drink, I'll have another."

"Do you think your mother would like the linen? And the silver plate and crystal?"

"You're insane. What will you do with your Irish setter?"

"I can shoot him. And the mynah bird."

"You ding-a-ling. Don't you touch that mynah bird!"

"I'll take the drink."

"Tell me again what the voice said," urged Tracy as she handed her husband a glass. "I never did get it straight."

"I think something about judgment in two days and about Noah's ark. I didn't—"

"Noah's ark! Yeah! What about that old tub that's sitting down there at the marina with a broken crankshaft? Are you going to give that away too, I hope?"

"I forgot about it." Frank made a note on his pad.

"I think Noah's ark would be better. He's got better insurance." Tracy headed for the master bedroom. "I'm going to be gone for a couple of hours. Got a tennis date with Mary Ann."

Frank put down his glass, followed her into the bedroom, and grasped her roughly. "Don't leave me, Tracy," he pleaded, a catch in his voice. "This thing has me climbing the wall. We've got to think about it together. Think about your jewelry. . . ."

Tracy managed to disentangle herself and slipped into her tennis shoes. "Take it easy, Frank. You've got my word, nothing's going to happen. There's Danish and stuff in the refrigerator."

Her husband watched as she worked her way into a pull-over sweater. "I don't know where to start," he muttered. "There's my credit cards, and the saving bonds, and the mortgage. What about the swimming pool?"

"Well, you can't take it with you, that's for sure," said Tracy, checking her purse. "Maybe you ought to go jump in it."

He pulled out a roll of bills from his pocket. "Look at this stuff. What good is it?" He gave a short, hysterical laugh and threw the roll on the carpet.

"I'll manage to find some use for it," said Tracy, stooping and gathering up the bills. She turned and faced her husband. "You know, if I really got the idea that this was the day of reckoning, I'd be thinking about something besides swimming pools."

"Like what?"

"I'd be thinking about my soul." She tucked the bills in her purse, took a last look in the mirror, picked up her tennis racket, and walked to the front door. "Don't shoot the dog," she said.

"Who'll I leave my suits to?" Frank asked, following her.

"Better keep your summer clothes, you may be going to a hot climate!" Tracy broke into a laugh, then checked it. "And leave my mynah bird alone!" she added fiercely.

As she slammed the door, a loud squawk emerged from the kitchen. Frank slumped into his reclining leather chair and studied his gold watch. As soon as he heard the Mercedes leave the driveway, he finished his drink with a gulp and got to his feet. The olive coloring was back in his cheeks. He went through the kitchen to the back door, where his Irish setter nearly smothered him with affection.

Ignoring the animal, Frank uncovered three plastic garbage cans in the yard and hauled them into the center of the white-carpeted living room. Then, in a savage burst of energy, he began dismantling the room, tossing a variety of treasures, ornaments, and *objets d'art* into two of the cans. Erotic French line drawings, Indonesian seascapes, Chinese carvings, and leather-bound early first editions were dropped in, along with a framed diploma, a strongbox, some thick insurance policies, a video cassette recorder, a small computer, and an elaborate stereo set. Several trips to the garage resulted in the third can being filled with skis, poles, golf clubs, tennis equipment, jogging gear, weights, fish-poles, and house tools.

When the cans were full to overflowing, Frank slipped off his wedding ring and tossed it in. Finally he picked up the gold watch, studied its engraved case intently, blew his nose, put the watch back in the box, and added it to the pile.

Exhausted but exhilarated, Frank then dragged the heavy cans out the front door and down the ramp to the sidewalk. Surveying the avenue of well-trimmed eugenia hedges, he saw no one except two little girls playing in a driveway across the street. From a pine tree in his front yard, a gray squirrel began scolding him. Looking straight at the squirrel, Intercontinental's ranking pilot began to bellow in a hoarse nicotine voice, "All right, everybody, come and get it. Time's running out. Here you've got it, the biggest windfall in town. Take it away! It's all free and it's all yours. Hurry! Take it! Take it! Take it all!"

Across the street a door opened; the two little girls were seized by strong female hands and dragged into the house.

Around a bend appeared a beige-colored Cadillac which cruised slowly past the house, the cans, and the agitated man with sunglasses. Peering at him through rolled-up windows were an elderly white-haired couple. As their car continued along the street, the woman kept alternately pointing at the cans and beating on the driver's shoulder with her small fists.

Shortly after the Cadillac left the scene, a sheriff's patrol car arrived from the opposite direction and slowed down alongside the gesticulating Frank.

"Help yourself, Officer," he shouted to the patrolman from

the sidewalk. "The gig's up and everything's beam ends. I almost made it, but the dice were loaded against me."

"What's going on?" asked the patrolman easily.

"Nothing. It's going off. I don't know if it's the Russians or what, but I got it right from the Source." Using his index finger, Medeiros pointed upward.

The patrolman pulled his car to the curb and got out slowly. *This guy's a nut,* he thought to himself, *and I've got to get him in the car. But what about the cans?* He flipped a switch to the outside speaker, got out, and took a pad from his pocket, and sauntered over toward Medeiros. As he did so, the car radio began blaring, "Unit 44 request backup for 10-36 at The Ark amusement park. Front entrance, red light and siren. . . ."

16

"I'm sorry, Reginald," announced Maybelle Lewis as she emerged from the ladies' room behind the "Land of the Giants." "The weather seems to be changing, and I don't like the looks of it. Anyway, I wore the wrong shoes and my feet are hurting. I think we'd better start back."

"You can't do that, Grandma. Please! We just got here. Those clouds will blow over. Don't you want to go on any of the rides?"

"Heavens, no. I might settle for a cup of tea if I could find one." Maybelle looked around the park dubiously.

"I bet they got some tea bags over at that Ham's Burger place."

"No, thank you. It sounds ghastly."

Reginald kept his tone innocent. "I saw some dolls."

Maybelle looked sideways at him. "You sly dog. I know you. What kind of dolls?"

"Looked like a Shirley Temple in the window."

"All right, lead the way."

As they wandered past the Ark, Reginald stopped to read the sign. "You can't go in there," his grandmother scolded him. "You have to be under two cubits. Are you under two cubits?"

Rather than press his chances, Reginald escorted Maybelle to the "Dolls of the Valley" concession. After promising to return in half an hour, he headed for the Ark and was walking past the latticed arbor when he heard what sounded like an altercation going on inside. The longer he listened, the more curious he became. Through the open squares he was able to make out the macho-looking man Mary knew only as "Lennie's friend." He was wearing an open shirt, gabardines, and expensive cowboy boots. Two gold chains hung around his neck, and a touch of silver adorned his sideburns. At the moment he was talking to the four people seated at the table. Reginald stepped closer.

"Sorry to interrupt the party, Mary," the man said in a gravel voice heavy with sarcasm, "but you're coming with me."

"I'm afraid she's not, sir," replied Ralph Epstein, rising quickly. Arvie, seated beside her, put his arm around Mary protectively.

"Back off, juicy fruit," said Lennie's friend to Arvie. "You don't want to get hurt. She owes me money." He reached out suddenly, seized her blouse, and ripped it. "These are my clothes," he announced. Mary screamed and covered herself, while Arvie leaped to his feet and shoved the man back.

"Get lost!" Arvie shouted.

"I'll call security," said Epstein.

"You don't seem to understand," said the gravel-voiced one, blocking Epstein's way. "I'm her banker. She works for me."

"Not any more, she doesn't," said Arvie.

"Look, I don't know who you people are," said the man, "but I'm not going to fool with you. She's just a two-bit trick that sneaked in on the plane two days ago. She owes my partner a lot of money, and I gave her an advance on her wages."

"That's a lie!" said Mary.

Reginald shifted his position for a better look. On the plane two days ago? Which plane? He couldn't see Mary's face, but when Sally turned her head he recognized her immediately. She was the stewardess! Then were all these people on that flight? What brought them here? Was it because of—? But his reflections were broken up by Arvie, who was now eyeball-to-eyeball with Lennie's friend. "Let's step out here a minute," he said. "Maybe we can work something out."

"There's nothing to work out," said Lennie's friend, but he backed away and stepped outside.

"He's got a gun!" warned Mary, noticing a bulge in his shirt. Reginald ducked behind a palm tree.

Arvie took out his checkbook. "What kind of money does she owe you?"

"Forget the money," said the man. "Just keep away from her."

"You the guy that beat her up?"

"I run a business. I don't beat people up."

"What kind of business?"

"None of your business! Look, don't waste my time. Split before you get hurt. You don't want to mess with that piece of baggage."

"She's a human being."

"So'm I."

Arvie looked at him steadily. "I wouldn't say so."

"Move!"

"I'm to look after her."

"Who—" But the man's question was never finished, for at that instant Mary slipped out of her seat and bolted toward the park gate.

A philosophy of life can be expounded in seven volumes of prose, or it can be crammed into a split second of action. Arvie Erickson's twenty-one years of existence were now on center stage. Ever since the death of his father he had dedicated himself to the personal pursuit of excellence. To achieve his goal he had worked his good looks, mental and physical talents, easygoing charm, and his mother's friends to bring about a string of brilliant successes. But the death of his mother at the peak of the college tennis season left him stunned, and his rhubarb with Brenda had further shaken him. Suddenly he was alone. Campus popularity had turned into a sour crabapple, and life into a cul-de-sac. Brenda had talked about a "mighty purpose in the universe," but it had baffled him. "Go out to the hills and talk with God," the minister had said, and his words had taken effect. After climbing to the top of the crag, with the wind in his face, Arvie sensed at last that God was real, despite all the ancient declamations of Lucretius. He caught a glimpse of a purpose that lay outside himself, that was relational and had nothing to do with his ego identity. It was at that moment that Mary Zlibin came into his line of vision. He discerned somehow that whatever it might be that God wanted of him, it had to do with Mary. Now the moment of decision had come.

At the instant Mary made her move toward the park gate, Arvie responded. He sensed what was going to happen, though how much of his reaction was based on perception and how much on raw instinct, he never had to decide. He saw Lennie's friend turn and sprint after the girl and immediately took off after him, caught him, and brought him down from behind with a flying tackle. Ralph and Sally raced past the struggling pair in pursuit of Mary. The man on the ground then turned on Arvie with a .32 pistol he had drawn from his shirt. There was a loud report, followed immediately by the wailing of a siren that Reginald set off in his handbag. The man jumped to his feet and sprinted toward the west entrance, tossing his gun into the moat as he ran.

Hearing the gunshot, Ralph Epstein turned back and encountered a crowd gathering around Arvie, who was lying on the ground and bleeding at the mouth. Sally now returned with Mary, who pushed hysterically through the crowd, grabbed Arvie's hand, and began kissing it repeatedly. Ralph tried to move the crowd back. In less than a minute the security guards arrived, but instead of trying to disperse the crowd that had grown considerably, or tracking down the fleeing gunman, they went for Reginald and his siren.

Raindrops began to fall, and the sky grew blacker. From the distant Topatopa Mountains a clap of thunder could be heard. A slight tremor shook the ground and caused some concessions to sway.

17

Nick Gavrilovich, the tattooed solitaire player on Flight 803 who dared to rebuke Charlotte Embree for her behavior, muttered to himself as he shuffled along Los Angeles' Sixth Street on his way to the Sailors' Rest Home. He noticed the sallow, bearded young man who was crossing the street toward him. The man's clothes were grimy from travel and his sneakers were stained. On his back was a typical small khaki pack. He chanted his refrain to Nick: "Sir, can you spare me a piece of change so I can catch the bus?"

Ordinarily Nick would have dismissed the man with a gesture. As a merchant marine pensioner he had little enough. But it so happened that on a bus trip to Las Vegas a month earlier he had lined his pockets with the oblations of several wage-earners and a dealer who had attempted to clean him at blackjack. Studying the young man's bloodshot eyes and straggly hair, Nick demanded, "You been shooting up?"

The man clasped and unclasped his hands nervously. "Not me. I swear to God I been clean for a week."

"Bilgewater!"

"Please, mister. I'm so hungry. I ain't eaten for two days. A dollar. Two dollars."

Nick pulled a roll of bills from his pocket, and the young man's eyes bulged like a Chinese pug's. Peeling off an Alexander Hamilton, Nick held it in his hand. "How long d'you expect to live?"

"I O.D.'d last week," was the eager reply. "My heart stopped, but they started it again. They won't take my blood anymore. I ain't eaten—"

"You're lying."

"No, honest to God I ain't."

"You goin' back on?"

The young man coughed and crossed himself. "No way."

Nick pointed to a sign across the street. "FINAL DAYS!" it announced. "EVERYTHING HAS TO GO!" "See that?" he asked. He looked up at the suddenly darkening sky. "You know what? I think it's all goin' down the scuppers. It's the end. I mean *everything!* I got the word. It's goin'!"

The young man looked greedily at the bill in Nick's hand. "What do I care? I been sleepin' out by the freeway."

"I don't care neither," said Nick.

The man coughed again. "I ain't gonna make it another night."

"How do you know?" demanded Nick. "You God or somep'n?"

"I know."

"You don't know nothin', but I do." The young man turned away, but Nick grabbed his arm. "Here," he said gruffly. And putting the ten-spot back in his pocket, he handed the rest of the thick roll to his panhandling suppliant. The young man took the bundle of bills in total disbelief, while Nick continued his stroll along Sixth Street, carrying on a soliloquy with himself. Crossing Broadway, Nick walked into a seedy-looking pet shop and was greeted by the woman behind the counter. "Hi, Nick. Come in. Started to rain yet?"

"It's comin'."

"Sure looks black. Welcome home! Maynard's been looking for you."

Nick walked up to a cage containing a large green parrot which had wrapped its formidable beak about one of the cage wires. "Hi, Maynard," he said. The parrot gave him a beady look as he fumbled in his pocket for a piece of cracker and poked it into the cage.

"Arrr."

Nick turned and left, causing Maynard to drop the cracker. "Bilgewater," it squawked.

Nick turned and waved as he went out the door. He walked over to Pershing Square, where Major McCorkle was opening a Salvation Army street-meeting with prayer. The circle was made up entirely of uniforms: Mrs. McCorkle with her cornet, Clarence with his tuba, Gary with his bass drum, and a few other soldiers. Frances was there also, one arm in a sling, the other holding a songbook. Suspended from her neck was a chain holding the cross Gus had been wearing, now cleansed of bloodstains. It seemed to glisten despite the threatening sky. The prayer ended, she began a solo in a strong, clear voice, while the curious and indifferent park-sitters watched and listened.

*"Then He'll call me someday
to His home far away
where His glory forever I'll share."*

Nick looked up. The rain was beginning to fall.

The Bellflower singers finished their number, and the delighted Sunday afternoon audience in Griffith Park demanded they sing it over again. Three members of a male quartet addressed the first tenor and pushed a chair at him. "Sit down, brother!" they sang, to which he replied,

*"Can't sit down.
I just got to heaven and I
can't sit down!"*

The Reverend Jordan Foster looked out from the platform at the colorful gathering with a sense of overwhelming gratitude. His church had shown mercy toward him; Vivian had tentatively agreed to try to mend the broken home; his estrangement from his mother was ended. His hand went to his head, where a grubby teenager had fulfilled, as he believed, an inspired prophecy. The music ended, and he stepped to the podium to read from Scripture: "Where is the wise? Where is the scribe? Where is the disputer of this world? Hath not God made foolish the wisdom of this world. . . ?"

The heavens opened and the rains came. Griffith Park began to tremble ever so slightly.

18

The Reverend Jordan Foster winced, shifted his position, and reached a hand to his neck. He was intensely uncomfortable. After a moment's disorientation, he opened one eye warily and discovered to his astonishment that he was riding a bus. He fumbled for the control, elevated his seat-back, and looked around. It was a new, cream-colored Sceni-cruiser, and it was climbing steeply and swinging around one hairpin turn after another.

"Hey!" he sang out, "what's going on?"

Across the aisle another sleeping person was just beginning to wake up. To Jordan her features seemed familiar, and when she sat up he knew: she was the flight attendant on Friday's plane. He turned and scrutinized some of the other passengers who were beginning to stir. They, too, were recognized from Flight 803. A weird sense of unreality gripped him—as if he were wandering through a Charles Williams novel. His senses were playing tricks. Nothing fit together. Had he been drugged? he wondered. He decided not, for his head was clear and his body had recovered except for a throb of hunger in his stomach and a lingering crick in his neck.

He found he could lower the window, and quickly did so. The mountain slopes were lush and bathed in sunshine. Daisies and bluebells were opening out to the clear sky, bumblebees were humming, meadowlarks were singing, woodpeckers were tapping, and the earth smelled sweet.

No one had responded to his remark, but now Jordan noticed that people were beginning to talk to each other. He heard a man say in a loud voice, "Driver, don't you think it's time we were clued in as to what this is all about?" A chorus of agreement echoed his query. The driver responded through a microphone without turning his head. "Please, folks, we will be arriving at our destination in a few minutes and you will be fully briefed."

"What happened to Griffith Park?" called out Jordan. "I was there ten minutes ago!"

"Still there," said the driver imperturbably.

Nick Gavrilovich barked, "Where in hell are we?"

The driver chuckled into his mike. "Not exactly. We're climbing up Mount Todos de los Santos del Cielo y de la Tierra, sometimes called Mount Todos. We'll be stopping at an information center, something new. They just opened it a hundred years ago."

"This better be good," muttered Rick Ramsey.

"Oh, very good," said the driver. "The man in charge, Mr. Columba, is an outstanding gentleman. In the sixth century of our Lord he was considered the greatest living person in both Ireland and Scotland."

"What did he do?" Rick wanted to know.

"Everybody in Scotland knows Saint Columba," declared Alison Pitt-Barr. "He crowned the king of Scotland and built hundreds of churches."

"Never heard of him," said Colleen Phillips.

"I have, if it's the same man," said Sally Carstairs. "There was a Mr. Columba on our flight."

"That's correct," said the driver.

The road became less winding and leveled off. The bus began rolling through mountain meadows dotted with pine and cedar. Inside, gloom settled over the passengers as the word of Arvie Erickson's murder was passed along the aisle. Commissioner Hilliard, already suffering asthmatic symptoms, was more distressed than the others, but kept silent about the fate of Gus Krieger. After a while the passengers tried to shake their despondency by describing to each other precisely what they were doing when they were suddenly and miraculously transported aboard the bus. Alison Pitt-Barr, however, was curious about the

events that occurred in the amusement park, and kept pressing
Ralph Epstein for more details about Arvie. What kind of person
was he? What was his connection with Mary?

"I really don't know," said Ralph. "I can tell you we all liked
him. Seemed a very fine young man. A tennis star. I think he just
met Mary on the plane, found out she was in some kind of
trouble, and tried to help her. Wanted to drive her out to her
aunt's place."

"Do you think he was a Christian?" asked Alison.

"I wouldn't know. The only real conversation I had with him
in the park was about Lucretius."

"Who?"

"The Roman poet. Apparently Mary kept asking him about
death, and Arvie had been studying this man's philosophy."

"About death?"

"Yes. It just happened I knew something about Lucretius.
He was mentioned in a deposition we took last year for a suit
against a New Jersey school district, and I had to read the
poem. Lucretius says there's nothing after death and don't worry about it. This bothered Arvie."

"What did you tell him?"

"I told him I thought Lucretius had an unhealthy materialistic streak. It shows up in his writing. I remember Arvie said he
had been researching atomic theory, and of course that started
with Lucretius. So I told him what the old guy had said about
love, that love was all nonsense. Arvie had read that. But then I
added that Lucretius was supposed to have poisoned himself by
drinking a love-philtre, and I wouldn't take him for an authority
on death or anything else."

"What did Arvie say to that?"

"He seemed satisfied." Ralph shook his head. "Such a terrible thing. Such a loss."

Now the vehicle rounded a bend and entered a tunnel, and
the driver flicked on his lights. A quarter of a mile further and
they emerged into daylight, but not before something quite
remarkable happened to all fourteen passengers. To their amazement they found themselves freshly attired in white linen, some
in robes, some in slack suits with chic tailoring, still others in
uniform.

Rennie Lopez, who was in a front seat, looked up from an examination of his wardrobe to shout, "*Mama mia!* We're sitting on a cloud!" A white, swirling mist covered the surface of everything as far as the eye could see. But it was clean linen, not the surrealist terrain, that had conversation buzzing aboard the bus. The driver braked to a stop and addressed his passengers.

"End of the line, folks. You'll notice we've entered a new space-time zone, but there's no change in temperature. We'll be here just a short time and then head back. Please take with you the things you'll need and leave by the front entrance." He was cheerful enough, but his auditors were in varying stages of bewilderment.

"You say it's safe to get out?" asked Maybelle Lewis.

"Perfectly safe. Whenever you're ready."

"Then what?" asked Epstein. "We talk to this information person, and get back on the bus, and then what?"

"Save your questions, please. I'll be waiting here. You can, of course, come back to the bus any time you wish."

Stepping gingerly, the passengers descended into the knee-deep fluff, but relaxed on finding their footing solid. They quickly congregated around a rangy, impressive-looking man, seated on a high wooden stool. He was wearing blue jeans and flannel shirt, and was holding a primitive lyre in one hand and eating a taco with the other. His feet were in sandals. Despite the informality of his dress—or perhaps because of it—there was a look of nobility, even royalty about him. His heavy black beard was shot with gray.

The man finished his taco while questions were tossed at him from all directions. At last he held up his hand. In a musical Irish lilt he said, "Yes, my name is Columba, and I was on that famous flight with you. Don't ask what I was doing; we get these assignments and do what we can with them. If you can believe it, my last detail was in the animal kingdom. I do apologize for the inconvenience of bringing you up here and popping you into these garments. It's an old tradition. I wish they'd do away with it."

"How did you pull it off?" inquired Reginald. "Did you spray us with ectoplasm? What a breakthrough! We were just sitting in a hotel room, and whoosh! we're on a bus."

244 / The Doomsday Connection

"And I hadn't finished my second cup of tea," said Maybelle.

"Sorry about that," said Columba. "We've got some punch."

"Why are we trussed up when you ain't?" demanded Nick.

"I'm afraid there are a lot of questions I don't have answers for," said Columba, his Irish face crinkling in a grin.

"Dress rehearsal, maybe?" suggested Epstein.

"Maybe. But you'll be going back down, in your own outfits, and life will go on. No ectoplasm. I'm sure you learned in school that space travel is also time travel. It's in the New Testament."

"Where?" demanded Rick Ramsey.

"In the ninth chapter of the second Gospel. Which, by the way, explains me."

"Did you wear those clothes when you were a monk on Iona?" Alison wanted to know.

Columba smiled. "What is it you people say? 'Blessed are they who adapt, for they shall be communicators.' "

"Is this supposed to be heaven, all this white stuff?" asked Sally.

"No, this is not heaven. Now, if you will not interrupt, I will explain how you happen to be brought here. Please be seated." A row of white upright chairs suddenly emerged out of the mist, arranged in a circle. The passengers sat. "First of all," Columba began, "I will ask my ingenious namesake, Reginald St. Columba Tibbets, to bring his bag to me."

"Why? There's nothin' in it," Reginald objected with a nervous laugh. "Just electronic junk."

"Bring it to me."

"It's my private stuff."

"Reginald!" said his grandmother forbiddingly.

Reluctantly he handed the bag to Columba, who then lifted out an assortment of tape recorders, batteries, earphones, language tapes, a cordless switch, and accessory devices. "This, my friends," Columba announced in a solemn voice, "is the source of the voice you heard in the skies over Colorado!"

While Reginald turned beet red, gasps went up around the circle of white chairs. Vasily Mechikoff shook a huge fist at

Reginald and swore a fervent Slavic oath that managed to top all the anti-Arian anathemas of the 318 bishops of Nicaea.

"My husband knew it was a fake," declared Colleen Phillips. "I didn't believe him."

"Neither did anybody on campus," said Rennie Lopez.

"One moment!" Columba held up his hand. "I have more to report. But first, perhaps we ought to let Reginald tell you why he thought you needed to hear that message."

Reginald gulped. "It seemed like everybody was talking about the world coming to an end, and I wanted to find out whether people really believed it. The plane just happened to give me a chance to try it out. My idea for the experiment was perfectly innocent. I didn't mean anything by it."

"But it foozled," said Nick.

"You broke federal law," said Sally. "That's a crime."

"The prisons are full of people who thought they were innocent," observed Ralph Epstein.

"So is hell," added Columba.

"I swear I didn't want to make any trouble," protested Reginald, his eyes brimming.

"A man is dead," said Jordan Foster.

"Well!" said Columba. "And now for something so important and significant that we had to bring you all the way up here to tell you about it. I really don't know where to begin. This is something that has just happened in the universe, and not only is it touching your lives, it is affecting the destiny of planet earth. Do any of you remember, in the Book of Genesis, the story of Abraham interceding before the Lord to spare the destruction of Sodom and all its evil citizens for the sake of such good people as might be living in the city? Do you? Let me see your hands if you do."

The three Bible college students, together with Jordan Foster, Alison Pitt-Barr, and Maybelle Lewis, lifted their hands. The rest looked blank and uncomfortable.

"I seem to recall it vaguely," said Ralph Epstein.

"It's in Genesis 18," said Rick, taking a paperback Bible from his pocket.

"Then you may remember," Columba went on, "that Abra-

246 / The Doomsday Connection

ham put the question to God: if there were fifty righteous people in the city, would He spare it? Would He destroy it? And then He kept putting more questions: If there were forty-five, would God still spare it? And then forty, and thirty and twenty, and finally ten."

"And each time," added Foster, "God said yes, He would spare the city for the sake of the righteous ones in it."

"Now you've got it," said Columba, "but is it clear? Do you understand it? Because if you don't, you'll never understand what I'm going to tell you."

"This 'righteous' thing," spoke up Vasily Mechikoff. "What is a righteous? Who is righteous?"

"Nobody is righteous," said Ralph Epstein.

Columba grinned. "Spoken like a lawyer. Gentlemen, let's stay out of theology, do you mind? I'm trying to say something. On a human level, where people are, righteousness is simply a way of behaving. It's a relationship. Not what you are, but what you do—the way you live, the way you treat people. And that's what Abraham meant. Are you with me?" Hearing no response, he continued, "Now I am going to say something so shocking, so unbelievable, that you will have a hard time grasping it. But at least you will understand why you, of all the people in the world, were brought here to hear it. You see, Reginald was right. Yesterday was the moment in the history of the universe when the Sovereign God of Creation intended to send judgment on the earth."

A look of horror froze on Reginald's face, leaving him white and speechless.

"Mother!" whispered Jordan Foster. "She had it right all the time."

"Yes, she did," said Columba. He turned and looked grimly at Reginald. "Son, when you brought that demon into your bedroom, and heard it tell you to pick a date, in the councils of heaven that date had already been picked."

"Was that why the sky went black a while ago?" asked Maybelle, trembling. "I was terribly frightened."

Columba nodded. "Did anyone feel the quake? That's how close it was."

"And those little notes I sat up writing to everybody—they told the truth after all?" asked Alison earnestly, but no one seemed to be listening.

"Something must have happened," said Rennie.

"I bet God changed His mind, like you said," guessed Linda.

"Oh, now, just a minute," interposed Commissioner Hilliard. "I must say I'm not sure I'm following this. The One who inhabits eternity is beyond our petty speculations. He is immutable. His reign is from everlasting to everlasting, and He never changes His mind. 'I am the Lord, I change not!' "

More exclamations followed, and again Columba held up his hand for quiet. "The commissioner is right," he said quietly. "God's Word is forever, and He does not change His character. But Scripture does say that God changed His *mind* more than once on the question of judgment. Abraham was told that God would gladly save the wicked city if He could come up with some righteous people in it."

"Right on, brother," murmured Jordan Foster.

"I've seen a lot of miracles," continued Columba, "but I'm having trouble believing this myself. Yesterday afternoon, as the archangel was preparing to sound his trumpet and pronounce the Final Judgment, and the people of God were to be gathered up, something beautiful happened. A strong, pure act of righteousness was taking place on the earth. A young man whom the Father loved very much gave his life for a girl whom it seemed nobody loved. It came through in the councils of heaven as a sacrificial act of self-giving. And that young man was honored, and the planet earth was honored because of him."

From somewhere came the ethereal sound of a harp. Mary Zlibin, not knowing what else to do, stood up. The blotches were gone from her complexion and the bruises from around her eyes. Her hair, usually gnarly and untidy, now fell in soft waves over her shoulders. She was stunningly beautiful in white, but her true beauty was in the expression of her countenance. She was smiling.

"My Lord and my God!" exclaimed Ralph Epstein softly.

"Hallelujah!" breathed Jordan Foster.

"Jesus!" said Rick Ramsey, his voice equally hushed.

"It's like something out of *Pilgrim's Progress*," said Commissioner Hilliard to Columba warmly. "Valiant-for-Truth crossing over, and the trumpets on the other side."

"But not the last trumpet," said Columba as he walked over and gave Mary a hug. "Not quite yet. Today the earth is full of the mercy of God. Grace before judgment. But don't expect people to believe you."

"Some will be disappointed," Jordan Foster suggested. "Like Mother, they've got their bags packed and they're ready to go."

Two "Amens" rang out from the lips of Maybelle Lewis and Alison Pitt-Barr.

"What about that story in the paper?" demanded Alison. "Will we get some advance word—I mean a real word—or is that just poppycock?"

Columba shook his head. "Neither the *New York Times* nor Prester John nor the Vatican nor anybody else will be giving out that information. I certainly won't. But I keep remembering that line in Browning's poem, 'Who knows but the world may end tonight?'"

"What's Arvie doing now?" asked Sally, wiping her eyes.

"He's fine. He's with us."

By now a number of the passengers were sitting quietly, unable to comprehend fully, or even partially, what had happened. But they were aware of the fact that they had been on the edge of an awesome mystery. A few were weeping, including Vasily Mechikoff. It seemed the most natural thing in the world when Jordan Foster stood and began to sing very slowly,

"Gabriel will warn you,
some early morn you
will hear his horn . . .
it's not far away,
lift up your head and say,
it's gonna be a Great Day!"

The song concluded, Columba clapped his hands for attention. "Before you get on the bus," he said, "help yourselves to tacos and punch!"

19

The engine of the Sceni-cruiser was idling as the fourteen passengers moved toward the open front door. Columba stood alongside to say good-bye to each as they climbed aboard. First in line was Maybelle Lewis.

"I guess I'll never really understand what happened until I get to heaven," she said to him. "I remember that young man. He seemed so nice. I'm going to have to read again about Abraham."

"Do that," urged Columba. "You like dolls, I understand."

"Oh, it's just a hobby. Really, I'm a Christian first. But that was a terrible thing Reginald did. Sometimes I just give up on him."

"You haven't given up on Henriette, have you?"

"What do you mean?" Maybelle paused on the step in alarm.

"You haven't broken her head? Ripped off her arms? Tossed her out the window?"

"Good gracious!"

"Of course you haven't." Columba squeezed her hand. "All I meant was, don't you lose faith in that boy. Pray for him."

Maybelle sniffed. "Thank you. I already do."

Columba grinned as he greeted Commissioner Hilliard. "Are you feeling any better?"

"It's quite gone, thank you. But I'm still in shock from what you said."

"It's all true."

"Coming on top of what happened to Augustin . . ."

"Don't worry about Gus, he's doing great. Tell them that at the funeral."

"Yes, of course."

"And tell Frances he's waiting for her," added Columba, turning away. "Comrade Mechikoff. How are you, *tovarich?*"

"It is most regrettable." Mechikoff spoke rapidly in a thick accent. "To be the victim of a schoolboy prank!"

"There was more here than a prank," replied Columba.

"Ah, yes. Your religious fables. I cannot commit myself to them."

"The earthquake . . ." began Columba, but Mechikoff interrupted.

"You forget that our brave cosmonaut, Comrade Gherman Titov, returned from his pioneer trip into outer space and told the world he saw neither God nor angels. So much for fairy tales."

"Yes, but we saw *him!*"

Vasily seemed not to understand. He reached into his pocket and drew out the well-worn snapshot. "My daughter Anna. She is my god."

Columba studied the photo. "Yes. Lovely. Looks like her grandfather."

Vasily was astonished. "Her grandfather? My father?"

"Of course. He's well-known up here."

Vasily shook his head. "Please, don't tell me these things. I am a man whose life is destroyed. And there is nowhere to hide."

"I have told you the truth, comrade. I know what you face. But listen to me. Christ is risen! Just for once, are you willing to take your eyes off yourself and your predicament, and fix them on that which Gherman Titov did not see?"

For a long minute Vasily Mechikoff stared at Columba. Then he bowed his head. "I have no choice."

Columba gave him a Russian bear hug, then slipped a card into his hand. "Call this number. It's a Molokan church. . . ." He turned to greet Colleen Phillips.

"If what you say is true," she said, "that God is holding back the judgment, then maybe—"

"Maybe what?"

"Maybe He'll hold it back on me!"

"He'll do better than that."

"How do you mean?"

"He overcomes sin with grace."

"I've heard all that. But when you do what I did—"

"You meant it for bad. He meant it for good."

"That's impossible."

"Only because the world is topsy-turvy."

Colleen shook her head. "It sounds weird. I don't get it. I still feel guilty."

"Look, Colleen, they kicked me out of Ireland a long time ago for starting a war. A lot of fine people died. I think I know how you feel."

"Yes, but you're somebody. I'm nothing. I can't even pray."

Columba placed his huge hands over both of hers. "I can give you this word," he said. "Your tears will give place to joy."

She looked at him, and the tears came, but she smiled. "What about my husband?"

Columba pulled at his ear. "As long as he lives, there is hope." He reached out a hand and grasped Ralph Esptein's. "Hey! I don't know what happened in that synagogue, but you've been doing some beautiful things."

"Two questions," said Ralph briskly. "What are you going to do about Reginald, and what are you going to do about Mary?"

Columba grinned. "And I have a question or two for you: What are you going to do about Charlotte? And Irwin?"

For a moment the lawyer was left without a rebuttal. Columba laughed and clapped him on the back. "Things are moving! They're moving in your own life, Brother Epstein."

"As a matter of fact, they are."

"Glad to hear it. *Y'shua Meshyah*. . . . Say, I've really wanted to shake your hand," he said to Alison Pitt-Barr, the next in line. As Alison curtsied he added, "The granddaughter of Frazer of Tain! How's *your* daughter?"

Alison flashed a smile. "A real sugarplum. But sir, have I done the right thing?"

Columba laughed. "Why is it everyone wants a report card?

Let's see—tax fraud, employer implicated, resigned position, spread notes around the hotel illegally, escaped from bathroom—what do you mean, the right thing?"

"I mean, if Charlotte loses that restaurant chain—"

Columba shrugged. "Up here restaurant chains and daisy chains all weigh the same. I wasn't sent here to judge you. Go and have a good time with your daughter. She sounds fantastic. . . . Ah, the Reverend Jordan Foster!"

"I'm deeply honored," said Jordan, bowing.

"What a mother you have, Pastor. And how they love her up here!"

"Isn't she something? The rest of us were picking blackberries and she saw the burning bush."

"We're expecting great things at your church."

"I don't know about that. You've got a pretty weak reed to lean on."

"Well, you're the man who said that God hung something on nothing and told it to stay there!"

Foster laughed. "It's wonderful to have my family back."

"Do you know who we're praying for up here?"

"Who?"

"Paula Marie! . . . Well, Sally, I owe you a huge debt of thanks. Did you ever get that book on heaven?"

"Right here!" Sally smilingly pulled it out of her handbag. "But it didn't answer one question. What happens to divorced people when they get to heaven?"

Columba ran his hand across his bald spot. "You know, it's only on earth that relationships get confused. Not here."

"So there's really no difference. That's what you're saying? And that lets me in."

Columba's eyes narrowed. "Did I say that?"

"It sounded as if you were making it pretty easy."

"It cost more than you'll ever know."

Sally stared at him. "You mean—"

"I mean in heaven it's not what we've done, Sally, it's who we know. That reminds me. Have you talked with his pastor?"

Sally's eyebrows went up. "Whose pastor?"

"Your husband's."

"Randy's? He has no pastor. Are we talking about the same person?"

"We are. It's possible, Sally, that for you heaven may start out in North Dakota. . . . Well, Nick, how's my buddy?"

"You gonna get me outa this stupid rig?"

"Soon as we get you into the tunnel. What are you doing for money?"

"I'm making out. All money ever did was send me over the side."

"It'll do that. Anything else?"

"Yeah. That kid. Too smart. Full of bilgewater."

Columba laughed. "O.K. . . . Well, here we are!" He greeted the three Bible college students by picking up his lyre. "Let's make some music!" He brushed the strings and Linda began to sing softly, the others joining in:

> *"Seek ye first the kingdom of God*
> *and His righteousness*
> *and all these things shall be added unto you.*
> *Alleluia."*

They finished to the sound of applause from the others. "Of course," said Columba, putting down his lyre, "you deserved to go to jail. You know that."

"I felt all the time that we should have kept quiet," declared Rick. "Everybody misunderstood us."

"Wait a minute," countered Columba, "you told the truth. You just went about it the wrong way."

"But we didn't know," protested Rennie. "Nobody knew anything, really."

"As a rule, the Holy Spirit does the best job of witnessing," said Columba. "He can handle the zeal factor. So often all we do is race our engines."

"How did you get us out?" asked Linda.

"The dean posted your bail. By the way, I like that Jennifer, Rick."

"So do I."

Columba's expression changed as Mary Zlibin approached and held out her hand. "God bless you, Mary," he said. "Got any plans?"

Mary's face was calm; only her eyes continued to glow with a new and different look. A thin gold cross hung from a chain around her neck. "I'm going home for a visit," she said. "Sally's going with me. Mr. Epstein gave me the fare."

"He's a generous man."

"He also helped me with a statement I had to give to the sheriff."

"What about your aunt?"

"I'm coming out to stay with her after that. I may take a job. There'll be the trial and all that."

"Will you be going to see her now?"

"Not till after the funeral. Arvie's sister called me and wants me to come over."

"I'm glad."

"You know something Arvie said to me Saturday night?"

"What?"

"He said he was going to be my angel."

Columba shook his head in wonder. "Incredible!" As Mary turned to enter the bus he asked, "Any other questions?"

She shook her head and pointed upward. "They've already been answered." She stepped aboard.

Columba now faced the only person left. "And here," he declared, "is the voice of the future and the hope of the human race, my dubious young namesake, Master Reginald Tibbets!"

20

"Do you think God will punish me for what I did?" asked Reginald timidly.

Columba stroked his beard. "You mean drop you in a shredder?"

"I just mean, is He angry?"

Columba's eyes flashed. "God is angry with the wicked every day."

"But—hey, wait up!" The driver had swung the door shut, and the bus was beginning to move through the ground mist. Reginald raced alongside and banged on the glass. "Oh, no, you don't!" he yelled. "Stop this thing!" He turned to Columba. "Tell him to stop. You can't leave me here!"

But Columba had walked back to his stool and was picking up his instrument. Reginald chased after the bus as it disappeared into the fog. In a few minutes he came back to Columba, panting, his face pale. "You did that, didn't you?"

Columba was seated on his stool and was singing,

"Behold, I stand at the door and knock
and if any man hear My voice . . ."

Reginald shouted at him. "You're gonna finger me because I made fun of God, aren't you?"

Columba stopped. "I didn't say you made fun of God."

"And now you're gonna ship me to hell."

Columba put down his lyre. "Son, I couldn't stop that bus."

"Don't give me that!" With a quick movement of his foot, Reginald hooked a leg of Columba's stool and jerked it, causing the man to lose his balance and fall into the ground mist. Columba righted himself, reached for the lyre, and examined it. It was broken.

"You double-crossed me, just like my folks did," lashed out Reginald. "I told you I was sorry." Columba remained silent. "You send me to hell and I'll computerize the place!" More silence. "You want me to be like my little brother, don't you? Make my little trip to the altar and give my heart to Jesus. Well, let me tell you something, last spring Dad and Mother and Grandma and Dick—all of us—went to this big outdoor rally in Albany. They had a preacher and when it was over Dick said he was going down front. He wanted to hear what the guy had to say. I went along just because I wanted to check out the cables and stuff. So I was fooling around under the platform when I heard my dad's voice. I didn't know he had followed us down, but I saw his legs, and he was talking to some character who had a Bible. I heard him use my name. He was telling this guy he had to travel a lot, and then he said he really wasn't my father at all, and I didn't belong to him, and then he said, 'You know, this bothers me.' When I heard that coming out of his mouth after all the stuff he had snowed us with, about God and church and everything, I puked right while they were having a prayer."

"So you decided to play games."

"Nope. That came to me in a dream."

"Don't blame your dreams, boy. The demon didn't corrupt you. You had already corrupted yourself."

"So Dick's good, and I'm evil, and God's mad, and I'm going to hell." Reginald stuck his thumbs in his ears, wriggled his fingers, and stuck out his tongue. "And that's the good news for today."

"You're using what happened under the platform at that rally as an excuse, son," said Columba. "You've been on an ego trip all your life. When you wired that plane, you didn't even think about the other people on board."

"That's not true."

"Isn't it? Two people are dead. I'm not saying how much you had—"

"All right!" Reginald interrupted him excitedly. "Suppose I make a deal with you. I'll stop hacking and close down my lab. I won't make any more video games. I'll quit my computer research. And instead of Pacific Tech, I'll sign up for Bible school next year. How's that?"

Columba looked at his broken lyre. "Try it on the monkey demon. See what he says."

Reginald couldn't believe what he heard. "What do you mean? Isn't that your price? What you wanted?"

"I have no price."

The boy's face was contorted. "I hate you!" he screamed. "I hate you, you stinking rotten two-faced fink!" He reached clum-

sily for the stool again, but Columba thwarted him. Reginald
buried his face in his hands in frustration. "You're no Christian,"
he said in a choked voice. "A real Christian would have prayed
with me and talked about love and forgiveness. I think the Devil
sent you here."

"You ought to know," said Columba.

"Didn't I tell you I was ready to make a change?"

Columba looked away. "What you say you're going to do is
peanuts. What is the Lord God going to do for you? *That's* the
issue. What's He going to make of your life?"

Reginald shook his head. "I don't know what He's going to
make of me," he sobbed. "I've never felt the love of God." His
knees buckled, and he sank up to his chest in the mist.

Columba stooped and laid a hand on his shoulder. "You've
never felt it," he said, "because you never felt the need of it.
You've thought for years that just because you're smarter than
other people, you're better than they are. But you're not."

Reginald shook his head. "I know I'm not."

"In fact, you're worse. You've been fooling around with
wickedness in high places. You think we're going to ship you
out and make you the new face in hell? You'll ship yourself out!
But suppose I told you that right now, right this minute, heaven
is your friend. Wouldn't you say that was love?"

"I'd say it if I felt anything, but just because you or somebody says it doesn't make it so. I've heard it all before."

"You've heard it because it's true."

"Maybe it is. It isn't true for me. It never got through. I keep
asking, what did God ever do for me except make me a bas-
tard?"

From his pocket Columba took out a small New Testament
and slipped it into Reginald's jacket, his voice suddenly tender.
"Tell Him your beef. He wants to hear from you."

"Naw, He doesn't. He knows what I'm like. He'd rather
hear from my brother Dick."

"I don't believe it."

"What would I say?"

"Say whatever you want."

Reginald stood up and looked around at the landscape. The

mist around their feet had dissipated, exposing a patch of green grass and a path that appeared to wind down a slope toward the road. "I meant that about a deal," he said. Columba did not answer. Reginald waved his hand in a gesture of resignation. "O.K., Jesus," he said.

"About your parents?" demanded Columba quietly.

"What about 'em? I love 'em." He glanced at his flight bag. "D'you want this thing?"

"Not really."

"I'm sorry about the strings."

"No problem. Jubal will fix them up."

Reginald turned around impulsively and hugged the man, then held him at arm's length for a scrutiny. "Now I know where I saw you—in the hotel. What were you doing? Tailing me?"

"I was on the plane with you, too."

"Where?"

"Up near the front."

"I mean, why? What was the deal?"

"You do carry my name, Reginald."

"It was the monkey demon, wasn't it? That's what got me a guardian angel."

"Except that I'm no angel and no saint. Just Columba. The bus is waiting for you down at the tunnel. Follow that trail."

"No kidding." For the first time Reginald broke into a smile. "Now I'll tell you something. Of all those people down there, I was the one that wasn't ready!"

"Tell them that."

The boy nodded, picked up his bag, and started down the trail. Before he had gone a dozen steps he slung the bag as far as he could across the bare slope. It arched a high trajectory, landed fifty feet away, and exploded. He turned and waved. Columba laughed and responded, then gathered up his lyre as a ponderous African elephant plodded toward him out of the mist. Astride its back were two figures who turned out to be Gus Krieger and his five-year-old daughter Julie, both dressed in white. Julie was wearing a wild rose in her hair. "Are you ready?" she called.

"Just closing up shop," replied Columba. "Let's go, Hannibal." The pachyderm reached out with its trunk, lifted the man, and deposited him on its back in front of Julie and Gus. As it padded slowly into the mist a red-tailed hawk dropped onto Columba's shoulder and a Bengal tiger emerged and came trailing after them, much to Julie's delight.